A Forever Love

BOOK FIVE IN THE WANTED SERIES

FROM *NEW YORK TIMES* AND
USA TODAY BESTSELLING AUTHOR

Kelly Elliott

Other books by Kelly Elliott

Wanted Series

WANTED
Saved
faithful
Believe
a novella
Cherished

Full-length novels in the WANTED series
are also available in audio.

Broken Series

BROKEN
Broken DREAMS

Contents

1950s Slang

The following includes some terms you will see throughout this book.

candy-ass—a wimp

cool cat—a nice guy

ditz—a female idiot

easy—a girl who will sleep with anyone

eat your heart out—be jealous of me

fast—a girl/guy who will sleep with anyone

flog your log—to masturbate (masculine)

fuzz—the police

heat—the police

knuckle sandwich—a fist in the face

on the stick—someone who is bright, prepared, and pulled together

paper shaker—a cheerleader

passion pit—drive-in movie theater

sides—vinyl record

square—someone who is not cool

stacked—big breasts

swapping spit—kissing or making out

thicker than a five-dollar malt—someone who is not very bright

virgin pin—a pin a father gives his daughter for her to wear until she is married, a promise to remain a virgin until married

wazoo—rear end

what's your bag?—what's your problem?

1 Garrett

I sat down at the kitchen table and looked at all of them. Ten faces were staring back at my beautiful bride and me.

"So?" Ari said as she wiggled her eyebrows up and down.

"So...what?" I flashed them all a smile. I knew why they had come over. "You're all kid-free tonight, and you're sitting here with two old people."

"Speak for yourself. You're as old as you feel, and honestly, I feel like I'm only fifty," Emma said as she sat down next to me but not before she kissed me softly on the cheek.

"Oh, don't play innocent with us. I think we've all waited long enough to hear the ultimate love story. Come on, Gramps, you once told me that your and Grams's love is a forever love. Spill it," Gunner said as he glanced at Ellie and then back at me.

"Now, why do y'all want to hear our story?" I raised my eyebrow at them.

Ari let out a laugh. "Please. I know you two still keep a quilt in the back of your truck, old man. There's a reason you have a sixth sense when it comes to sex."

"Ari!" Ellie, Heather, and Amanda said at the same time.

I chuckled as Emma reached over and grabbed my hand. I peeked over at her, and when she smiled at me, my heart skipped a beat. It took me back over fifty years to that moment when I'd realized I would do whatever it took to see that smile every day for the rest of my life.

"Well, I can tell ya one thing. This woman sitting here put up one hell of a fight," I said as I winked at Emma.

"I was just playing hard to get, that's all," Emma said as she looked at the kids.

"Gramps, tell us what it felt like the first time you saw Grams," Gunner said with a slight smile.

I let out a chuckle. "Y'all want a story, huh?"

"Yes!" they all said at once.

Emma and I both started laughing. I glanced over at her, and she nodded her head.

"Well, if we're going to tell this story, I need a beer and a sweet tea," I said.

Ellie and Ari both jumped up and scrambled to get the drinks. My sweet Ellie handed me a beer and flashed her beautiful smile at me.

Oh, how she reminds me of my Emma.

Ari placed a sweet tea down in front of me and another one in front of Emma.

I took a drink and looked around at each of them. I loved them all like they were my own, and my dream was for them to have the kind of love that Emma and I had been blessed with.

"I'll never forget the first time I ever laid eyes on Emma Rose Birk. I'm pretty sure my heart stopped beating, and I fought like hell to catch my breath." I closed my eyes and could still see her piercing gray eyes staring back into mine, like it had happened just moments ago. "It was 1956, and I was seventeen…"

Mason, Texas

Summer 1956

I jumped out of Billy's truck and made my way over toward the drugstore. It was another hot summer day in Mason, and I was exhausted from burning thorns off the prickly pears.

"Garrett, are you sure you want to take over your dad's ranch someday? I mean, we could move to Austin and have completely different lives than what our dads had growing up in this little town."

I smiled as I shook my head. Billy was like a brother to me, but he and I had very different ideas on where we saw our lives going.

"I want to be a cattle rancher. It's my dream."

"All right, but don't be jealous while I'm in Austin getting laid by different girls every other day."

I let out a laugh and hit him on the back. "Keep dreaming."

We walked into the drugstore, and I couldn't wait to get something cold down my throat. I glanced around, and my eyes were immediately drawn to the blonde girl sitting at the counter. She was in between Margie and Anna, and I couldn't help but notice Wayne standing there.

Anna glanced up and smiled.

Shit. I was hoping that Wayne would have made Anna forget her crush on me, but it looked like that wasn't happening.

All Anna ever did was tell everyone how I was on the stick, and we would make great babies with her blue eyes and mine. We were both smart, organized, and good-looking.

"Why, if it isn't Garrett Mathews," Anna purred.

The blonde spun around, and that was when her eyes met mine. I was pretty sure my heart had just dropped to the floor, and I was having a hard time breathing for a few seconds.

"Mathews? What in the heck is wrong with you?" Billy asked as he slapped me on the back.

As she slowly smiled, I shook my head and about dropped down to my knees. No girl had ever had such an effect on me.

None.

I had already had my fair share of girls. None of them had meant anything to me though, and the fact that they had all been easy turned me off.

"Wow…check out the new girl," Billy said.

I smiled back at her, and I was positive her reaction toward me was the same one I'd just had. She quickly looked down and then back up at me. She gently bit on her lower lip and turned back to face Margie, who whispered something into her ear. The blonde snapped her head up and gave me a funny look before glancing over at Billy.

"I think I just got a woody," Billy said with a chuckle.

I quickly looked at him. *Jerk.*

"Come on, Mathews. Let's go say hi."

I drew in a deep breath and started to make my way toward everyone. When I saw Anna jump up, I gave Wayne a look, and he grabbed her and started talking to her. Just the fact that a guy had his hands on her caused her to forget about me. She just wanted to suck in all the attention. Everyone talked about how Anna had slept with half the school. She and I had hooked up earlier this year, and then she'd quickly moved on to my three best friends—Raymond, Billy, and Wayne. Now, she was back to me, trying for a repeat, but one of the biggest mistakes of my life had been screwing Anna King in her bedroom when her parents were in Fredericksburg.

Margie stood up and smiled at me. "Garrett, Billy…I'd like you to meet my cousin, Emma Birk. Emma, these are some good friends of mine, Garrett Mathews and Billy Bauer. We've known each other since…what? First grade?"

Billy let out a loud laugh. "Something like that."

He reached out his hand, and Emma shook it as she smiled. When she glanced over at me, I momentarily forgot how to talk. Finally, I tilted my head and tipped my cowboy hat. I held out my hand, and she stood up.

"It's a real pleasure to meet you, Miss Birk." I gave her the smile that I knew drove the girls crazy.

She bit down on her dang lip. "The pleasure is all mine, Mr. Mathews."

Oh dear God.

She had the voice of an angel. There went my stupid heart again, and now, I could hear ringing in my ears.

What in the hell is wrong with me?

I stood there, like an idiot, and just stared at her. She was beautiful with blonde hair and bluish-gray eyes that pierced my soul. I glanced down at her soft pink lips. I'd do anything to taste her lips and see if she was as sweet as she looked.

She couldn't be more than five-three, but she had a figure on her that was to die for. The pink ribbons in her hair screamed her innocence. The moment she placed her hand in mine, I felt a jolt of electricity, and I was positive she'd felt it, too, because she sucked in a breath of air. I smiled, which was a mistake. She knew I'd seen her reaction, so she quickly pulled her hand away and sat back down. She turned her back toward me and acted like she was listening to something Wayne was telling Anna.

"What can I do you for, Garrett?" Mr. Horster asked.

"Root beer, please," I said with a slight smile.

I looked at Margie, and she gave me a wink before sliding down a seat, leaving the seat next to Emma empty. I quickly sat down before Billy could. He shot me a dirty look, and I pretended I hadn't noticed it. There was no way I would let Billy anywhere near my Emma.

My Emma?

"You look a little lost there, Garrett," Margie whispered in my ear.

I snapped my head over at her and shot her my crooked smile. "I'm never lost, Margie. You should know that."

She let out a small laugh as she gave me a look my mother would give. Margie was like a sister to me. She had wavy long brown hair and green eyes. She was pretty enough to get any guy she wanted but classy enough to keep her legs closed. She did have a thing for Billy though. I was pretty sure if they had the chance to be alone, they would end up together. They both liked each other, but neither would ever admit it. They always put me in the middle of their messed-up friendship, and I was getting tired of it.

"I know I've never seen that look on your face before. You seem a little…shall we say, smitten with my cousin?" Margie said as she glanced over my shoulder at Emma.

I turned around, only to see Emma's back was still facing me as she played with the straw in her strawberry milkshake. When I looked back at Margie, she had one eyebrow raised, and a chill ran up and down my body.

"Don't give me that look, Marg. You look evil when you do that, and it doesn't suit your face."

Margie tilted her head and said in a hushed voice, "Garrett Thomas Mathews, I saw the way you looked at Emma. Don't deny it to me. I'm one of your best friends and like a sister to you. I'm probably the only girl in Mason County who can say she's seen your penis and about threw up. Don't bullshit me."

I rolled my eyes and shook my head. "Are you ever going to forget that day? Ever?"

She slowly smiled. "Nope," she said, popping the P sound. "It was your idea to go swimming in the tank on my daddy's ranch. It wasn't my fault you got a fish caught in your drawers, and no one but me would help with it."

Good God. The memory of me ripping off my britches and Margie standing there, staring at my dick, still made me sick to my stomach. Then, when she'd opened her mouth and said, *I'm impressed, Mr. Mathews. I'm very impressed, but put your snake away*, I'd wanted to crawl under a rock for the rest of my life.

"We made a vow—a vow, Margie—that we would never talk about that day. Do you know what a vow is?" I asked as I quickly looked around.

I smiled at Mr. Horster as he set my root beer down.

Margie glanced around also before looking back at me with her evil little smile. "I know what a vow is. You're not the only smart one in our class."

"Hey, Garrett. What are your plans for tonight?" Anna ran her tongue across her upper teeth.

She was probably the only girl in Mason County who gave blow jobs out like she was passing out Halloween candy.

I gave her a weak smile. "I've been burning thorns all day, Anna. I'm probably going to go home and go to bed early."

She pouted her lip. "That doesn't sound like fun."

I couldn't help but notice that Emma was watching me. Billy was talking to her, but her eyes were on me. I tried not to look at her, but a part of me liked that she was staring at me while he was talking to her.

"So, what do you say, Emma?" Billy asked.

Emma sat up a little and cleared her throat. "I'm so sorry. What were you saying?"

Billy let out a laugh. "We're all going to the passion pit tonight. Are you going with Margie and Anna?"

Emma crinkled up her nose and giggled. "Passion pit?"

"Drive-in theater is what he meant," I said as I shot Billy a dirty look.

Emma glanced over at Margie and then looked at me as she tilted her head. "Are you going, Mr. Mathews?"

I didn't know what in the hell came over me, but before I could stop myself, I said, "Yes."

Anna's mouth dropped open. "Hey, you just said—"

"What a great way for Emma to get to know everyone. This will be fun!" Margie said, cutting Anna off.

I tried not to look at Anna, but I quickly peeked at her. She practically had steam coming from her ears as she looked back and forth between Emma and me.

Great. Just great.

I sat there for a few more minutes, listening to Billy, Margie, Anna, and Wayne make plans to meet at the drive-in tonight. I was exhausted and not in the mood to go see a picture show, but if it meant spending time with Emma, I would do it.

Margie stood up and bumped me on the arm as she smiled. "I'm going to kick you in the wazoo if you don't show up tonight, Garrett Mathews."

I chuckled. "I'll be there, I promise."

Emma stood up and smiled. "Wayne, Billy, it was very nice to meet you both."

When she turned to face me, I got up and held out my hand. I glanced down and saw my hand was shaking.

Oh, man. Get it together, Mathews. It wasn't good that a girl had me so nervous that I was shaking.

She slowly let her smile move across her face. "Garrett, it was a pleasure meeting you. I'll see you tonight?"

I smiled back and tried my best to make her melt.

Nothing.

Her face never budged. She stared me in the eyes, and I had to quickly turn away before looking back at her.

"Yeah, I'll be there. The pleasure was all mine, Emma."

Her eyes lit up when I said her name, but other than that, she had no response. I watched as Wayne walked out with the girls, and he began talking to Emma. I knew what the jerk was thinking—new girl, new chance to score. There was no way in hell I would let that happen.

"You got your eye on the new girl?" Billy asked as he pushed my shoulder, causing me to stumble into the stool.

I turned to face him and shrugged my shoulders. When Billy let out a laugh, the people sitting farther down the counter looked at him.

He leaned closer to me and said, "Did you see how stacked she was?"

I instantly felt my face get hot. I grabbed on to him and pulled him closer to me. "Don't ever talk about her like that again."

His smile faded, and I gave him a good push away. I threw money down on the counter and thanked Mr. Horster.

Billy followed me out. "I'm going to take that as a very clear response that you've got your eye on Emma Birk."

I smiled as I jumped into Billy's truck.

Neither one of us said a word as Billy drove me back home. His family owned the ranch next to ours, and we had been best friends for as long as I could remember. I thought this was the first time we hadn't spoken a word to each other on this daily drive. I got a funny feeling in my gut that maybe Billy liked Emma also. The last thing I wanted to do was ruin our friendship over a girl. No girl was worth that.

"You want me to take you all the way down?" Billy asked as he pulled up to my family's gate.

I looked up at the big M on the gate and smiled. *Someday, this will all be mine.*

"Nah, I need to clear my head, so I think I'll just run home," I said as I got out of his truck.

He nodded his head and glanced around before looking back at me. "I like her, too, Garrett," he said.

My stomach dropped. "All right. How do you think we need to handle this, Bill?"

He shrugged his shoulders. "I don't know. I saw the look on your face when you first saw her, Garrett. In an instant, I knew you were attracted to her. I gotta ask…is it just a sex thing? Or is it something more?"

Just the idea that he was asking if I was interested in Emma for only sex pissed me off. "What is it for you?"

He looked down and then back up at me. "Honestly?"

I nodded my head and got ready for his answer.

"At first, it was just the idea of getting her alone, but the more I talked to her, the more I liked her. She's different than the other girls around here."

I looked down and kicked the dirt. *We really need rain to get out of this drought.* My heart was aching now, more than it ever had before. I'd already been worried about my family's ranch because of this drought, and now, I was worried that my best friend and I were about to go head-to-head over a girl.

I simply said, "Yeah."

I looked at Billy, and we both smiled at each other.

"Gentlemen about this?" I asked.

Billy nodded his head and said, "Always."

I hit the side of his truck. "I'll pick ya up in a couple of hours."

I stood there and watched as my best friend drove away. I turned and climbed over the gate before taking off toward the house. Maybe a good, hard run would help me figure out these feelings floating around that I'd never experienced before. As I ran faster and faster, I couldn't seem to shake the blue-gray eyes from my head as I thought about what Billy had said.

I hated to admit this, but I was ready to fight my best friend to the death for Emma.

My Emma.

2 Emma

"Did you meet anyone today, darling?" my mother asked as she gave me a sweet smile.

I smiled and nodded my head. "A few people, but no one like my friends back home."

My mother gave me the you-better-watch-out look.

I sat down and let out a sigh. I had planned to hate Mason. Moving from Fredericksburg to Mason had been bad enough, but the thought of making new friends had pained me. My only saving grace was Margie, my cousin. When she had introduced me to Anna, I'd liked her almost immediately. It hadn't taken me long to figure out that the girl was a sexpot and a ditz, but she was funny and actually very sweet. She did like the boys though. Then, I'd met Wayne. He was a typical guy.

Nothing new there.

"So, did you meet girls and boys or just girls?" my mother asked, drawing me out of my thoughts.

"Both."

There was no sense in lying because I'd seen my mother and aunt walking by the drugstore. They'd looked in when I was saying good-bye to Garrett.

Garrett Mathews—that boy has me confused for the first time in my life.

My mother let out a little giggle. "I saw you talking to Garrett Mathews. He's a nice boy."

My mouth dropped open. "H-how do you know Garrett?"

My mother was from Mason, so I didn't even know why I'd asked that question. She probably knew his parents or something.

She turned and began cutting up sirloin for sauerbraten. "I went to high school with his parents. I might have had a crush on his father at one point before I met your father."

I felt my face blush just from my mother admitting to liking another man besides my daddy. "Mom, can I ask you something?"

She set her knife down and wiped her hands on her apron as she leaned against the counter. "Of course you can."

I took in a deep breath and said a quick prayer. "When did you know you were in love with Daddy?"

She smiled so big that it caused me to smile. "The first time I saw him. I was walking with my friends to class, and I saw him walking toward us. The moment he looked into my eyes, my breath caught, and I got a weird little feeling in my stomach. I'd never felt like that before, not with any of the guys I went to high school with…not even Thomas Mathews," she said with a wink.

I let out a giggle and shook my head.

My parents had met and fallen in love in college. My father had been studying to be a doctor, and my mother had been going to school to be a nurse. They had lived in Fredericksburg ever since Daddy got out of college. He had worked there since I was a baby, but once an opportunity had opened up in Mason for a doctor, my mother hadn't even had to ask twice. My father had known how much she loved home, and he'd moved us here, so she could be closer to her parents.

I looked at my mother and smiled. "Love at first sight?"

She giggled again. "Yes, Emma Rose, love at first sight. Your father turned around and followed my friends and me for a bit while we walked to the café for lunch. Before we walked in, he asked to talk to me. We spoke for a bit. Then, he asked me out, and I said yes. The rest is history."

"Your love story is different though," I said in almost a whisper.

I thought my parents' love story was one of a kind.

I'd figured out that all guys just wanted one thing. I'd had a crush on Nelson Wells for so long, and once he'd asked me out, I'd thought I was in heaven. Of course, it was right before we'd moved. Nelson and I had gone to see a movie with a bunch of friends. When he'd started sliding his hand up my dress, I'd quickly learned his idea of true love was nothing like mine.

Jerk. He's lucky I never told my father about what he tried.

My mother gave me a very serious look. "Why do you say that, Emma Rose?"

I shrugged my shoulders. "I don't know. It just seems your love with Daddy is one of a kind."

"Your father and I have a true love, a strong and wonderful love."

I smiled and nodded my head. "You do. I know this. It's just…well, it seems like all boys are just interested in making out."

My mother put her hand up to her chest and let out a gasp. She quickly looked around and then back at me. "Emma Rose! Do not let your father hear you say that. If you want to have somewhat of a normal life, don't ever tell him that, or he will never allow you to even think of dating."

I let out a laugh as my father walked into the kitchen.

"Hello, my two beautiful loves. Maria, my love, I missed you." He kissed my mother first on the lips, and then he reached across and kissed me on the forehead.

I loved that my parents showed affection in front of me. My father wasn't afraid to take my mother into his arms and passionately kiss her. That was what I wanted—someone to passionately love me and not just in a sexual way. I wanted to be romanced. I wanted to be swept off my feet. I wanted to feel like I was walking on a cloud.

I'd felt that way when Garrett Mathews smiled that stupid crooked smile at me. My heart had melted and then slammed over and over in my chest. I closed my eyes and could picture him perfectly. He'd tried to play it cool, but I'd seen the way his eyes couldn't get enough of me. It'd caused a sensation in my lower stomach that I'd never felt before. It had felt so strong that I almost needed to touch myself to ease it. I'd told Margie about it after we left the drugstore. She'd told me that a boy she really liked affected her the same way, and when she'd been alone, she had given herself an orgasm with her hand. The thought of it had intrigued me more than I wanted to admit.

Then, there was the way Billy had talked to me. He hadn't ignored me like Garrett had when he was talking to Margie the whole time. Billy was handsome and funny. Something about him had made me smile, but I hadn't gotten the same feeling I had when I looked at Garrett…or talked to Garrett…or thought about Garrett.

There goes that feeling.

"You are off in a faraway land, Emma."

I snapped my eyes open to my father's voice. "What?"

He raised his eyebrow and looked at me.

"I mean, excuse me?" I jumped up and began helping my mother with dinner.

My father chuckled. "Ladies, do you need any help?"

My mother smiled and shook her head. "Go relax. It's not often you are home early."

As my father turned to leave, I mustered up the courage and got ready to give him my puppy-dog eyes. "Daddy?"

He turned around and looked at me.

"Margie is going to the drive-in this evening with a bunch of her friends. Girls and boys will be there. They've invited me to go along, and I'd really like to, so I can make new friends and all."

My father smiled and nodded his head as he glanced over at my mother. "I don't have a problem with it since they are Margie's friends. Let's keep it to an early evening though. No staying out too late. Your mother and I have to head to the country tomorrow. Some friends of hers have invited us out to welcome your mother home and to introduce me to some other folks. I think it's their way of getting to know the doc."

11

I wanted to jump up and down. I was so happy. My father was usually much stricter, but I was guessing that he didn't mind because I'd mentioned Margie would be there.

I nodded my head. "Yes, Daddy. I won't be out too late. Margie is picking me up in about two hours."

My father smiled. Then, he turned and headed into the living room. I peeked back toward my mother.

She was smiling at me. "By that smile on your face, I'm going to guess that this has something to do with a certain young man with the last name of Mathews?"

I felt the blush on my cheeks as I quickly looked away. "Nope. I actually kind of like this guy named Billy. At least he talked to me while Mr. Mathews talked to Margie. Margie said they are best friends, but clearly, I think he likes her." I tried to sound convincing, but I had a feeling I failed.

"So, this Billy…you like him then?" Mother asked as she dropped the beef in the pan.

The sizzling sound caused me to look at the pan and then back at her.

Do I really like Billy? He is no Garrett Mathews. I shrugged my shoulders. "I don't know. He's okay. I just really want to hang out and meet some new friends. The last thing I want to do is get involved with a boy. I just want to focus on my last year of high school and get ready for college."

My mother smiled. "I like your thinking. Schoolwork first. You will have plenty of time to date."

I nodded my head and noticed the uneasy feeling moving through my body. I pushed it aside as I continued helping my mother with dinner.

The moment I got out of Margie's car, I started scanning the whole area. We had stopped and picked up Margie's friend Peggy on the way. Now, Peggy and Anna were whispering about some boy who had walked by. Anna was already making plans to sneak off with him.

"Of course, if I happen to get lucky with Garrett again, I won't need that cowboy."

I spun around and looked at her. "Get lucky with Garrett?" I asked.

Anna gave me a wicked grin. "Yeah, you know, have sex, do the deed, swap spit…and other bodily fluids."

"Knock it off, Anna. That's gross, and we don't want to hear about how you have a problem with keeping your legs together," Margie said as she hooked her arm with mine and started walking.

"Eat your heart out, Marg. Your cherry won't ever get popped at the rate you're going," Anna called out.

Peggy started laughing.

I turned to face both of them and then looked back at Margie. "Are you really going to let her talk to you like that? What a bitch."

Margie started laughing. "Hearing you swear is weird, Emma Rose," she said as we walked up to the concession stand. "Don't worry about Anna. She has been after Garrett for some time, but he doesn't want anything to do with her."

I glanced over my shoulder and then straight ahead. The moment I saw Garrett, I sucked in a breath of air and stopped walking.

"What's wrong?" Margie asked.

I tried to look away, but his eyes had caught mine. Then, he smiled, and I couldn't help but smile back. When I remembered what Anna had said, my smile vanished. Garrett looked confused at my sudden change of moods. I noticed Billy was also standing there, talking to another guy.

"Did Garrett really have sex with Anna?" I asked as I looked at Margie.

Her eyes widened, and she peeked over toward Garrett and then back at me. "Does it matter?" she asked.

Great. He did.

"To me, it does," I said.

Margie took in a deep breath and slowly let it out. "Yes, he slept with her, but before you go judging him, Anna has slept with every guy she has ever laid eyes on."

My heart dropped, and I looked back at Garrett. He was now talking to some brunette paper shaker. He threw his head back as he laughed, and my heart started beating faster as I balled my hands up into fists.

"Emma Rose? What is wrong? You look like you are ready to hurt someone," Margie said, pulling me out of my moment of rage.

What is wrong with me? I shook my head and tried to smile. "Nothing is wrong at all. Shall we?" I motioned for her to walk ahead of me.

As we walked up to Garrett, Billy, and Wayne, they all stopped talking. They turned to face us, and they each grinned. My heart skipped a beat when I saw Garrett's smile, but then he turned and kissed the paper shaker on the cheek. My heart stopped, and I felt like I couldn't breathe. When Garrett looked back at me, I shot him a dirty look before turning to look at Billy. He had a beautiful smile, and it made his green eyes brighten—but it didn't have the same effect on me as stupid Garrett Mathews. I smiled at Billy as I stopped just in front of all three guys.

Margie grabbed my arm and turned me to a guy I'd never seen before. He was the tallest out of Billy, Garrett, and Wayne. He was built just a bit bigger than Garrett, who had muscles that made me weak in the knees.

Farm boys were always built the best—or at least that was what Margie always said.

"Hey, Emma. How are you?" Garrett asked.

I gave him the dirtiest look I possibly could. "Fine."

I turned to Billy and flashed him the sweetest smile. When he smiled back, it hit me. I was flirting with him just because I was mad at Garrett.

What are you doing, Emma?

Margie cleared her throat and turned me back toward the taller guy. "Emma, this is Raymond. Raymond, this is my cousin, Emma."

I nodded my head and grinned. "It's nice to meet you."

"Nice to meet you, too, Emma. Welcome to Mason," he said as he gave me the biggest smile I'd ever seen.

I couldn't help but laugh. "That's the best welcome I've gotten yet," I said with a giggle.

"That's my boyfriend—always so welcoming," Peggy said as she jumped into Raymond's arms.

When they began kissing, I had to look away, and the first thing I saw was Garrett staring at me. He gave me a weak smile, and when I didn't return one, a confused look came over his face.

"So, what movie are we going to see?" Anna asked as she walked up to Garrett.

I couldn't help but notice how Wayne moved himself in between Garrett and Anna, and a part of me was happy to see that Garrett clearly didn't want to be around Anna.

Billy took a bite of popcorn. "Well, considering the only two movies playing are *The King and I* and *Lady and the Tramp*, I'm going with *The King and I.*"

I did a little hop. "*Lady and the Tramp?* I've been wanting to see that."

Everyone turned and looked at me with their mouths dropped open—that was, everyone but Garrett. He was smiling that stupid smile at me. I didn't want to, but I smiled back slightly before I looked away.

"Are you kidding?" Anna said. "You're kidding, right?"

I just looked at everyone and gave a small smile.

"Sorry, I'm not watching a cartoon," Anna said, grabbing Wayne's hand and pulling him off toward his car.

Billy gave me a slight smile and said, "Yeah, I'm not watching a baby show."

I glanced at Margie, who was just about to say something, when Garrett said, "I'll watch it with you."

My heart started beating faster as I asked, "Alone?"

He tried to hold back his smile, but he failed miserably. "I promise, I won't bite."

I thought about the girl he had just kissed a few minutes ago. "What about your little friend?" I asked, sounding like a total snob.

"What friend?" Garrett asked.

"Please," I said as I faced Margie. "Marg…please?"

Margie rolled her eyes. "Fine, but I'm not going to enjoy it. Garrett, you want to go in my car or yours?"

Wait, why is he coming?

"Garrett can't come!" I shouted out.

I looked at Billy and Garrett, and they exchanged a look. Garrett seemed devastated, and Billy seemed almost relieved.

"Why can't Garrett come? He just said he would go see the movie with us," Margie said.

Garrett took a few steps closer to us. "Yeah. Why can't I go?"

The way he was looking at me was driving me insane. *Why does my body react this way around him? I really don't like him. I do not like him.*

I squared off my shoulders and dug deep down inside. "You can't go because I'm sure your little friend, the one you kissed earlier, would be upset that you're watching a movie with two girls." It was out of my mouth before I could even stop it.

Garrett looked totally confused before recognition crossed his face. "You mean Melanie?"

I didn't say a word. I wanted to scream, *Yes, the cheerleader, you idiot!*

"The girl I kissed good-bye on the cheek? That's my cousin, Melanie."

I felt the heat move up my neck, across my cheeks, to my ears, and all the way up to my forehead. *His cousin? I got jealous over his cousin? I can't believe I got jealous at all.*

I watched as Garrett took in my every move. He wanted to smile. I knew he did. Billy and Raymond started laughing as they walked off with Peggy.

Garrett gave me a sexy smirk before he walked toward Margie's car.

I stood there, trying to regain my thoughts. I wanted to crawl under a rock. I'd let this guy get me so worked up that I totally just embarrassed myself in front of everyone.

Margie grabbed my arm and started leading me to her car. "Emma Rose Birk, were you jealous?" she whispered.

"No! Not at all."

We got into Margie's car and drove to the screen. By the time we ordered drinks, I was feeling somewhat better. Garrett and Margie got out of her car, and they climbed up to lie on top of the hood, leaning against the glass. There was plenty of room for all of us. When I went to climb on, Margie moved to the middle. She kept talking to Garrett about the football team this year and how good they were going to be. My heart sank when it dawned on me that if I had just kept my mouth shut about being alone with Garrett, I would be next to Garrett and not Margie.

I couldn't even enjoy the movie. The whole time, I was daydreaming about what Garrett smelled like, the feel of his touch, and what his favorite movie, favorite song, and favorite thing to eat was. When Margie and Garrett both let out a laugh, I was snapped out of my daydreams.

I glanced over at the two of them. Garrett was honestly trying to watch the movie, but Margie wouldn't shut up. She'd said she didn't have feelings for Garrett, but it sure seemed like she did to me. I couldn't even concentrate on the movie with all her talking. Leaning up, Garrett looked over at me and smiled. I wasn't sure why, but I turned away.

I just want to go home. "I'm not feeling so well, Margie. I hate to ask, but do you think you could take me home?"

Garrett slid off the hood and walked over to me. "What's wrong? Do feel like you're going to be sick? Should I get you some water?"

I tried to smile and thank him, but all that came out was, "No. I just want to go home."

"Really, Em? It's still so early, and I hate heading home so early."

I looked over at my cousin as she took a sip of her soda. "Yes, Margie, really! I feel sick."

Garrett lightly touched my arm, and I jerked away, surprised by the strange feeling running through me.

He quickly held up his hands and took a step back. "I was just going to help you down."

My heart was beating so hard in my chest that I was sure he could hear it. I held out my hand, and then he took it and helped me down. I had the strangest sensation that I just wanted to walk right into his arms.

Then, Margie walked in between us. "Come on, Emma. I'll take you home."

I smiled slightly at Garrett, and he gave me a smile that about dropped me to my knees.

I really need to stay away from him—far, far away from him.

3 Garrett

"Did you get all the chores done, Garrett?" my father asked as he walked into the kitchen.

I was sitting down, drinking a glass of tea, after I'd spent most of the morning mending a fence. "Yes, sir, I did."

My father smiled and nodded his head. "You taking care of your heifer? Treating her good and loving her more?"

I let out a chuckle. My father had a way with words, and for him to use the same advice for a female cow as he did with a female girl made me laugh. He would always tell me, *Son, when you find the right girl, treat her good and love her more.*

"Yes, sir, I am. I'm treating her like a princess."

My mother rolled her eyes and continued cutting up apples.

My father laughed. "Good. Now, help your mother here with the fruit while I go clean up. Our guests will be here soon."

I walked over to where my mother was. I grabbed an apple and began cutting it up. "So, who is coming over again?"

My mother smiled. "The new doctor in town. We wanted to welcome him and his family to Mason. Your father and I know the doctor's wife. She went to school with us. It will be good to see her again."

I nodded my head and cut up a few more apples before my father walked up next to me.

"Garrett, we need to talk."

He motioned for me to head outside. I set the knife down next to the apple and followed my father down to the barn. We walked in, and he pointed for me to have a seat.

"So, what is this I hear about you running around with Anna King?"

I looked up at my father. "Excuse me, sir?"

"Garrett, I'm not stupid. I was your age, and I did the same things you're doing. I'm not going to sit here and preach to you about how you can't have sex until you're married. Hell, I was fourteen when I lost my virginity to my sister's best friend."

I rolled my eyes and looked away. "Dad, did I really need to know that?"

My father let out a chuckle as he sat down on a barrel and looked at me. "Garrett, don't be running around with the town whore. She's gonna end up getting pregnant, and the poor schmuck who ends up marrying that girl will be struggling for the rest of his life because she is like her mother. They come from money, and Anna's gonna want the world on a silver platter."

My father was sitting here, talking to me about our school tramp, and all I could think of was how in the hell he knew I'd had sex with Anna.

"Dad, how did you know?"

My father smiled. "Billy's daddy saw you and Anna sneaking off. He followed y'all and saw you going into her house. He knew her parents were gone for the weekend."

I instantly felt my face go red.

"It took me so long to talk to you about it because...well, honestly, son, I just didn't know how to talk to you about it. I do want you to be careful. Son, someday, you're going to meet a girl who will change everything. She'll make you want to be a better man."

My father shook his head and smiled. I knew he was thinking about my mother.

"She'll be the reason you wake up every morning and push through another day. She'll be your everything."

I nodded my head and kicked the dirt. "How will I know it's her, Dad?"

He smiled so big. "Trust me, you'll know. You won't be able to think clearly when she is anywhere near you. You'll find yourself having a hard time breathing when she walks into a room. You'll think about her all the time, and you'll want to do nothing but make her happy for the rest of your lives."

"When did you know Mom was the one?" I asked.

The light in his eyes danced. "The first moment she ever looked at me, I couldn't move. I couldn't breathe. I knew right then."

I thought back to yesterday when I'd walked into the drugstore, and my reaction had been the very same when Emma looked at me. I cleared my throat and got the nerve to ask the next question. "How old were you and Mom when you first met?"

He chuckled and winked at me. "I was fifteen years old."

"Fifteen? You knew you were going to be with Mom for the rest of your life at the age of fifteen?"

He nodded his head and stood up. "Garrett, love doesn't know age." He turned and walked out of the barn.

I sat there for a few minutes and thought about Emma. She was so sweet and innocent, such a firecracker. I smiled and shook my head, remembering how she'd reacted when she thought I had kissed another girl.

Next time I see Emma Rose Birk, I'm asking her out to eat.

I heard a car pulling up, so I stood up and walked over to Mary Lou—my paint horse I'd gotten for Christmas from my parents. I gave her a good scratch before heading out to meet the new doctor. I turned the corner and started making my way back to our white clapboard house, and then I stopped in my tracks.

Emma?

What is Emma doing on our ranch? Oh shit. She's fixin' to eat dinner in my house…at my kitchen table!

I just stood there, unable to move. She was dressed in a purple poodle skirt and white collared shirt. Her hair was pulled up into a ponytail with a purple-and-white piece of fabric tied in her hair. She was smiling as our parents were greeting each other. My father looked up, and when his eyes met mine, I was almost one hundred percent sure he saw the fear in my eyes.

He smiled and shook his head. "Garrett? Come on over and make the proper introductions."

Emma turned and looked at me. Her smile instantly faded. My heart dropped. I was beginning to think that Emma Birk didn't feel the same way about me as I did her. Maybe Billy had been right. Maybe he was the better guy for her. I flashed her a smile and started to walk toward everyone.

I put out my hand as I introduced myself to Emma's father. "Hello, sir. I'm Garrett Mathews. It's a pleasure to have you here in Mason." Looking at Emma's mother, I took her hand in mine and kissed the back of it. "Mrs. Birk, it's an honor to meet you."

She let out a little laugh. "My goodness, you have certainly raised him right, Thomas and Julia."

My parents both chuckled. I turned to Emma and held out my hand for hers, but she didn't move.

I dropped my hand to my side. "It's a pleasure to see you again, Emma."

She gave me a tight smile and looked away.

Yep, I don't need any more signs. Emma Birk is clearly not interested in me one bit.

Fall 1956

I walked off the football field and let out a curse. I was sick of chasing after someone who couldn't care less about me. When I glanced up into the stands after the game, I couldn't help but notice that Michael Draft was sitting next to Emma, talking to her. She was laughing and seemed to be having fun.

I walked up and asked her out—again. And she turned me down—yet again.

I threw my helmet down and slammed my locker. Someone hit me on the shoulder, and I turned to see Billy standing there.

"She say no again?"

I nodded my head. "Yes. I'm about ready to just give up. I've never chased after a girl as hard as I have with her."

Billy let out a laugh. "That's why I moved on weeks ago."

I smiled as I sat down, and then I looked up at him. "Margie, huh?"

His face turned red. "Don't even start with me, Mathews. It's just one date to see how it goes."

I nodded my head and laughed. "If you say so, but I'm pretty sure the two of you have had a thing for each other for some time now."

After I changed, I made my way out of the locker room and to the parking lot. I saw Emma leaning against Margie's car, and Michael was still talking to her. When she looked over at me, I didn't give her my normal smile. Her smile faded a bit, and I turned my head as I walked toward my truck. I didn't have the energy today to deal with any more rejection from Emma.

Reaching my truck, I threw my stuff in the bed and opened the door. One quick look behind me showed that Emma was watching me. When she lifted up her hand and waved good-bye, I ignored her and jumped in.

I slammed my head back against my seat and let out a curse word. "Now? Now, she decides to give me some sort of response." I shook my head and closed my eyes as I thought back to the Halloween dance when I asked her out.

"Emma, you look darling as a ghost!" Margie said with a laugh.

I smiled as I watched Emma come skipping out of her house. She was dressed up as a ghost for a Halloween party we were all going to.

"Thanks! My mother helped me with it," Emma said as I held the door open for her.

The whole way to Peggy's house, Margie and Emma talked about school.

I rolled my eyes and said, "Can y'all, for once, not talk about school?"

Margie laughed. "Who are you going to ask to dance with first, Garrett?"

I smiled. "Emma."

Emma let out a laugh. "I think I'm going to sit out dancing today since I would have a hard time dancing in this outfit."

I shook my head and said, "We'll see."

Three hours later and after ten attempts to get Emma to dance with me, she finally gave in. "I Want You, I Need You, I Love You" by Elvis Presley began playing, and I walked up and took Emma's hand in mine. I brought her out to the makeshift dance floor. She didn't say a word, so neither did I. When the song ended, I pulled back and looked into her eyes.

She smiled slightly. "Thank you for the dance, but I really need to get back home. I have a test I need to study for."

I closed my eyes and quickly opened them. "Emma—"

"Garrett, please. I'm not interested in dating anyone. I like you, but—"

"But what? Emma, I really like you…a lot, and I'm not going to stop asking you out until you say yes."

Her smile faded. "Garrett, you're wasting your time."

She turned and walked away, and I stood there gutted—again.

Someone knocking on my window snapped me out of my memory. I looked over to see Billy standing there.

I rolled the window down. "What's up?"

"Party down at the wall tonight. You coming?" Billy asked with a smile.

I glanced back at Emma, and she was no longer looking in my direction.

"Who's all going?" I asked, not looking at Billy.

"Everyone! Raymond scored some alcohol."

I looked back to Emma as Michael was reaching down, saying something in Emma's ear. Emma nodded her head, and as he turned and walked away, she looked over toward my truck.

What game is she playing?

"Is Emma going?" I asked as I watched her get into Margie's car.

Margie called out for Billy.

Billy glanced back and yelled, "Give me two seconds, and I'll be right there." He turned back and placed his hand on my shoulder. "Garrett, don't stop fighting for her. Margie said she knows for a fact that Emma likes you."

I gave him a weak smile. "Yeah, I don't think so, but whatever. I'll go tonight."

He said, "Yes! By the way, Emma will be there."

I started up my truck and put it in drive. "I'm sure she will. Looks like her and Michael just made plans."

Billy took a few steps back, and I floored the gas, peeling out before making my way home.

I spent the whole night watching Emma talk to everyone but me. I ran my hand through my hair and took a drink of beer. My father was going to kill me for drinking, but I didn't care. I needed to let loose once in a while. I had been sitting on the old rock wall, watching everyone dance and talk. I even watched some couples make out before sneaking off to probably have sex in a car or in the woods. Wall parties were rare, but when we did have them, everyone would go all out. Booze, sex, and more booze were usually involved.

Billy's truck was pulled up and parked near the wall, and the radio was blasting so loud that it sounded as if it were right by my ear. I jumped off the rock wall and made my way over to Raymond to get another beer.

"Garrett! Man, awesome playing on the football field tonight," Wayne called out. He was already on his way to being drunk.

"You driving, Wayne?" I asked.

He shook his head. "Nope. Anna is driving, and she knows better than to drink anything, or her daddy will take her precious car away."

I laughed and nodded my head. I quickly looked around and saw Emma talking to Margie, Peggy, and Billy. I made my way over, and I heard "Love Me Tender" by Elvis starting to play.

"Emma, would you like to dance?" I asked, expecting her to say no.

She smiled and nodded her head. She held out her hand, and I took it in mine. I moved us a little bit away from everyone. I brought her into my arms and held her the closest I'd ever had her.

"Why do you fight me so much, Emma?" I felt her stiffen in my arms.

"I don't know what you mean," she said as she pulled back and looked into my eyes.

I smiled and pulled her to me again. As I listened to the song, I prayed she would give in to me.

The song ended, and Emma pulled back slightly and smiled.

"Emma...I've been in—"

Then, someone started yelling out, "Fire!"

I quickly looked up and saw Hank Hunter running toward us.

He stopped right in front of me. "A wildfire is heading straight toward your family's cattle ranch."

"What?" Emma and I said at the same time.

I took off running to my truck as I heard Billy yelling at Margie to get home. I didn't even stop to think about anything or anyone else. I needed to get to the ranch.

The next six hours were spent fighting the flames to keep them from jumping the river and hitting our ranch. I wasn't sure how we'd managed to get that fire under control, but we did. I was sitting against a tree when I felt someone kick my boot. I opened my eyes and saw my father standing there.

"I'm proud of you, Garrett. You showed me today what I've always known."

I slowly stood up and smiled. His words meant more to me than my father would ever know.

"I'd rather die than see anything happen to this ranch," I said.

He threw his head back and laughed. "Spoken like a true rancher. Now, get your butt home. Get yourself cleaned up, and get some sleep. Your mother is probably worried sick, and when she sees your face, she is probably going to get after me for letting you get hurt."

I nodded as I touched my forehead, and I let out a gasp. I brought my hand down and saw that it was covered in blood. "I didn't even know I was hurt," I said.

"Get on home, son," my father said.

I was not about to stand there and argue. I was exhausted and more than ready to get some sleep.

I made it back to the house and climbed out of my truck. I glanced up to see a bunch of women gathered on our porch. I didn't even bother to scan them all to see who they were. I just needed a hot bath and my bed.

Then, I heard her laughing. I walked up the stairs and saw Emma doing something to Billy's arm. I knew he had cut it pretty bad earlier, and my father had told him to head here and have it cleaned up. When I saw Emma place her hand on the side of Billy's face as she smiled at him, my heart dropped to my stomach. I was frozen, unable to move at all.

She turned, and her eyes met mine. She was still smiling, but when she saw me, her smile immediately dropped. She brought her hands up to her mouth and shook her head. She walked up to me, and she was about to reach out and touch my face when I took a step back.

"Don't touch me," I whispered.

She looked confused. "What?"

I looked back at Billy, who looked at me funny.

"Garrett, oh my gosh! You're bleeding," Emma said as she reached out to me again.

I took another step back and bumped into someone. The next thing I knew, my mother was all over me. She rushed me over to Emma's father. She never left my side as Dr. Birk stitched up my forehead.

"Garrett, go clean up, and get some rest," Dr. Birk said.

I nodded my head. "Yes, sir." I made my way past everyone and headed into the house. As I began climbing the stairs, I heard the screen door shut.

"Garrett?"

I turned to see Emma standing there.

"I just wanted to say I'm glad you're okay and that the fire didn't make it to y'all's ranch."

I didn't have the energy anymore. I smiled slightly at her and said, "Thanks," before turning and making my way upstairs.

I'd never been so tired in my life.

"Garrett, please go do something with your friends. It's your Christmas break, and all you've done is help your father with the ranch. You need to have fun. Billy called and asked—"

I stood up as I grabbed my cowboy hat and looked at my mother. "I'm sorry, Mom. I don't mean to be disrespectful, but I'm not interested in doing anything with my friends." I started making my way to the front door.

"Is this because of Emma? Garrett, is that what's bothering you?"

I stopped just short of the door. Just hearing her name hurt my heart. Both my mother and father had seen how I'd reacted to Emma last summer, and they were convinced I was head over heels for her. It was too bad Emma didn't feel the same way.

"No," I said as I opened the door. I gently closed it behind me, and I made my way down to the barn.

I just needed to ride. I needed to go for a ride and clear my head. I would be leaving and playing football for Texas A&M next year, and I would forget all about Emma. At least, that was what I kept telling myself.

After I saddled up Jack, I hopped on him and took off to my favorite spot on the ranch. Once there, I jumped off of Jack and let him roam while I went and sat against the giant oak tree. I loved it here. It was quiet, and I could really think. I closed my eyes and thought back to the other day.

Billy walked up to me and gave me a weak smile.

I smiled back as I put my books away in my locker. "What's going on? You look like someone died," I said with a chuckle.

Billy looked down. "Garrett, are you ever going to ask Emma out again?"

My heart dropped, and I knew what he was about to say. "I've asked her out a dozen times, and every time, she says no."

He looked me in the eyes and then glanced back down. "This morning, Michael asked her out to go skating."

God, please no. "What did she say?"

"Yes."

I stumbled backward just a bit and hit my locker. "What?"

I looked past Billy, only to see Emma and Peggy walking up. Both girls were laughing.

"You're going out with Michael?" I asked before I could stop myself.

Emma's smile faded, and she quickly glared at Billy and then turned back to me. "Um…"

I shook my head and let out a laugh. "I've been asking you out for months, and you keep turning me down. He asked you one time, and you agreed?"

She swallowed hard and stared into my eyes. I almost thought I saw regret in her eyes, but I knew that was wrong. This girl had been pushing me away since the moment I met her.

"Um…well…"

I pushed off against my locker and stood right in front of her. "I got the message loud and clear."

As I turned to walk away, Emma began calling out for me, but I kept going until I was out the door and to my truck. I jumped in and took off for home. For the first time in my life, I cried, and it was for losing something I never even had in the first place.

"Garrett?"

I slowly opened my eyes to see Margie sitting on top of my mother's horse.

"Marg? What are you doing here?"

She slid off the horse and walked over to sit down next to me. "Wayne, Billy, and Raymond asked me to come talk to you. I guess you haven't been hanging out with them very much, and they were getting worried about you."

I laughed and shook my head. "I'm fine. I certainly don't need them sending you to check up on me."

"You're fine? Really, Garrett? We never see you anymore. You go to school, football practice, and then home. You never come out or hang out with us. What is going on?"

I let out a long breath. I wasn't in the mood to get into this with Margie. "Marg, I'm fine. I've just been busy. I'm trying to help my father with the ranch and—"

"Bullshit. What is your father going to do when you go to college? I know he has a few ranch hands who help him. You're just avoiding her."

I snapped my head over and looked at Margie. She always knew my true feelings. Everyone thought we had something going on, but she really was like my sister.

I looked away and mumbled, "I don't know what you mean. I'm not avoiding anyone."

Margie jumped up and kicked the shit out of my leg. I flew up and began jumping around, holding my leg.

"What in the hell, Margie? Why did you kick me? You bitch!"

She stood there with her hands on her hips, trying to look serious, when I knew she wanted to laugh.

"Why, Margie? I thought we were friends."

I began walking off the pain, and she followed behind me.

"Garrett, she went out with him only once."

I was pretty sure my jaw dropped. "How do you know that?"

She rolled her eyes and shook her head. "She likes you and only you. She's just afraid to admit it to herself. I think it scares her how much she likes you."

I shook my head, confused. "How do you know she likes me? I've been asking her out for months, only to have her turn me down time after time. Michael asked her out once, and she was all over it."

"It wasn't like that, Garrett. She doesn't like him like that."

I started laughing. "Then, why did she go out with him, Marg? I'm done talking about Emma Birk. I'm moving on, and I'm just going to worry about college. Emma can go out with anyone she wants. I don't care anymore."

"Right. Keep telling yourself that." She smiled just a little. "Are you going to the sock hop tonight?"

I shook my head as I turned around and whistled to call Jack back over. Jack and my mother's horse came walking up to us. Margie and I both quietly climbed up onto each horse, and we began slowly heading back to the barn. We were silent for the next ten minutes or so.

"Please come tonight, Garrett, just to hang out with your friends. Please. I need someone to dance with."

I started laughing because Margie didn't dance. In all the time I'd known her, I'd never seen her dance.

"You gonna dance with me tonight if I go?"

She gave me an evil smile and said, "Only if I get to dance to that Elvis song you like so much."

I threw my head back and laughed. "'That's All Right' is the name of the song, Margie, and Elvis is the coolest cat around."

Margie chortled and nodded. We continued riding back in silence, and the only image that kept running through my mind was of Emma dancing with another guy. I would have to really keep it together since just thinking about it made me mad.

After Margie and I took care of the horses, I walked her to her car.

Before she got in, she gave me a serious look. "You know, I never thought I'd ever see you giving up on something you truly wanted, Garrett. Please don't give up."

I smiled weakly. "Yeah, I know, but it's hard to fight for someone who doesn't feel the same." I glanced up and saw my mother standing on the porch.

Margie turned around and gave my mother a wave before getting into her car. I shut the door and leaned down to say good-bye.

"She really doesn't like him, and she only went out with him the one time. And, Garrett?"

"Yeah, Marg?"

She looked away and then back at me. "Please don't stay away from your friends."

I gave Margie a weak smile and nodded my head. "I promise, I'll be there tonight."

She smiled and wiped a tear away. I wasn't sure why she had gotten upset, and I began to worry that she knew more than she had told me about Emma. I stood there and watched as Margie drove off before I turned to face my mother.

"Garrett, was Margie upset? Did you say something to make her upset?"

Walking up to my mother, I shook my head. "No. To be honest with you, I'm not really sure what's going on anymore, Mama. The only thing I do know is that women were placed on this earth to drive men insane, and I don't really give a shit about them anymore."

My mother placed her hands on her hips. "Garrett Thomas Mathews, I should wash your mouth out with soap."

"Sorry, Mama. I've never felt so twisted in my life. I best go help Dad with some stuff, so I can head to the dance this evening."

She nodded her head and gave me a knowing smile. That was one of the things I loved about my parents. They trusted me and knew when not to push. I didn't want to tell my mother that I had been chasing Emma Birk for months, only to have her turn me down time and time again before going out with a dick like Michael.

I turned and headed to the barn. My head was spinning, and I couldn't figure out what I should do. Tonight, I was either going to walk away from the idea of Emma Birk or give it one last go.

I had a funny feeling this night was going to change the rest of my life. I just didn't know if the night would change my future for the better or for the worse.

4 Emma

Margie hadn't been acting right since she walked into my bedroom and sat down on my bed.

"What did you do today?" I asked as I looked in my closet to grab a skirt.

"I, um…I went to see Garrett."

I stopped for a brief second to catch my breath. Just hearing his name did weird things to my stomach. *Play it cool, Emma.* "Oh, really? What did you go see him for?" I tried to sound like I was not really interested in her answer.

"His mom called my mom, asking for me to come talk to him. I told him the guys were worried about him. She has been worried about him because he has been pretty much sticking to himself ever since…"

I closed my eyes and held my breath. The moment I'd agreed to go out with Michael, Garrett had stopped talking to me. He'd stopped doing pretty much everything, and I knew his friends all blamed me.

I slowly turned around. "Ever since what?"

Margie bit down on her lip and tilted her head. "Can I ask you something?"

My hands started sweating, and I could hear my heart beating in my ears. I slowly nodded my head.

She took a deep breath and said, "Do you like Garrett?"

That was not what I had expected her to ask me. "Excuse me?"

She stood up and put her hands on her hips. "I see the way you look at him. You practically have to catch your breath every time he walks into a room or comes anywhere near you. Why are you fighting your feelings for him when he has been doing nothing but trying to win your heart?"

I stood there with my mouth dropped open. *How dare she assume such a thing!* But every word she'd said was true. I turned and grabbed the first skirt I could find. It didn't really matter how I looked at this point. I knew Garrett wouldn't be at the sock hop, and I'd already told Michael I wasn't interested in going with him.

"I'm not interested in a relationship, especially one with Garrett Mathews. The way he has been looking at me lately is like he hates me. He doesn't smile at me anymore, and he wouldn't even let me touch him when he got hurt from the fire. Besides, earlier today, Anna mentioned that she was fooling around with Garrett again."

Margie's mouth dropped open, and she just stared at me. "Do you hear yourself? Honestly, Emma, you are coming up with every excuse under the sun to deny your feelings for Garrett! And what in the hell do you mean about Anna? That was months ago!"

I shook my head. "No, Anna said she—"

"I don't give a crap what Anna said. Garrett is not interested in her. He is interested in you! Why are you denying how you feel for him? You are totally pushing him away."

Now, I was getting angry...but I wasn't sure who I was angry with—Margie or myself. I'd been so stupid all these months.

"Why do you care anyway, Marg? Let's talk about you and your sex life, shall we?"

The door flew open, and Peggy came walking in. She quickly shut the door behind her.

"You are thicker than a five-dollar malt, Emma. I could hear you down the hall. What if your parents heard y'all talking in here? I don't even want to think about what your mother and father would do to you, Margie. You'd be wearing more than that virgin pin you have on all the time. Now, what is this about Margie's sex life?"

I looked at Margie and whispered, "How can you even wear a virgin pin when you're not a virgin?"

Peggy started jumping up and down. "Oh my, when did you lose your cherry? And who was the lucky bastard?"

"Shh! For the love of all things good, Peggy, shut up!" Margie said as she grabbed both of us and pushed us down on the bed. She looked right at me. "I can wear it because I am a virgin."

Peggy's whole body slumped down, and she fell back onto my bed. "Damn, I thought we were going to get a good story out of this."

I stared at Margie. "I thought y'all had sex."

Peggy sat up quickly. "What? You and Billy finally bumped uglies?"

Margie hit Peggy on the arm as she sat down. "Shut up, Peggy. We are not talking about me! We are talking about Emma denying her feelings for Garrett."

Peggy winked at me. "Now, come on, Emma. Have you looked at Garrett's body lately? Tell me you haven't dreamed of wrapping your legs around that boy."

I jumped up off the bed. I let out a gasp and yelled, "You have a boyfriend! You can't talk that way! And you most certainly can't talk that way about Garrett. What dreams I have about him are none of your business!"

"Emma Rose, what is all the yelling about? Is everything okay?" my mother asked after opening my bedroom door.

Never taking my eyes off of the two giggling girls on my bed, I said, "Everything is fine, Mother. We're just playing around."

"That's fine. Just keep it down. Inside voices, okay?"

I nodded my head as I glanced back at my mother, smiling sweetly. I let out a giggle. "Okay, Mom. Sorry."

She grinned and shut the door. I quickly looked back at Margie. For some crazy reason, I pictured my legs around Garrett while he was making love to me. I felt my cheeks instantly flush. Peggy and Margie both started laughing.

"I'm getting a good story after all," Peggy whispered.

Margie stood up and dropped open her mouth. "Oh my gosh. You *do* want Garrett, don't you?"

I started to shake my head as I took a step back and bumped into my dresser.

Margie started jumping up and down. "Tell me about your dreams with Garrett, Em. You know he's coming to the dance."

I let out a gasp.

Peggy said, "Yep, this just got really good."

I spun around and looked at Peggy. "Please. No comments from the peanut gallery."

Margie smiled. "Emma?"

I rolled my eyes and whispered, "Fine. I might have had a dream…or two about Garrett."

I turned and walked the few steps to my bed. I face-planted onto it and began yelling into the mattress as Peggy and Margie did the same. We all rolled over onto our backs and looked at the ceiling.

Then, I sat up, turned, and looked at Margie. "Was Billy the guy who made you give yourself an orgasm because he turned you on so much?"

Peggy sat up and yelled out, "What?"

I slammed my hands over my mouth.

Margie sat up with a shocked look on her face. "Emma Rose! I told you that as a secret because you said you felt like that after you met Garrett!"

"This just got so much better. Have you wanted to do the same, Emma?" Peggy said.

I stood up and looked back and forth between them. "Um…" I dropped open my mouth. "I'm not, um…I'm not answering that."

Peggy grabbed my hand and pulled me back down onto the bed. "Please. We've already established you have a thing for Garrett, and he makes your little girl parts tingle."

I rolled my eyes and pushed Peggy back. Margie started laughing, and then I started laughing. Before I knew it, we had all fallen back onto the bed, laughing until we were almost crying.

When we finally got ourselves under control, I let out a sigh. "Okay. Tonight, I'll tell Garrett that I like him…maybe."

Peggy said, "Emma, you are going to march your little self up to Garrett and tell him how you feel. Better yet, just ask him to dance. He won't expect that. Make it a slow song, and dance as far away from the chaperones as you can get. If the coast is clear, push yourself into him. Make him so crazy that after the dance, he has to flog his log."

I sat up quickly and looked at Peggy. "You did not just say that!"

Peggy smiled and winked at me, and then we all started chortling. We laughed for at least another ten minutes before my mother called for us to stop goofing around and get ready for the dance. We frantically began looking through my closet for the perfect dresses to wear. After picking them out, we fixed each other's hair and put just a tad bit of rouge on.

When I looked at myself in the mirror, I couldn't help but smile. I had my favorite flower-print skirt on with a white collared shirt. I slipped on my saddle shoes and looked in the mirror one more time.

Peggy came up behind me and placed her chin on my shoulder. "You ready to make Garrett Mathews the happiest guy at the dance?"

I laughed and pushed her away.

She tilted her head and gave me a wicked smile. "Then, are you ready to change Garrett Mathews's world?"

I felt my cheeks blushing, and I closed my eyes. I could almost feel his lips on my neck and his hands on my body. *Yep, I'm totally ready.*

"Shit, I'm going to take it you're ready. Please open your eyes. It pains me to think what your ass is thinking about right now."

I giggled and looked at Margie as she was walking out of my bathroom. She looked breathtaking. Her brown curls looked perfect, and the little bit of makeup she had on highlighted her beauty.

"Shall we, ladies?" Margie said as she walked past us, wiggling her car keys.

We giggled like little girls all the way down the stairs. I kissed my parents good-bye, and then the girls and I headed out to Margie's car. I couldn't wait to see Garrett, and my sweaty palms were evidence of that.

"Stop fidgeting, Emma. Everything is going to be fine. This night is going to change your future," Peggy said with a wink.

When we walked into the high school gym, "Rock Around the Clock" by Bill Haley and His Comets was playing, and everyone was dancing. I instantly wanted to dance. I loved dancing, and I would do it all the time if I got the chance. Peggy yelled out and ran into Raymond's arms. I smiled and shook my head. Those two were for sure in love. I looked behind Raymond and saw Michael.

"Hey, Emma," Michael said as he walked up to me.

"Michael, can we step outside, so we can talk?" I asked.

He nodded his head. "Sure, it's a beautiful night, and I actually wanted to talk to you, too."

It was pretty warm for being December in Texas, but something in the air gave me a chill.

I turned and looked at Michael. I didn't want to give him the chance to start the conversation, so I just started talking, "Michael, I'm so sorry. I didn't mean to lead you on by going out with you. Honestly...I have feelings for someone else." I couldn't believe I'd just blurted that out.

Michael closed his eyes and smiled. When he opened them, he said, "Thank God, Emma. I just didn't feel a connection. I didn't want to be a jerk and just drop you, but...I kind of like someone else, too."

We both started laughing.

"Emma, I'm glad you are finally admitting your feelings for Garrett."

I stopped smiling. "What? How did you know I was talking about Garrett?"

Michael shook his head and grinned. "It's hard not to notice. Anytime he is near, you can't keep your eyes off of him, and the same goes for him. I know you only went out with me to hide from your feelings."

I nodded my head. "Well, starting right now, I'm not hiding anymore."

Michael laughed. "Me either."

I giggled. "Then, get in there and go ask a girl to dance!"

He grabbed me and quickly hugged me. When we stepped back from each other, I glanced toward the door and saw Garrett standing there. My smile faded when I saw the hurt on his face. I guessed that Michael must have seen Garrett, too, as I noticed how he'd tensed up.

"Garrett, it's not what you think," I said.

Garrett gave us a weak smile and turned to walk back into the gym.

"Let me go talk to him," Michael said.

I grabbed his arm. "No, I need to be the one to talk to him. Thank you though."

I ran up the steps and made my way into the gym. I looked around until I found Garrett. He was leaning against the wall, trying to look like he was listening to Wayne talking about something. I took a deep breath as I walked right up to him.

I smiled. "Garrett..."

He smiled, and my heart melted. Only he could make me feel this way. It would always be only Garrett. My parents would probably tell me I was crazy and that I needed to live my life before making such a decision, but in this very moment, I knew that Garrett Mathews was the only man I'd ever love, and I was done fighting it.

"Hi, Emma."

"Will you dance with me?" I bit down on my lower lip and looked up at him through my eyelashes.

My mother always told me that I had the most beautiful long lashes, and if used properly, I would be able to get any man to do anything I wanted.

He nodded his head and took my hand before leading me out to the dance floor. When he gently brought me into his arms, I felt like I was finally home. "Only You" by The Platters began playing, and I looked up into Garrett's eyes. The way he was looking at me caused me to hold my breath. It felt like a million butterflies were flying around in my stomach, and all I wanted was for him to kiss me. I quickly looked around to see who was watching us. I looked back up into his eyes, and he started laughing.

"You must be thinking the same thing I am, Buttercup," he said as he winked.

Every hair on my body stood up. I gave him a slight smile. "And what exactly are you thinking of, Mr. Mathews?"

"I wish you weren't dating Michael because I'd really love to kiss you right now."

My smile dropped, and I felt my eyes beginning to water. I licked my lips. "I'm not dating him. I told Michael that I had feelings for someone else, and he told me the same thing."

The look on Garrett's face was one I knew I would never forget for as long as I live. It almost appeared to be relief. As the song was beginning to end, Garrett looked down at my lips. I had never wanted something so badly in my entire life. I was practically willing him to kiss me. He began to lean down, but then someone started calling out his name.

"Garrett! Garrett, you have to come right away!"

We both instantly jumped back from each other. Garrett smiled that crooked smile, and I about dropped to the floor. I put my hand on my stomach to settle my nerves.

Garrett and I both turned and looked at the older gentleman running toward us. Billy, Wayne, and Raymond were running behind him.

"Uncle Pete? What's wrong?" Garrett said.

The older gentleman was attempting to catch his breath. "You've got to get to Dr. Birk's house. Your dad…he was holding his chest…fell…I drove here as fast as I could."

Garrett just looked at his uncle. "What?"

Billy walked up and quickly glanced at me before looking at Garrett. "Garrett, you need to get over to Emma's house. Uncle Pete took your dad there. Something is wrong. Um…your dad passed out while he and Pete were trying to shoe a horse."

Garrett stood there. "What do you mean, something happened?"

I grabbed Garrett's hand and began running out of the gym, pulling him behind me. I yelled back at Billy, "Who drove?"

"Garrett did."

We ran to Garrett's truck as Pete, Wayne, and Raymond ran over and jumped into what I guessed was Pete's truck.

I turned to Garrett. "Garrett, Billy needs your keys."

He looked back and forth between Billy and me. Garrett reached into his pocket and handed Billy the keys. I opened the passenger door and jumped in. Garrett followed behind me. Billy ran around and got into the driver's seat. As Billy started driving to my house, I grabbed Garrett's hand. He looked at me and gave me a weak smile.

He leaned down and said, "I'm going to give you that kiss…soon."

I smiled and nodded my head. "I'm going to hold you to that."

His smile faded, and he whispered, "Promise me."

"I promise."

Garrett looked out the window and didn't say another word. I had the most terrible feeling in my stomach. As soon as his Uncle Pete had mentioned Mr. Mathews holding his chest, I knew he must have had a heart attack. I closed my eyes and silently prayed for him to be okay.

Billy pulled up to my house, and Garrett jumped out of the truck before Billy even came to a stop. I started crying when I saw my father stepping out onto the porch. He stopped Garrett from going any farther.

I threw my hands up to my mouth and started saying, "No. Oh, please, God, no."

"Emma?" Billy grabbed my hand. "What's going on?"

I knew from the look on my father's face that something bad had happened.

"Billy…Garrett is going to need you. Go! Get out of the truck, and go!" I slid over and jumped out of the truck.

I quickly walked up to Garrett and my father. I looked through our front window and saw Mrs. Mathews. My mother was holding her while she cried.

"Garrett, your father had a heart attack," my daddy said.

I tried not to, but I started crying.

"Is he okay, Dr. Birk? Is he going to be okay?" Garrett asked, his voice breaking up.

My heart was breaking for Garrett, and I felt so incredibly helpless.

My father stepped closer to Garrett. "Garrett, I need you to listen to me, okay?"

Garrett nodded his head as he looked at my father.

"I'm sorry, son, but your father passed away. I tried everything I could to bring him back, but I just couldn't do it."

I slowly felt my body falling, and then two arms wrapped around me. When I looked up, I saw Raymond was holding me.

"No," Garrett whispered. "No. He can't leave us, Dr. Birk. He can't leave me alone like that."

My father closed his eyes and shook his head. When he opened his eyes, he looked directly at me and then back at Garrett. "Garrett, your mother needs you to be strong right now. I know what I'm asking from you is a lot. I know what it is like to lose your father at such a young age. But your mother in there has just lost the love of her life, her soul mate, and she needs you, son. She needs you. Now, I want you to walk around to the side of the house. Let it out before you go in there to see your mother."

I was taken aback by what my father had said. He was giving Garrett mere minutes to grieve the loss of his father.

Garrett nodded his head, and then he turned to me. He walked up to me and grabbed my hand. I looked back at my father, and he simply nodded at me. Garrett and I began making our way around to the side of the house. On the way, he grabbed Billy by the shirt, and Billy followed us. My heart was beating so loudly that I was sure Garrett could hear it. I tried to calm myself down.

What is Garrett going to do? How can I help him?

When we got around the house, Garrett dropped my hand and started yelling out, "No! Son of a bitch, no!"

I jumped and attempted hold back my sobs.

Over and over again, he just kept yelling out, "No!"

Billy walked up to him, and Garrett started pushing him away.

"Billy, no! My God, he was my world. Who's gonna run the ranch and take care of my mother while I'm at college?"

I swallowed as the realization hit me. By the look on his face, it must have hit Garrett as well, but he didn't say a word.

"Garrett, I'll help you. Raymond and Wayne will help, too. We're all going to help," Billy said.

Garrett put his hands on his knees and began crying. He tried to take in air at the same time. Billy looked at me with pleading eyes. I nodded as I walked over and placed my hand on Garrett's back. He jumped and stood up straight. The moment he looked into my eyes, he cried harder. He reached for me and pulled me into his arms.

He whispered, "I'm so sorry, Emma. I wanted to give you the world. I'm so sorry."

My heart slammed in my chest, and I knew exactly what he'd meant. *Our future.*

He had been thinking of our future. I didn't think it was possible that my heart could hurt even more. I'd wasted all those months, hiding and denying my feelings.

I held on to him harder. "Shh…I'm here for you. Garrett, I'm here for you."

Garrett sucked in a deep breath and stepped back from me. He looked at Billy and then at me. The tears running down his face gutted me, and when I looked at Billy, I knew he felt the same way. Turning back to Garrett, I went to say something, but he shook his head and turned back toward the house.

He quickly wiped away his tears and stopped. He turned around and looked at us. "Nothing will ever be the same."

I shook my head and reached out for him, but he took a step back.

He whispered, "Nothing."

5 Garrett

I walked up the porch stairs and stopped at the door. I could hear my mother crying inside, and I wanted to turn around and throw up. I took a deep breath and opened the door. Dr. Birk was standing there, talking to my uncle, Wayne, and Raymond. I wanted nothing more than to just run as far away from here as I could. I knew Billy and Emma were right behind me, and the last thing I wanted to do was see Emma. If I saw her, I would just be reminded that the future I wanted with her was now gone.

Dr. Birk looked up and gave me a sympathetic smile.

I better get used to those.

I walked into the front parlor, and the moment I saw my mother sitting on the sofa, crying, I knew what I had to do. I straightened up my shoulders, pushed all my feelings deep down, and walked up to her. Mrs. Birk glanced up at me with tears rolling down her face. She stood up, so I could sit down next to my mother. I sat down and took her into my arms, and she began crying harder.

"Garrett…oh God! Garrett, I can't live without him. What are we going to do? Thomas, no…please come back to me."

My gut tightened up, and I had to take a few deep breaths to calm myself. I held her closer as I began talking to her, "Mama, it's going to be fine. I promise, I won't let you or Dad down. I'll take care of you and the ranch."

My mother pulled back and looked at me. "Garrett, he left us. He left us…"

She broke down crying again, and I pulled her back to me and began rocking her. I glanced up and saw Billy's father, David, standing there. He was white as a ghost, and I knew this had to be hard on him. He and my father were best friends, and David had lost his wife a few years ago.

I closed my eyes and tried to make sense of everything that was happening. Just a little bit ago, I had been about to kiss the girl of my dreams and tell her how much I cared about her, and the next moment, my whole world had been torn apart.

Why, Dad? Why did you leave us? Why?

I had been going over everything that had happened the last four weeks in my head, still trying to make sense of it all.

"Garrett? Son, are you listening to me?" David said.

I was pulled out of my daydream. I cleared my throat and nodded my head. "Yes, sir. I'm sorry. My mind was wandering."

David nodded his head and looked back toward the house. My mother was busy, working in her garden and getting it ready for spring planting.

I'd been trying to be strong for my mother, but today, I wanted to just run away from all of this.

The coach from Texas A&M had been over for a visit, and he'd talked to me about my decision not to attend college and play football. He had pulled me off to the side and said they would help find ranch hands to help my mother out. They would do whatever it took to get me to play.

The sounds of my mother's nightly cries had filled my head. I'd shaken my head and said, *I'm sorry, sir. I need to stay here and take care of my mother and our family ranch.*

He'd nodded as he'd given me that same damn pathetic look everyone had been giving me. *Son, let me ask you something. What would your father want? I think he'd want you to go to college and get your degree, so you could be better suited for running a cattle ranch like this.*

I'd given him a weak smile and said, *My father didn't have a degree, and he built this cattle ranch with nothing but hard work and determination. I intend on making it even bigger and better. I'm staying here. Thank you though for driving all the way out here. I appreciate it very much.*

After our conversation, he'd left, and David had told me it was time to get to business.

So, here we were, going over everything in the barn.

David cleared his throat. "One of the main things you always need to remember is to keep good records on everything from breeding, calving, culling, and weaning to your purchase and sales. Everything needs to be recorded, and you need to do it the day of. Don't think that you'll write it down the next day because I guarantee that you'll forget."

I nodded my head. "Yes, sir. My father showed me all of that about a year ago. I was in charge of keeping records of all the feed, hay, and fencing supplies."

David smiled and shook his head. "Damn. Your father was already getting you ready to take over the ranch, wasn't he? He was one smart man."

I smiled weakly. "Yes, sir, he was."

"What do you think would be the next important thing you need to concentrate on?"

I didn't have to think long on this one. "Fences. Broken fences mean lost cattle, and that means lost money."

David's smile spread across his face like he was the proudest man in the world.

Billy started laughing. "Now, you are talking like my dad here talks." We all laughed.

David slapped me on the back. "Next?"

"Machinery needs to be checked daily in order to make sure everything is running. If something isn't running, then it means loss of work time, which equals loss of money."

"Your father did a good job, Garrett. You'll want to also manage your grazing and your feeding. With us being in this drought, I'm sure your daddy told you that you only feed during times of need. Most of the time, the cattle are fine with hay."

I nodded my head. I glanced back at the house when I heard a car pulling up. *Emma*.

Dr. and Mrs. Birk had been by a few times to check on us, and each time, Emma had come. I'd seen her the first two times, and every time since then, I'd taken off on my horse and just vanished. I couldn't bear the idea of seeing her and having to tell her that I wasn't going to college, so I had no real future to offer her. She probably wanted to move to a big city, like Austin, and live in a big house with lots of babies. I couldn't give her that. I'd never be able to give her that.

"Keep up to date with vaccinations. That's real important for healthy cattle."

I nodded my head as I stepped back just enough to where I could see Emma, but she couldn't see me.

"Also, be sure to fully prepare for calving season. Now, your daddy already has the breeding season managed and down."

I glanced over toward Billy, and he looked at me. He had just jumped all over me this morning. He'd said Emma was worried sick about me and kept asking him if he had spoken with me. I hadn't gone back to school yet, but that was all about to change. Mother had said she would stop eating if I didn't get myself to school, so Monday would be my first day back.

"Always take care of your horses and stock dogs," David said, snapping me out of my thoughts yet again.

"Yes, sir. Take care of the horses and dogs," I said halfheartedly.

David followed my eyes to where I was looking, and he let out a laugh. "Garrett, you can't keep avoiding her."

I snapped my head over to Billy, and he just shrugged his shoulders. Never taking my eyes off of Billy, I said, "I'm not avoiding her. I just...I just don't know what to say to her. I mean, she deserves more than what I can give her. I can't give her anything."

David grabbed me by the shoulders and turned me to face him. "Excuse me? You can't give her anything? What about love? Respect? A beautiful home sitting on one of the most beautiful countrysides God has graced us with. So, you're not going to college. I didn't go to college, and your daddy didn't go to college. Do you think your mother would have been happier if your father had a law degree?"

I swallowed hard. "No, sir, I don't think she would have been."

David looked back out and motioned with his head. "You're not even going to give her a chance to decide for herself? Son, you don't make decisions about a woman's feelings—*ever*. You let her decide on her own. They are her feelings, and only she knows them."

I turned back to David and smiled as I whispered, "That sounds like something my father would say."

David's eyes began to fill with tears. He quickly wiped at his eyes and then looked me square in the eyes. "No one will ever take the place of your daddy, but I want you to know that I'm here for you, Garrett. You're like my own son. I'll always be here for you."

My heart began beating harder in my chest, and for the first time since I'd held my mother in my arms on that fateful day, I wanted to cry. I nodded my head and barely said, "Thank you, sir. Thank you."

Billy stood up and walked up to us. He slapped us both on the back. "Well, hell, this is nice and all, but you better get your ass out there, Garrett, and show that girl how much you care about her."

I stuck my hand out and shook Billy's hand and then David's.

Billy started laughing. "Now, maybe we can go on a double date—you and Emma with Marg and me."

I let out a laugh and turned to make my way out of the barn. Everyone had gone into the house by this point. I walked up the stairs as I wiped my sweaty hands on my pants. I took a deep breath and opened the door. I walked into the living room, and Emma was standing at the window, looking out at the west pasture.

She slowly turned around and smiled when she saw me. It wasn't the same smile I'd been getting from everyone else. It was different. Her eyes sparkled, and her face flushed.

"Your mama's packing up a picnic. I thought maybe we could go for a ride, if you're up to it," Emma said as she tilted her head.

She gave me a look I'd never seen before. My dick jumped in my pants, and I had to shake my head to clear the thoughts I was having.

"That, um…that sounds, um…" *Holy shit, what is wrong with me? I can't even think clearly.*

"Yesterday was my birthday. The least you can do is take me on a picnic, Mr. Mathews."

My mother and Mrs. Birk came walking up behind me, and it was the first time in weeks I'd heard my mother laughing.

"Why, Garrett Mathews, you're a mess. Run and clean up, and I'll have Pete saddle up some horses for you and Emma Rose."

I winked at Emma and turned to face my mother. "Yes, ma'am."

Five minutes later, I was walking Emma down to the barn. I helped her up onto my buckskin horse, Jack. I loved that damn horse, and if I ever had a son someday, I was going to name him Jack.

"What's this guy's name?" Emma asked as she got atop the horse.

"Jack," I said with a smile as I handed her the quilt.

"Jack. I like that name."

Yep, I just fell in love with her even more. Wait, am I in love with Emma? We've never even been on a date. How in the world could I possibly love her?

I grabbed the basket and tied it onto the back of Jack's saddle. Then, I led him and Buttercup out of the barn. When I got on Buttercup, she started getting feisty with me.

"Whoa, Buttercup girl. Settle down."

Emma looked at me with a shocked face. "Your horse's name is Buttercup?"

I wanted to laugh because I knew she was thinking back to the night of the dance when I'd called her Buttercup. "It sure is. She is feisty but still a lady, stubborn but sweet as hell, and strong but gentle, too. She's my Buttercup."

Emma gave me a crooked smile that melted my heart on the spot. There wasn't anything I wouldn't do to make her smile like that every day for the rest of our lives.

As we made our way to my favorite oak tree in the west pasture, I let Emma do all the talking. She had an amazing sense of humor, and for the first time in weeks, I felt alive and happy.

We rode up to the big oak and Emma let out a gasp. "What a beautiful oak tree."

I smiled and nodded my head. "I know. This is my favorite place to come. I could sit here for hours and just think."

"A thinking spot, huh?" Emma said with a giggle.

"Something like that," I said with a wink.

I helped Emma lay out the quilt she had brought, and then we set out all the food my mother and Mrs. Birk had packed up. I'd never laughed so hard in my life as I listened to Emma tell me about the first time she swam in a river.

"I did. I screamed the whole time. I don't like swimming in water I can't see through."

I chuckled. "Why?"

She shrugged her shoulders. "I don't know. Maybe it's the fear of not knowing what's in the water. Oh, and don't get me started about the snakes."

"No wonder your friends wouldn't let you go back with them to the river." I took a sip of the sweet tea my mother had made.

I watched as Emma drank her tea, and afterward, some of it was still on her lips. She used her tongue to get it off, and my heart dropped to my stomach.

I began praying, *God, please give me the strength to take my time with this girl. She means so much to me.*

She slowly smiled and began chewing on her lower lip. "Garrett?" she whispered.

I swallowed hard and said, "Yes."

"I'm still waiting," she said with a small smile.

I shook my head, confused. "Waiting?"

She nodded her head. "The promise."

My heart began beating so fast that I was sure she could hear it. I put down my tea and moved closer to her. I'd never been so damn nervous in my life. It wasn't like I'd never kissed a girl before, but Emma...Emma was different. She slowly began lying back as her beautiful gray eyes locked with mine. I moved my eyes over her body. Her chest was moving up and down so fast.

Don't mess this up, Mathews.

I looked back into her eyes and whispered, "I want to make all your dreams come true, Em. I want you to take me into your heart, like I've taken you into mine. I never want to be apart."

She smiled and whispered, "Garrett, I'll be yours till the end of time."

I leaned down and brushed my lips against hers. I tried my best not to let out a moan. I slowly began kissing her as I moved my tongue along her bottom lip.

Shit. I can taste the sweet tea on her lips.

She reached her hand up and pushed it through my hair. She let out the sweetest sound and opened her mouth more for me to explore it. Our tongues moved slowly at first as we learned each other. It didn't take long before the kiss turned passionate. I wanted to crawl into her body and stay there forever. Every bad memory of the last month completely vanished the moment I tasted her. I couldn't try to describe what she tasted like. It was heaven...just pure heaven.

She grabbed a fistful of my hair, causing me to moan.

Then, she pulled her mouth away and gasped for air. "Touch me, Garrett."

I shook my head and looked at her, confused. "I am touching you, Buttercup."

She smiled, and the flush that covered her cheeks about killed me on the spot.

"Touch me, Garrett. Please touch me. I need to feel your hands on me. I need you to ease the feeling I get every time you are near me."

I pulled back and stared at her. "Emma, I…"

I watched as she began pulling up her shirt. I didn't think my dick would ever be as hard as it was in this moment.

She looked into my eyes and whispered, "I've never…I've never been touched before. I want you to touch me, Garrett. Please."

"Emma…are you sure you want to do this?" I asked as my voice cracked.

She took my hand and moved it down her chest, her stomach, and then even lower until she stopped when my hand was on the inside of her thigh. I closed my eyes and prayed to God that I wouldn't come on myself as soon as I touched her. I moved my hand closer to her knickers, and she held her breath as she closed her eyes. I instantly stopped, and her eyes snapped open.

"Please don't stop."

I slowly moved my hand up until I felt her silk knickers.

"Garrett…oh God."

"Emma, I don't know if I can…"

She ran her hand through my hair and smiled at me. I slipped my hand inside her knickers and brushed my fingers across her soft lips.

"Emma…" I whispered as she pushed her hips into my hand. I slowly slipped one finger inside her. "God, Em…you're so…"

"What? I'm so what?" she asked as she panted.

I licked my lips as I looked at her lips. "Wet. You're so wet, Emma. I should stop."

She thrashed her head back and forth. "No! God, no…please, Garrett."

I closed my eyes and gently pushed another finger inside her. She was so tight, and I could practically feel her pulling my fingers in. I leaned down and began kissing her neck.

Then, I moved my lips up next to her ear. "Emma," I whispered.

I stretched her a little, and she whimpered. I stopped, and she thrust her hips into my hand.

"Garrett, do something…please…"

Do something? What does she mean, do something?

I slowly slipped another finger in and began moving in and out faster.

"Oh…that feels…I've never felt anything so good. Faster, Garrett. Go faster."

I was pretty sure if my heart beat any faster, I was going to pass out. I brushed my thumb across her clit, and she bucked harder against my hand.

"Yes!" she called out.

I did it again, but this time, I kept my thumb there. I rubbed it against her clit as I moved my fingers in and out of her body. I wanted nothing more than to be inside her. I wanted to feel what it would be like to make love to her.

"What's happening? Oh God...Garrett."

Her eyes locked on mine as she began to call out my name. I couldn't take my eyes off of her. She was so beautiful, and the fact that I was giving her an orgasm, her first one, made this moment even more beautiful. I leaned down and began kissing her since she was calling out my name so loudly. The last thing we needed was for someone to hear her. She pushed her hands into my hair and kissed me back with such intensity that I wanted to strip off my clothes and just take her as mine. I could feel her squeezing down on my fingers, and I'd never in my life been so turned-on.

She slowly stopped moving her hips, but I could still feel her body reacting to her orgasm. I pulled back and looked into her eyes. The smile on her face caused me to smile. I leaned down and kissed her neck as I took my fingers gently out of her.

I moved my lips next to her ear and whispered, "I love you, Buttercup. I want to make you feel that good always."

When I lifted my head to see her face, she had a tear rolling down her cheek.

Fuck. I knew I shouldn't have done it. I knew it.

"Say that again," she whispered.

I looked at her, confused. "Say what?"

She let a small sob escape her as she reached her hand up and placed it on the side of my face. "Tell me that you love me."

I let out the breath I had been holding as I sat up and pulled her up with me. I pushed her skirt down and brought her onto my lap. When she felt my hard-on, she raised her eyebrows, and a beautiful rosy blush moved across her cheeks.

I pushed a piece of hair back away from her eyes and smiled at her. "I love you, Emma Rose Birk. I'm going to marry you someday, and I'm going to have my wicked way with you anytime I want."

She moved a little against me, and I moaned.

"Garrett, should I...I mean...would you like me to make you feel good?"

I laughed just a little and shook my head. "Don't worry about me, Em. I'll be okay. We better head back before your father comes looking for us."

Emma stood up and fixed her hair, and then she smoothed down her skirt. I started gathering up all the food and putting the containers back into the basket, but all I could think about was Emma and the way she'd called my name as she had that look in her eyes. I needed to get home and get away from her as fast as possible, or her father would be able to see on my face how much I wanted her.

After I tied the basket onto the back of Jack's saddle, I turned to see Emma holding the folded quilt. She was biting on her lower lip.

I walked up to her and placed my finger under her chin. "Emma, look at me. Do you regret what just happened?"

Her eyes widened, and she said, "No. My God, no. I've been dreaming about that for months. You don't know how badly I've wanted to touch myself to ease the feeling I get in my lower stomach every time I think about you."

I smiled and tilted my head. "You've wanted that, Em?"

She nodded. "I've had dreams about you—very descriptive dreams of us…making love. Each time I woke up, I was touching myself, but I quickly stopped because I wanted it to be you. I wanted you to give me my first orgasm. Garrett, I have to be honest with you. I don't think I can wait until we are married to make love. I want to feel you inside me."

Jesus…I've died and gone to heaven. "Emma, you're gonna kill me."

She let out a giggle and held up the quilt. "I want to make love on this quilt for the first time. I made it a few months ago, and the whole time I was making it, I had thoughts of you and me…" She stopped talking and looked away.

I brought her face back to me and pierced her eyes with mine. "What's wrong?"

She began crying, and I brushed away her tears with my thumbs.

"I feel so guilty because the whole time I was pushing you away, I just…I just…"

I held my breath. "You just what?"

She closed her eyes and then opened them again. "I just wanted to be with you."

I took her in my arms and began kissing her. When she let out a small moan, it traveled through my whole body, and I trembled. I pulled her closer to me and pressed myself into her stomach. I needed her to know how much I wanted her.

That was when I heard someone clear his throat. I slowly pulled back and stepped away from Emma. I turned to see David sitting on top of his horse, looking at us.

"Emma, go on, and get onto Jack. Garrett, take Emma on back now. I'm sure her parents are waiting and ready to go. After they leave, I'd like for you to meet me in the barn."

Emma quickly walked up to Jack, and I ran over to help her up.

Then, I jumped up onto Buttercup and looked at David. "Yes, sir. I'll be there as soon as I can."

As we rode back to the house, Emma looked over at me. "I'm so sorry if I got you in trouble, Garrett, but I'll never be sorry for what we did. It was…magical."

I smiled at her. "I'll never regret it either, Emma."

She giggled and looked away.

"What's so funny?" I asked.

She looked at me through her beautiful long eyelashes. "Do I look different? Will my parents be able to tell?"

I threw my head back and laughed.

"Do not laugh at me, Garrett Mathews. It was an honest question."

I shook my head and said, "No, Buttercup. You don't look different, except for the beautiful flush that has been on your cheeks since you came on my fingers."

She let out a gasp. "Garrett Mathews, you shouldn't talk to me like that."

I smiled and looked ahead. When I peeked over at her and saw the smile on her face, I knew she had liked what I just said to her. I made a note to myself that I would be romantic as hell the first time I made love to her, but the second time…the second time I was going to see just how naughty my Emma truly was.

After putting the horses up we walked back up to the house, holding hands, I glanced up and saw Mrs. Birk and my mother sitting on the porch. They were both smiling at us, but my mother's smile faded for a brief second before returning.

That's weird.

"Did y'all enjoy the picnic?" Mrs. Birk asked.

Emma did a little jump and said, "Yes! We enjoyed it very much. Garrett took me to his favorite oak tree, and we laid out the quilt and had a lovely time talking." She glanced back at me and winked.

I was pretty sure my face turned bright as the sun.

The screen door opened, and Dr. Birk stepped out. "Ladies, I do believe it is time to leave." He turned back and shook Uncle Pete's hand. Then, he walked up to me.

I reached out my hand and said, "Thank you for allowing me to take Emma on a picnic, sir. It really helped me to spend some time with her. She makes me laugh with her stories." I looked at Emma.

"I'm not surprised. The girl has always been good at telling stories. Even as a little girl, she knew how to make us laugh."

Emma looked down. "Daddy, please, you're embarrassing me."

Emma's mother giggled and said, "Charles, don't embarrass your daughter."

Dr. Birk let out a loud laugh. "Now, I don't mean to embarrass you, sweetheart. Come on, ladies, we need to be heading on back."

After everyone said their good-byes, I watched as they left down our long driveway. I could still feel Emma's kiss on my lips, and I reached up to touch them. When I felt a hand on my shoulder, I jumped. I quickly turned to see my mother standing there.

"Garrett, don't do anything stupid. I see the way the two of you look at each other." She smiled slightly and said, "It's the same look your daddy and I shared when we were your age."

I smiled as I took my mother's hand and kissed the back of it. "Mother, I would never do anything to hurt you or Emma. I promise."

My mother looked over my shoulder and nodded her head at someone. She turned and walked back toward the porch. I spun around to see David leaning against the barn door.

I took a deep breath and walked up to him. He put his hand on my shoulder and led me to the back of the barn into the foreman's office.

He pointed at a chair and said, "Sit down, Garrett."

I sat down and looked up at him as he shut the door.

He sat down on the edge of the desk and let out a sigh. "I'm going to ask you something, and I don't want you to lie to me. I was eighteen once, so I know what a pretty girl can do to you."

I nodded my head. "I would never lie to you, sir."

He spit out his tobacco and nodded his head. "Did you and Emma…well, did y'all have sex, Garrett?"

I shook my head. "No, sir, we did not have sex."

He let out a sigh of relief as he dropped his head. He slowly looked up at me and said, "Do you have condoms, Garrett?"

I nodded my head. "Yes, sir, I do."

"I want you to start carrying them with you at all times. A moment will come when you both won't be able to stop. When that time comes, you protect her and yourself. Do you understand me, Garrett?"

I swallowed and nodded my head.

"I'm not giving you permission. Understand that right now. I'd like for you both to wait until you are married, but what I rode up on today…" He shook his head and let out a chuckle. "Hell, boy, it was like looking in a mirror and seeing me and my Dorothy all over again."

I gave him a weak smile.

"I promised your mama I'd watch over you. I don't want you thinking that having sex with Emma will take away any of your other pain. You just need to know that, son. You can't hide from it."

"I'm not hiding from it," I whispered.

David stood up and pushed one hand through his wavy blond hair. "Good. Just be careful. Her daddy would snap you like a twig if he found out you were touching his little girl the wrong way."

I instantly felt sick to my stomach.

He laughed. "Go on. Get on out of here, and do your chores."

I jumped up and headed out of the office.

I spent the rest of the afternoon and evening replaying every single sound and movement Emma had made. I closed my eyes and pictured her lying there, looking so beautiful.

I'll be yours till the end of time.

Yes, I was going to make Emma Rose Birk mine, and I was going to make her mine soon.

6 Emma

I walked into my kitchen and came to an abrupt halt. My mother and father were sitting at the table, and they both looked at me with serious faces.

"What's wrong?" I asked nervously.

My father cleared his throat. "Emma Rose, please sit down."

My heart started pounding. *Do they know what happened between Garrett and me yesterday? Did Mr. Bauer see us and tell my parents?*

"Yes, sir," I said as I slowly sank down into the chair. "What's wrong? You're both scaring me. Did I do something wrong?"

My mother and father both smiled at me, and my mother reached for my hand. "No, darling. You didn't do anything wrong, but I'm afraid we have a bit of bad news."

My eyes began to sting from trying to hold back the tears. *Garrett…something happened to Garrett.* "Garrett?" I barely said.

My mother shook her head but looked away. "Garrett is fine, darling. This has to do with us—as a family."

I nodded my head. "Okay."

My father took in a deep breath. "We're moving to Austin. I've been offered a position with Brackenridge Hospital. This is a wonderful opportunity for us."

"No," I whispered. I began shaking my head. "You promised me. When we left Fredericksburg, you promised we wouldn't move again. I have friends here. I have…I have Garrett."

My mother turned back to face me and said, "I know you think you have feelings for Garrett, darling—"

"Think? No, Mother, I *know* I have feelings for Garrett. I love him. I want to marry him someday."

My father shook his head and pushed his chair back. "Emma Rose, please, you barely even know him. You've spent one afternoon with him, and you think you love him. That's impossible."

I felt the tears sliding down my face. "Why is that impossible, Daddy? I knew the moment I first saw him back in August. I tried to deny it because I was so scared."

"Why were you scared?" my mother asked.

I smiled at her and wiped away my tears. "I've never felt that way before. Just the way he looks at me does weird things to my heart, Mother. When he smiles at me, I have to catch my breath."

My mother dabbed a tear away before it had a chance to move down her face.

My father pointed at me. "You're only eighteen. You don't know what love is, Emma. Besides, what is going to happen when you go away to college? You'll have to leave Garrett behind. He is obviously going to make his living as a cattle rancher since he walked away from his scholarship at Texas A&M. He won't be able to provide you with a comfortable lifestyle. It would be a struggle your whole life."

I couldn't believe what I was hearing. "You don't know that, Father."

"We are in a drought, for Christ's sake, Emma!" my father shouted.

"Charles! Do not yell at your daughter," my mother said as she stood up and walked in front of my father.

I slowly got up and looked directly at my father. "So, Father, you are saying that Garrett is not good enough for me because he chose to stay home and be there for his mother, who had just lost her husband. He decided he wanted to take care of the cattle ranch his father had worked so hard to build instead of going off to college to play football and leaving it for other people to tend to. How selfish of him to pick his mother over football like that."

My father glared at me. "This has nothing to do with football. It has to do with going to college and getting a degree to better himself."

"So, because Garrett isn't going to college to *better himself*, I'm supposed to just walk away from him like he means nothing to me?"

My mother took a few steps closer to me. "Emma, honey, just listen to us for one minute."

I took a step back and shook my head. "I only have four more months of high school. Why can't I just stay with Margie and finish out school in Mason?"

My father let out a laugh. "The only reason you want to stay is because of that boy."

"Now, he is *that boy*?"

"You better watch your tone with me, young lady." My father pushed his hand through his hair and let out a long sigh. "Emma, I don't want to argue with you about Garrett. I think what he has done for his mother is very honorable. I truly do. But I want more for you. You are my only child. I want the world for you. Your mother and I are able to provide you with more than what a lot of girls your age have, and I won't allow you to walk away from a future. We are moving to Austin, and you will finish high school there. Then, you will go to college at the University of Texas, like your mother and I did, and you will get a college degree. Once you are finished, you may choose to do as you see fit with your life. Until then, this talk of marrying Garrett Mathews is done."

I put my hand up to my mouth and began sobbing. I shook my head as I looked at my mother and then at my father. I slowly dropped my hand and said, "I hate both of you, and I will *never*, ever forgive you for this."

My mother let out a gasp, and my father's mouth dropped open.

"Emma Rose Birk, you apologize for saying such a hurtful thing to your mother this instant."

I turned and started to run out of the house, and all I could hear behind me was my father yelling for me to come back.

I needed to get to Garrett right away. I needed to get as far away as I could possibly get from my parents.

"Emma, if I get caught, I'm never going to forgive you for this," Margie said as I stared out the window.

"I promise, you won't get caught," I whispered.

Margie had lied and told her parents she was picking up Peggy and going to the library for a few hours. She was really driving me out to Garrett's, and she and Peggy were going to meet Billy and Raymond down at the river for a few hours.

"Emma, your father called my father and asked if you were at our house. I've never lied to my parents, and today, I've already told them three lies for you."

I rolled my eyes and looked back at her. "You and Peggy are meeting Billy and Raymond at the river. I'm sure once y'all see them, you will forget all about the lies you told your parents."

From the backseat, Peggy let out a little squeal. "Don't be a square, Margie. This is going to be fun. As long as Emma doesn't get knocked up, we will all be okay."

I turned and looked at Peggy. "What?"

She winked at me. "Please. If my parents told me I was moving, the first thing I would do is give up my virgin pin to Raymond as a good-bye gift to myself."

Margie let out a giggle.

I turned back around and looked out the window. "I'm not saying good-bye to Garrett because I'm not leaving. I'll ask his mother if I can stay with them. I'll ask Garrett to marry me if I have to, but I'm not leaving him."

From the corner of my eye, I could see Margie turn and look at me. She pulled up to the Mathews' gate and put her car in park. "Emma Rose, look at me."

I turned to face her.

"I've known Garrett my whole life. I know the type of person he is, and he would never allow you to leave your family. He is going to want what is best for you."

I felt the tears building in my eyes because I knew she was right. Garrett would tell me to be a good little girl and do what my parents said.

I shook my head and looked straight ahead. "No," I whispered. "He gave me his heart. I won't leave him."

Peggy put her hand on my shoulder. "Emma, if he said that, he meant it. He'll wait for you. He is going to want what is best for you, but he is true to his word."

I quickly wiped the tears away and got out of the car.

"Where are you going?" Margie asked.

"I'll walk from here."

Margie jumped out of the car and ran around it. "Bullshit you will. That walk is a few miles long."

She pushed me back inside the car and then opened the gate before getting back in the driver's seat to head toward Garrett's house. Before she got to the house, she turned down another dirt road.

"Where are you going?" I asked.

"Billy was going to call Garrett and tell him to meet us at the barn. This road pulls up just shy of the barn. Mrs. Mathews won't know we are here, so she can't tell my parents that she saw me dropping you off."

I looked at Margie and then turned to look at Peggy. "Oh, I see. I take it y'all have snuck out before?"

They both laughed as Margie brought the car to a stop. She smiled bigger, and I followed her stare. Billy, Raymond, and Garrett were all standing there, talking. Billy waved as Raymond slapped Garrett on the back. Raymond headed toward the car as Billy said something to Garrett before turning and making his way over.

"Two hours, Emma. I'll give you two hours before we meet back here, and I take you home," Margie said with a serious look.

I nodded my head and got out of the car. Raymond jumped into the back with Peggy, and they immediately began necking. Billy winked at me as he took my seat, and then he shut the door. I watched as Margie turned the car around and took off down the dirt road. I spun around, only to see Garrett leaning against the tractor. My stomach began doing all kinds of weird flips as he stood there, smiling at me. I let out a sob and ran to him. His smile faded, and he caught me as I jumped into his arms.

"Buttercup, what is going on? Why the secret meeting? And why the tears?"

"Just hold me for a bit, Garrett. Please just hold me."

Garrett held on to me tighter and whispered, "Emma, you're scaring me. What's going on?"

In that instant, I knew what I had to do. I pulled back and looked into his eyes. "Make love to me—right now, right here."

His face dropped, and he took a step back as he looked at me with a stunned face. "What?"

My heart started pounding. *Maybe he doesn't feel the same way about me?* I did the only thing I could think of. I just started spitting everything out, "My parents are moving. I mean, we're moving. We're moving to Austin because of my dad. They're making me leave, Garrett. My father went on and on about how I needed to go to college and that if I stayed here, I'd get nowhere, or I'd end up marrying you and just be a housewife with nothing to show for, um…well, I mean…" I stopped talking the moment I saw the devastation in his eyes.

I closed my eyes and cursed myself for saying what I'd just said. When I opened them, Garrett was running his hand through his brown hair. His blue eyes were filled with so much sadness that I wanted to hit myself for hurting him.

"Garrett, I didn't mean—"

He held up his hand for me to stop talking as he gave me a weak smile. "You're moving to Austin? When?"

I shrugged my shoulders. "I don't know. I guess soon, but I didn't give my parents time to get that far. When I found out, I just kind of ran away. I needed to get to you right away. I don't want to leave you, Garrett. I…I love you."

His whole body slumped slightly as he let out a sigh and closed his eyes. He turned away from me and looked out onto the open field. I glanced up and couldn't help but smile. It was so beautiful out here. The hills took my breath away, and I wanted nothing more than to spend the rest of my life here with Garrett. I walked up to him and wrapped my arms around his waist.

I was just about to start talking when Garrett let out a small chuckle. "This is just my luck, I guess."

I pulled back when he turned to look at me. "What do you mean?" I asked as I tilted my head.

He smiled, and my stomach did a few twists and turns.

"Nothing. Emma, why did you run away? What were you thinking?"

"Well, I don't know. At first, I thought I might be able to stay with Margie, but I know my parents wouldn't allow me to be away from them. So…" I looked down.

Garrett lifted my chin with his finger. "So?"

I swallowed hard and said, "So, I had to see you. I don't want to leave"—I turned away before looking back into his eyes—"without us being together, Garrett. I don't want to lose you."

His smile faded, and the look in his eyes changed. "You think sleeping with me will make me wait for you?"

Darn it. That didn't come out right. "No. I mean, I don't know. Do you not want to be with me, Garrett?"

Now, it was his turn to swallow and suck in a breath of air. "Emma, I want to make love to you more than anything, but I don't want our first time to be me fucking you up against the side of the barn."

My stomach dropped, and it felt like I had a rush of water hit between my legs. The crude way he'd said that did things to me deep in the pit of my stomach. I was ashamed to even admit to myself that I loved the idea of Garrett doing exactly that to me. I looked his body up and down and licked my lips. *What would it feel like?* I'd heard the first time would hurt, but I bet Garrett would be so gentle.

"Emma, stop looking at me like that," he said as he moved closer to me.

"Garrett," was all I could manage to get out.

I didn't even have time to think before he was grabbing me and pulling me into the most passionate kiss I'd ever experienced. It was like he was trying to get as much of me as he could. He bit down on my lower lip, and the shock wave riding through my body had me whimpering.

"Please…Garrett, please," I said as I began trying to take off his T-shirt.

When I finally pulled it off of him, I let out a gasp. I'd known he was built, but his muscles were amazing, his chest—*oh my goodness, I think I might have just had my second orgasm*—was broad, and his stomach—*mother of God, I swear, I can see the definition of every single muscle.*

He pressed his lips against mine again, and this time, he kissed me like he was hungry for more of me.

Yes.

I began unbuttoning my shirt as fast as I could as his hand moved up my skirt. The moment he touched my leg, I jerked and let out a whimper. His touch drove me mad with desire, and I wanted nothing more than to be with him, for him to make me his.

I'll be his for the rest of my life.

"Oh…God…" I whispered as he moved his hand inside my knickers.

I pushed my hips against him to get him to touch me there. I needed to feel his touch.

Then, in an instant, the warmth of his body and his touch was gone. I opened my eyes, only to see him reaching down for his shirt before putting it back on.

I began shaking my head. "No, wait. What are you doing? Garrett, I want you. I need you."

He turned away from me. "Not like this, Emma. Not when you're scared and not sure of the future. I won't do that to you or to me."

I felt the tears building in my eyes. "You're rejecting me?"

He quickly spun around and looked me in the eyes. "No! I'm trying to do the honorable thing here, Emma. The only reason you want to do this is because you think you might never see me again. You know, there is a chance you'll go to college, meet someone else, and never look back."

I wrapped my arms around my body and began sobbing harder. "That's not true." I slowly shook my head back and forth. "I love you. I don't care that my parents think we are too young or that we don't know each other well enough for me to say that. I want to spend the rest of my life with you. I want to help you build this ranch up even bigger and better. I want to wake up every morning with you by my side and fall asleep every night with you making love to me."

Garrett closed his eyes and then turned away. He walked over to a bale of hay. He sat down and put his head in his hands as he let out a frustrated moan. "Jesus Christ, Emma. I want the same things, but I'm not going to take you here because you're moving. I'm not going to risk both your future and mine because you're leaving, and we might not—"

"Don't say we won't see each other again! Stop saying that!" I yelled out. I walked over to him and dropped to my knees. "Please, don't…don't say that anymore."

Garrett placed his hands on the sides of my face and gave me a weak smile.

"Okay, I won't say that again. Buttercup, you have to go with your parents. Your father is right. It's best if you go to school and get your degree."

"No," I whispered.

He nodded his head. "Yes. I won't let you give up on college and stay here just to be a housewife to some deadbeat cattle rancher."

I pushed his hands away and stood up. "Why does everyone think they can tell me what I want and what I don't want? Garrett, you're not a deadbeat cattle rancher. You're the most amazing man I've ever met, and I want to build a future with you."

He stood up and used his thumbs to wipe away my tears. Then, he pulled my lips to his, and he kissed me so tenderly. In an instant, I knew he was saying good-bye.

"Emma, you'll go to college and get your degree, and I'll wait."

I tried to shake my head, but his hands were holding my face, keeping me from moving. "Garrett, no…"

Leaning down, he sucked my lower lip into his mouth and gently bit down on it. Instead of it turning me on, it caused me to cry harder.

"I'll wait for you, Buttercup. I promise."

I threw myself into his body, and he wrapped his arms around me and held me while I cried.

"I promise, I'll wait for you, too, Garrett. I love you."

His hands moved slowly up and down my back. "I love you, too. I'll always love you."

Garrett and I sat in the barn, and I smiled as I listened to him making plans to visit me in Austin as much as he could.

"I'm scared, Garrett. It's such a big college, and I don't even know yet what I want a degree in. Maybe something to help you with the ranch? Business or something?" I said.

He let out a weak laugh. "Lord knows I don't have any business sense."

When I heard Margie pulling up, I jumped. "I'm not ready to leave yet!" I called out.

Garrett slowly stood up and took my hand in his. As he led me out of the barn, I tried to pull him back, but he just smiled and winked at me.

"I don't…I can't leave you," I whispered.

He leaned down and kissed me on the lips. He barely pulled away and whispered back, "You'll never leave me because you're forever in my heart."

I let a small sob escape my lips before Garrett kissed me again. This time, he kissed me like he knew something I didn't. It was so full of passion that I wanted to beg him to never stop. Then, he quickly stopped and took a few steps back as he raked his hand through his hair again. I smiled because he only did that when he was frustrated or nervous. I was secretly hoping he was frustrated with himself for not making me his own.

I glanced over and saw Billy and Raymond standing there. When I turned, I saw Margie and Peggy waiting for me in the car. I pointed to them to give me a second. I wanted to tell Garrett one more thing before I left. I turned back to face him, but he was gone. My heart began pounding, and I started to walk into the barn, but then I felt someone take my arm.

"Emma, you have to let him go," Billy said.

He began to lead me back to the car, and I began crying.

"No, Billy, no. He needs me, and I can't leave him. He needs me."

I slowly sank down to the ground, and Billy held me in his arms.

"I can't leave him. I just can't," I cried over and over again.

Margie and Peggy were next to me on the ground, saying something about how I needed to stand up.

I wasn't even sure how I'd made it back to the car.

I cried the entire way home. Margie walked with me as I made my way into the house.

I ran into my mother's arms. "I can't leave him alone. Mother, please!" I cried out.

As my mother held me in her arms, she softly said, "Shh…baby girl. I promise you, it will be okay."

I shook my head as I pulled back to look at her. "No, it won't. I'm leaving him when he needs me the most. I'm leaving him."

I had never cried as much as I did the next two days. My father and mother had our house packed up so fast, and before I knew it, I was sitting in the backseat of our car, crying yet again.

"Emma, it will get better. You're going to meet new people and then start college. Soon, you'll for—"

My father stopped talking, but I knew he was going to say that I'd soon forget about Garrett.

I looked out the window and whispered, "I'll never forget about Garrett—ever."

7 Garrett

December 1957

Raymond and Billy went on and on about Austin. I couldn't have cared less about it. It was too big with way too much traffic. There were people everywhere, and it smelled weird.

"Garrett, are you sure it's a good idea to surprise Emma? You even said yourself that y'all haven't talked in over a month," Billy asked from the backseat.

"I haven't seen her in almost a year. I want to surprise her, and I'm sure she's just been busy with school." I turned and saw Margie staring at me with worry in her eyes. "Marg? Are you hiding something from me?" I asked.

She shook her head as she started fiddling with her skirt. "No, I promise, but it's been a couple of months since I talked to Emma. The last time, she sounded pretty down."

I nodded my head and looked straight ahead. The last time I had talked to Emma, she had told me how much she missed me. I'd wanted to tell her that I was planning a trip with Margie, Billy, and Raymond during their Christmas break, but I'd wanted to surprise her.

"Blanton Hall you said?" Raymond asked as he pulled in and parked.

I nodded my head and wiped my hands on my pants. I looked at Raymond and then back at Margie and Billy. The two of them had been dating over a year, and I'd never seen two people so in love. I smiled and shook my head.

"Wish me luck." I jumped out and started walking toward the entrance. I reached in my pocket and pulled out the piece of paper that had Emma's room number on it. I walked in the building and smiled at the girl sitting behind the desk.

"May I help you?" she said as she looked me up and down.

I gave her my signature smile, which caused her to smile bigger.

"Yes, ma'am, I do believe you can. I'm looking for Emma Birk." I handed her the piece of paper.

She quickly looked at it and then back at me. "I know who Emma is."

I smiled bigger. "Well, I'm kind of here to surprise her."

The girl made a funny face. "Are you her boyfriend?"

I looked down at the ground and then back up at her. "I guess you could say that I am."

She looked at me with almost pity in her eyes. "Emma's not here. She left about an hour ago."

My heart sank, and I pushed my hand through my hair. "Shit," I whispered.

She stood up, and that was when I got a good look at her.

Damn.

Her shirt couldn't possibly get any tighter. Her tits were practically spilling out of it, and I couldn't help but stare.

I quickly looked back into her eyes and gave her a weak smile. "You wouldn't happen to know where she went, would you?"

When she put her index finger in her mouth and bit down on it, I wanted to roll my eyes.

She let out a laugh and said, "Oh yeah, I know where she is. When you leave here, take a right and walk for about two blocks. You'll see Johnny D's on the corner. I believe she said she was going to meet someone there for a burger."

I smiled. "What's your name?"

"Marcy," she said with a huge grin on her face.

I nodded my head. "Thank you so much, Marcy, for your help."

She winked at me. "The pleasure was all mine. If you, um…find yourself looking for some fun, be sure to stop back by in a few hours. I can…show you around Austin, cowboy."

My smile faded for a brief second before I took a few steps back. I turned and headed out the door. I jogged back to the car and tried to shake the uneasy feeling I had.

I opened the passenger-side door and jumped in. "Head down the road about two blocks to a place called Johnny D's. She's meeting a girlfriend there for a hamburger."

Raymond started the car.

Margie let out a little squeal. "I can't wait to see my cousin!"

I felt the same way. The closer I got to seeing Emma, the harder my dick got. It was going to take everything out of me not to make her mine this weekend.

After Raymond parked the car, we all piled out and started to make our way up to the restaurant. Raymond and I were talking about the traffic and laughing when I smacked right into the back of Billy.

"Shit, just stop in the middle of the damn sidewalk, why don't ya?" I said as I gave him a push.

Margie quickly turned to me, and the look in her eyes told me something was wrong.

"I don't see her. Let's just drive around and see if we can find her," Margie said as she tried to pull me back to the car.

"What? We haven't even walked in. How do you know she isn't here?" I pushed her hand off my arm and started to walk toward the entrance door.

Billy stepped in front of me and said, "She's not in there. Let's go."

I gave Billy a push back. "What's your bag? Why in the hell are y'all trying to keep me from going in?" Right after I asked that question, I looked through the window, and my heart stopped beating.

Emma. She looked beautiful. Her blonde hair had grown longer and was pulled to the side. She was laughing, and when my eyes followed to where she was looking, I almost puked.

I watched as Emma held the hand of another guy, and she was laughing at something he'd said to her.

I'll wait for you.

"She lied," I whispered.

Margie grabbed on to my arm and said, "No, Garrett. We don't even know who that is. I mean, they are probably just—"

"That's why Marcy told me to come back and see her. She knew Emma was here on a date." I slowly turned and looked at Billy.

For the first time in almost a year, I saw pity in his eyes. I hadn't seen it since my father passed away, and now, here it was again.

"Let's just go back to Mason, Garrett. She doesn't even need to know you're here."

I glanced back at Emma and this other guy. *Have they kissed yet? Maybe she's fucking him?*

I shook my head and pushed past Billy and Margie. "Now, why would I want to do that? We drove all this way. The least we could do is say hi."

"Garrett!" Billy, Raymond, and Margie called out.

"Shit!" I heard Billy say as he ran up behind me.

I pushed open the door and walked right up to the table. I stopped just behind Emma and said, "So, now I see what's been keeping you so busy the last few months that you couldn't call."

The dick looked up at me and gave me a strange look. He was a built bastard, and I was pretty sure he was a football player.

Emma turned and looked at me. "Garrett?" she said as she stood up. "Oh my God! What are you doing here?"

At first, she wasn't smiling, but then a huge smile spread across her face before it quickly vanished. She must have realized what was happening.

I looked her body up and down, and I wanted nothing more than to take her in my arms and kiss her. "I wanted to surprise you, but it looks like the surprise is on me, Em."

She looked back at the guy she was with, who was just sitting there, and then she turned back to me. She shook her head and said, "Um, Garrett…wait, no. Philip is…well, he is helping me with biology, and he's my—"

I let out a laugh. "No need to worry about explaining, Emma. You waited as long as you could, right? While I've been lying alone in bed at night, thinking about you, after working my ass off for fifteen hours a day…you've moved on, right? I bet your father is happy. Phil here will most likely give you that life your daddy wants for you."

Emma's mouth dropped open. "Garrett, that's not what's happening here. Philip and I—"

I took a few steps back. "Please, don't explain it to me, Emma. I saw the two of you through the window. It was really touching, seeing y'all holding hands." I looked at Philip, and he acted like he wanted to say something, but I didn't give him a chance. "Take care of her. She deserves the world."

I quickly turned and started walking out of the restaurant.

"Garrett!" Emma called out after me.

I picked up the pace, and by the time I got outside, Raymond was jumping into the car and starting it. I could hear Emma pleading with Margie and Billy to get me to stop and just listen to her.

"Margie, please! You know I would never—"

Billy was pulling Margie by the arm, and he pushed her into the car and jumped in next to her.

"Wait! Garrett, wait and let her explain. She said it wasn't what it looked like," Margie said.

"Drive, Ray," I said.

"Garrett, please," Margie said.

I slammed my hand down on the dashboard and yelled, "Drive, Ray! Margie, just stop! You saw what I saw. They were holding hands and having a grand time. There is nothing for her to explain."

Raymond backed the car out, and right before he pulled away, I glanced back at Emma. She was standing there, crying, and the jerk had his hands on her shoulders while he was saying something to her.

I looked straight ahead and said, "Head back to Mason, Raymond. I never want to set foot in Austin again."

New Year's Eve

I downed another beer and gave the empty bottle a good throw as Billy and Wayne argued about something. I was well on my way to getting drunk, and I didn't care. Emma had tried to call me every day for the last few days, and each time, I'd told Mother to tell her I wasn't around. I'd seen the worry in my mother's eyes.

She would hang up and ask me, *What happened in Austin, Garrett?*

I would say the same thing each time, *My eyes were opened, Mama, to my true future.*

"Hey, Mathews. Why the long face?" Anna purred as she walked up and looked down at me.

She was wearing a pair of tight pedal pushers and a black shirt that was tied just above her midsection. I licked my lips as I took in her body.

Wayne leaned over and said, "Don't do it, Garrett. You know you'll regret it the moment it happens."

I grabbed another beer and continued to stare at Anna. I could take her around the corner and screw her brains out, but it wouldn't help me forget about Emma. It could give my poor dick some relief, but that would be about it.

Anna leaned in and put her lips up against my ear. She whispered, "Let's bring in 1958 with a bang, shall we?"

I pulled back as I looked at her and shook my head. "I might be on my way to drunk, but I'm not drunk yet."

She gave me a dirty look and stood up straight. She smoothed back her hair and looked at me like she hated me. "Your loss, jerk." She spun around and made her way over to the next poor guy she was going to attempt to sleep with.

I felt someone nudge my shoulder.

"Come on, let's get out of here and hit the fields," Billy said.

Margie and Peggy started jumping up and down, and then they took off for Billy's car.

The fields were what they'd started calling the west pasture of the ranch. We would all hang out there and either shoot the guns or just sit there and drink. Billy always parked the car far enough away so that he and Margie could stay behind and have sex while the rest of us hung out. We'd been going there for the past six months whenever everyone came home from school, but it seemed like we'd been doing it every night for the last week. Ever since we'd gotten back from Austin, I'd been attempting to drink Emma away.

I stood up and felt a little dizzy. "You driving? I think I've had too much to drink."

Billy laughed. "I'll have Margie drive your car, and I'll follow."

I nodded my head. "Sounds good. I'll wait in the car." I made my way over to my car and crawled into the backseat.

I wasn't sure how long I'd been lying there before I heard Margie get in the car and start it up.

"Margie, Margie, Margie, let's go get drunk," I said.

I slowly felt myself falling asleep. As I drifted off, all I could see were Emma's beautiful gray eyes looking into mine while she was sitting on the quilt under our oak tree, smiling at me.

Why, Em? Why didn't you keep your promise?

My eyes snapped open when I heard the car door shut. I slowly sat up and tried to adjust my eyes. It was dark out, but the full moon lit up the oak tree perfectly. *Why in the hell did Margie park here?*

I slowly made my way out of the car and called out, "Marg, why in the hell did you park here?" I looked around and couldn't see or hear anyone. "Where's Billy?" I spun around and didn't see them.

"Margie? If you and Billy want to sneak off, fine, but don't leave me here! I don't want to be here."

"Why not? This is my favorite place on the ranch."

The moment I heard her sweet voice, my heart dropped to the ground. I turned around and saw Emma leaning against the tree, holding the quilt. I was so happy to see her, and my first instinct was to walk up and kiss her.

"Emma? What are you…why are you here and not in Austin?"

Austin.

Philip.

The hurt rushed through my body again, and I took a few steps back. "What happened, Em? Your boyfriend break up with you before y'all could ring in the New Year together?"

I couldn't see her facial expression, but I could tell she stiffened up.

"I hope not. I was kind of hoping we would celebrate it together."

I let out a laugh. "You brought your boyfriend to Mason?" I pushed both hands through my hair and then leaned over. I felt sick to my stomach. I put my hands on my knees and took in a few deep breaths. "Fucking great," I whispered.

I jumped when I felt her touch my shoulder. I stood up and took a few steps away from her. I couldn't handle her touch right now. I couldn't even handle the sound of her sweet voice.

"I didn't have to bring him to Mason. He lives in Mason, and we've been apart for too long." She reached her hand out toward me.

I shook my head to clear my thoughts. "Emma, what in the hell are you talking about? Philip doesn't live in Mason."

The corner of Emma's lip rose, and then she smiled at me. She slowly shook her head and said, "No, Philip lives in Austin with my aunt and uncle."

Jesus, is it possible for the trees to be spinning around me?

"What?" I asked as I leaned back against my car. "Why does he live with your aunt and uncle?" *What type of messed-up relationship does she have with this guy?*

Emma slowly started to unbutton her white shirt as she took a few steps closer to me. "He lives with them because they are his parents."

"What? Did they adopt him or something?" I asked as I watched her take off her shirt.

She stood in front of me with nothing but a skirt and her white bra. My dick was so hard that I was pretty sure I would explode if she rubbed against me.

Emma let out a giggle and started removing her pencil skirt.

I held up my hands and said, "Emma, I won't let you do this."

She stepped out of her skirt and stood before me in her bra, white lace knickers, and a garter belt that held up her hose.

"Motherfucker," I whispered.

She walked up to me and stopped inches from me. "No, Garrett. Philip was not adopted by them. He's their biological son. I was having dinner with my cousin, who was helping me with a class I was struggling with. We hadn't seen each other in months. He has a wicked sense of humor, and that's why I was laughing so hard when you walked up to us."

Emma reached behind her back, and before I knew it, her bra had fallen to the ground. She stood in front of me, wearing nothing but knickers, her garter, and hose.

"I think I'm going to faint," I said as I looked her perfect body up and down.

"Garrett...touch me," Emma whispered.

My eyes snapped up to hers, and I felt the tears building in my eyes. "Emma...I'm so sorry. I thought—"

She pushed herself into my body and ran her hand through my hair. "Garrett Thomas Mathews, kiss me and put your hands on me before I explode from needing to feel your touch."

I did as she'd asked. I slammed my lips against hers, and the moment her tongue touched mine, I let out a moan. She tasted like cinnamon and honey—that was the only way I could describe it. She was so damn sweet. She grabbed my hand and moved it up to her breast. The instant I touched her, I jerked my mouth from hers.

She dropped her head back and moaned. "Oh God, I've dreamed of this moment for months." Bringing her hand up, she grabbed her other breast and began playing with her nipple.

"Emma...you're gonna kill me. I think you're trying to kill me."

She snapped her head back up and took a step back. I reached out to keep touching her, but she smiled and turned. She started walking back to the tree.

Holy shit. I could see the cheeks of her ass peeking out from her knickers.

She looked back at me from over her shoulder, and she used her finger to motion for me to follow her. I began walking toward her, and I watched as she reached down and began laying out the quilt. I stopped just short of the quilt and stared at her as she leaned up against the tree.

She slowly put her finger in her mouth and then let out a giggle. "I'm trying to seduce you, Mr. Mathews. Is it working?"

I couldn't help but smile. "I would say it's working very well, Miss Birk, very well indeed."

"Garrett?"

I looked her body up and down. "Yeah?" I pulled my shirt up and over my head and tossed it to the ground.

She held up a condom, and I about dropped to my knees.

"I want you to make love to me, Garrett. Then, after we make love, I want you to do something else for me."

My mouth was dry, and I fought like hell to speak. "Oh...okay. I'll do whatever you want, Buttercup."

She pushed off the tree and began walking over to me. She put the condom gently between her teeth as she reached down and started taking off my pants.

Don't touch me. Don't touch me. Oh God, please don't let me come from just her touching me.

She slowly began stripping me of my clothes. I lifted one leg at a time, and before I knew it, she was standing up and taking a step back. She ran her eyes over my body. The way she was looking at me had me grabbing myself, and I let out a moan.

She went to unclip her hose, but I quickly walked up and dropped to my knees onto the quilt. I began to open each snap. I placed my hands on her legs and listened to her breathing increase.

"Take off your knickers, but leave your stockings on, Emma."

I looked up at her chest heaving up and down. I'd never seen anyone move so fast in my life. Emma tossed her knickers on top of my clothes. I reached up and began rolling her stocking down her right leg. I placed my hands on her left leg and slowly began taking off that stocking. When she lifted her leg, I removed the stocking but put her leg over my shoulder.

"I want to taste you, Emma," I said as I pulled her closer to me.

She placed both hands in my hair and whispered, "Garrett…I'm scared."

I pushed my face into her and quickly flicked her clit with my tongue. She jerked her hips into me and let out a small scream. "Oh my God!"

She grabbed a handful of my hair and pulled my face into her more. I couldn't help but smile, knowing my sweet, naughty Emma liked this. I slowly pushed two fingers into her.

Damn…she's so tight.

I needed to make her orgasm as many times as I could before we made love. I gently moved my fingers in and out as I began sucking on her clit, and then I began my assault on her clit with my tongue. She started pumping her hips more, and before I knew it, she was clamping down on my fingers and falling apart as she called out my name. I didn't even care how loud she was. I was making her come in the most intimate way. I was about to make her completely mine. When she finally began relaxing, I quickly stood up and held on to her.

"Garrett…that was…oh my…that was amazing."

I smiled and kissed her as I gradually brought her down to lie on the quilt. "Please tell me you haven't had an orgasm since the last time we were on this quilt," I whispered against her lips.

She looked away. "I can't tell you that because it would be a lie."

I swallowed hard, and I was about to ask her when she turned back to face me. The moonlight caught her eyes, and I fell in love with her even more.

"I have dreams about you all the time, Garrett. When I wake up, I'm touching myself. I can't tell you how many times I've made myself orgasm because I was dreaming or thinking about you. I'm so sorry."

She went to look away again, but I placed my hand on the side of her face.

"Don't ever say you are sorry. Baby, I've done the same thing."

The smile that spread across her face would have dropped me to my knees had I been standing up.

"Emma, I need to make you come again, so when we make love, it won't hurt as bad," I whispered.

She nodded her head and gave me a wicked smile. "I never finished telling you what I want after you make love to me."

I chortled. "No…no, you didn't."

She began chewing on her lower lip as she slowly wrapped her legs around me and said, "Garrett, after you make love to me, I want you to…I want you to fuck me against the tree."

Holy…

Son of bitch…

Did she just say...
"Emma, I think I just came."

8 Emma

"What?" I pushed Garrett off of me and slammed my hands over my mouth. I was filled with regret for even saying what I had just said. Here I was, so close to Garrett making love to me, and I'd made him come before he even got inside me.

Garrett started laughing. "Buttercup, I'm kidding. Lie back down."

He gently laid me back down and buried his face between my legs again before I could even say a word to the cruel joke he had just played on me. I didn't care how dirty all the other girls had said this was. It felt amazing, and I would let Garrett do it anytime he wanted to. The way his tongue moved on me was wonderful. I tried with all my might not to come so quickly this time, but when he reached his hand up and began playing with my nipple, I lost it.

It didn't take long before I was calling out his name. "Garrett, oh my God! Oh God, yes! God, yes, don't stop!"

I couldn't believe how I was acting. It was like I had left sweet and innocent Emma in the car and found my inner sex goddess. I was pumping my hips into his face and begging for him not to stop.

When I finally began coming down from that intense high, I felt Garrett's kisses moving up my body. When he stopped and put a nipple into his mouth, I could feel another orgasm beginning to build. He stopped, and the feeling quickly went away. Then, he moved to the other nipple, and the feeling began building again. Right before I thought I was going to explode, he moved his lips up to my neck as he positioned himself between my legs. I could feel his dick looking for entrance into my body, and I was scared and excited at the same time.

He stopped right before my lips. "Can I kiss you after what I did?"

I slid my hand around his neck and pulled him to my lips. At first, the idea of it made me feel a bit unsure, but soon, I was lost in Garrett's kiss. He slowly began pushing against me, and I immediately tensed up.

"Emma, baby, I need you to relax."

I looked into his eyes and nodded my head as I whispered, "Is it going to hurt, Garrett?"

His eyes filled with tears as he gently kissed me on the lips. He pulled back slightly and said, "At first, but then it will feel good. I promise."

I wrapped my arms around him and opened my legs more to him. The moment he began seeking entry, I felt the burning sensation. I bit down on my lip and tried to relax.

Garrett started kissing me over and over. "I love you, Emma. I'll love you forever."

Then, he pushed in a little more, and I let out a gasp.

"I'm going to make you mine. You're completely and utterly mine."

"Yes!" I called out as he pushed in more. "Oh my God. I just thought you looked big, but…my God, I think you're huge. Is it…will it fit?"

Garrett began laughing as he looked at me. "That is the sexiest thing anyone has ever said to me, and yes, baby…it will fit."

I let out a giggle, and Garrett pushed in more.

"Oh God!" I cried out as he slowly began moving in and out. "Are you in all the way?"

Garrett began kissing me again as he moved gently and slowly. Each time, he pushed in more until I was positive that I wouldn't be able to take another inch of him.

"I'm all the way in, baby," he whispered against my lips. "I'm going to make love to you now, Emma."

My heart slammed in my chest, and I felt a tear slide down my cheek. He moved so slowly, and at first, it burned like hell, but then it began to feel amazing.

"Garrett, I never imagined it would feel so…amazing, so…beautiful."

As Garrett began to go faster and faster, I started to feel the buildup again. I instantly thought about Margie saying how Billy had yet to make her orgasm during sex. If it happened to me on my first time, I was going to rub it in.

"Garrett…can you go deeper? I mean…faster and deeper?" I reached over and grabbed the quilt.

I arched my body as Garrett picked up his pace.

He let out a grunt and said, "Emma…I'm so close."

I thrashed my head back and forth. "Garrett, oh God…I'm going to come…yes! Oh God, yes!"

The next thing I knew, Garrett was calling out my name as I called out his. I could feel my insides pulsing down on him. It felt so incredible, and I'd never experienced anything so moving in my entire life.

"I love you, Emma. I love you so much," Garrett said as he stayed on top of me.

He was still inside me, and I could feel him twitching. I smiled, knowing that Garrett would be the only person to make me feel like this for the rest of our lives.

"I love you, too, Garrett. That was wonderful. I can't believe how amazing you feel inside me."

Garrett jumped up and began swearing. "Motherfucker! Oh shit. No! Oh my God, no."

I sat up quickly. "What? What's wrong? Did I do or say something wrong?"

Garrett looked at me as he dropped to his knees. "Emma…I'm so sorry. I'm so very sorry. I can't believe…I didn't think…I got so caught up in everything, and I just…oh God."

He dropped his head on my chest, and I started to feel like I couldn't breathe.

What is happening? Why is he so upset?

Then, I looked down and to my right.

The condom. Oh no, Garrett forgot to put on the condom.

A part of me was overjoyed at the idea of possibly getting pregnant with Garrett's baby. The other part of me panicked. My parents had been mad enough at me when I told them I was leaving college. My father had told me if I walked away from school, he would never speak to me again or help me if I chose to go back to school.

The moment I'd seen the hurt in Garrett's eyes when he saw me with Philip, I'd known that I would never hurt him again. When I'd watched him drive away, I'd known I had to listen to my heart, and my heart had told me that I needed to be with Garrett.

I moved back some, so Garrett would look at me. "Garrett, please don't do this. It's okay. I promise, it's okay."

He shook his head. "No, Emma, that was so irresponsible of me. I promised David…I promised him that I would be careful. We just…oh my God, Emma. What if you get pregnant?"

I smiled. "Then, it would be a part of God's plan. Garrett, I'm here to stay. I love you more than life itself, and I'm not going back to Austin. I want to be with you—forever."

Garrett looked at me with a shocked expression on his face. "What do you mean, you're not going back to Austin?"

I took in a deep breath and slowly let it out. I knew Garrett was about to be upset with me, but I didn't care. "I saw the hurt in your eyes when you thought Philip and I were together. I vowed at that very moment that I would never be the reason you hurt like that again. I told my parents I was quitting school and coming back to Mason…coming back to be with the man I love."

When I saw the tear slide down his face, everything in that one moment changed. We were meant to be together, and nothing would ever keep us apart.

"Can I ask you something?" Garrett asked as he pushed a piece of loose hair behind my ear.

Then, he ran his finger up and down my arm, and it felt like a million little pricks were stinging me everywhere he touched.

"Always," I whispered.

"How many condoms did you get out of my drawer?" he asked with a wink.

My mouth dropped opened, and I slapped his arm. "How did you know I got them from your room?"

Garrett shrugged his shoulders. "Lucky guess."

I smiled and pulled him to me as I slowly began to lie back. I reached over and grabbed the condom. "I was looking for the quilt when I found them. I finally asked your mother where you might have put the quilt I'd made you, and she just smiled and said it was in your truck."

Garrett's face turned to panic. "Did she see you getting the condoms?"

"No! Of course not."

I looked down when I felt Garrett's hardness pushing against me. When I looked back up, he was ripping open the condom, and I watched as he rolled it over his thick, long shaft. I shivered with anticipation and opened myself to him. This time, Garrett wasn't as gentle, and I was surprised by how much I liked it. He told me to roll over and get on my hands and knees. It was much deeper this way, and I came almost instantly. Being with Garrett like this would forever be my favorite thing.

I rolled over, and right before Garrett came, he whispered in my ear, "Happy New Year, Buttercup." As he came, he then whispered my name and told me how much he loved me.

Garrett dropped to my side and tried to catch his breath as I wrapped myself up in the quilt. Tonight was warmer than normal, and I was ready to sleep under the stars with the man I would love forever.

Garrett held on to me, and his breathing began to slow and even out. I found myself being soothed by it. I had never felt so at peace in my life.

I fell asleep and dreamed of white dresses, puppies, babies…and Garrett making love to me against the tree and then the barn.

I felt Garrett moving his hand down my face, and I smiled. I was just about to say something when he covered my mouth. I snapped my eyes open and looked at him.

He put his finger up to his mouth and slowly shook his head. My eyes grew bigger.

Oh God, someone must be coming! My parents! Oh. My. God. My father. Garrett better run if he wants to live.

"Em, don't move. Stay perfectly still. Can you stay perfectly still?" Garrett whispered.

I swallowed hard and nodded my head.

He very carefully removed his hand from my mouth. "Don't make a sound."

I opened my mouth, and he looked at me.

"If it's my father...run!" I whispered.

Garrett looked at me, confused at first, and then he must have understood what I'd meant.

He rolled his eyes and smiled. "No, it's not that, but I do need you to be calm. Okay?"

"Calm. I can do calm," I said with a wink.

When I felt him against me, I immediately began grinding myself against him.

He peeked down and raised one eyebrow. "Em, this is serious."

I pouted. "What could be more important than you taking me against the tree?"

Garrett's eyes darted over my head and then back at me. "The rattlesnake near us is kind of taking top priority right now."

I smiled, but then it hit me. *Did he say...rattlesnake?*

"What did you say?" I said a little louder.

He held his finger up to his mouth. "Baby, I need you to very slowly start getting up after I get off of you, okay? Don't make any sudden movements or loud sounds, or the snake will—"

Oh. My. God. He did say rattlesnake!

I pushed him as hard as I could, somehow managing to throw him onto his back, while I let out the loudest scream humanly possible. I was pretty sure my arms where flailing about as I jumped over Garrett before making my way to the car. I jumped into the backseat, and for some reason, I was still screaming. I watched as the snake took off in the other direction. Garrett got up and quickly wrapped the quilt around him. He turned and just looked at me. I let out another scream and then another, but each one got quieter and quieter.

He shook his head as he walked over to the car and opened the door. "Damn, woman, you left me out to burn."

I threw my hands up to my mouth and started to laugh. "Garrett, I'm so...I'm so sorry, but I just panicked."

"You don't say?"

I bit down on my lower lip and felt the blush hit my cheeks when I realized I was still naked.

"I could have been bitten by a snake, and you just took off. Matter of fact, you pushed me out of your way *and* jumped over me in your escape."

I slowly dropped my hands and looked behind him to make sure the beast was gone. Then, I remembered my dream last night where Garrett had taken me against the tree.

"Garrett?"

When he gave me that smile of his, I knew I could go forward with this. I pushed him back and got out of the car. Now that it was daylight, I could really see him taking in every inch of my body, and the lust in his eyes turned me on even more.

I lifted my foot and began running it up and down my other leg. "I do believe you promised to…take me up against that tree."

Garrett dropped the quilt and grinned as I looked at him.

He pulled me to him and put his lips on my neck. "I do believe your exact words were that you wanted me to fuck you against that tree."

I let out a moan, and the naughty girl inside me was more than ready to come out and play. The only thing I could say was, "Yes…please."

Garrett picked me up, and I wrapped my legs around him. He reached down and picked up the quilt. He walked over to the tree and placed the quilt behind me before pushing me against the tree.

He was about to lift me up and slide me onto him when he stopped. "Shit! Condom!"

I let out a laugh as he slid me down his body. He turned to go get one, and then he stopped. He glanced back to me, and I was about to say something when he put his hand on my mouth again. My eyes widened, and he shook his head.

"Truck. A truck is coming!"

I pushed his hand away. "Oh my God!" I yelled.

We frantically began searching for our clothes.

Where in the heck is my bra? The car! It's by the car!

As I took off toward the car, Garrett jumped in front of me, and we ran right into each other. He started running in circles, and I couldn't help but start laughing. I found my bra and attempted to put it on. Garrett was now dressed in his pants and shirt, and he was helping me get my skirt on.

"It's getting closer, Garrett!" I said.

He picked up my garter and hose. We both looked each other in the eyes, and the next thing I knew, he was shoving them down his pants. Garrett spun around, and then he grabbed my hand and pulled me over to the quilt. He began spreading it out, and then he pushed me down on it.

"What are you doing?" I asked as I tried to sit back up.

"Trust me! Lie back down and just look up at the sky." Garrett lay down next to me and then said, "Shit! The condoms!"

He jumped up and kicked a bunch of dirt over them. Then, he sat down next to me right as the truck came around the bend. When I turned and looked at it, I noticed it was Mr. Bauer's truck, and sitting in the front seat was—

Oh no, my father.

Garrett grabbed my hand. "I'm glad we had last night."

I couldn't help but let out a giggle as I sat up and waited for what was about to happen.

When Mr. Bauer got out of the truck, he immediately looked at Garrett.

"If I die in the next two minutes, always remember, I love you."

I swallowed hard when my father got out of the truck. He looked at me and then Garrett.

I turned to Garrett and smiled. "Same goes for me."

9 Garrett

I reached down and grabbed Emma's hand as I watched David and Dr. Birk walk up to us.

"Emma, Garrett, are you enjoying the morning?" David asked as he looked at me.

He knows.

Dr. Birk walked up and looked at Emma. "Emma, Mrs. Mathews said you and Garrett left earlier this morning to watch the sun rise. Why in the world are you doing this?"

My mouth about dropped to the ground, and Emma squeezed my hand. I quickly looked at David, who winked at me.

Oh God, my mother knows Emma and I had sex. Dr. Birk killing me would be better than facing my mother right now.

"Daddy, I don't expect you to understand, but I can't be away from Garrett any longer. I gave school a try, and I'm not going back. I'm staying here with Garrett."

My heart started pounding as Dr. Birk slowly looked at me.

He nodded his head and turned to David. "Do you want to start, or should I?"

I stood up and stepped forward and cleared my throat. "Dr. Birk, before you begin, may I please say something?"

Emma's father turned and looked at me. "Yes, Garrett, you may."

I faced Emma and smiled. When she grinned back up at me, I knew what I was about to do was the right thing. I leaned down and gently kissed her on the cheek before facing Dr. Birk and David.

"Dr. Birk, I know you don't think I can provide a good future for your daughter since I gave up on school and all, but I promise you, I work my butt off every day on this ranch. My father built one of the best cattle ranches in the area, and I intend on making it even better. I want to give your daughter the world. I want to take her places where she's only dreamed of going. My goals in life are simple, sir. Work hard, build an even better name for this ranch, and wake up every day and thank God for what he has given me. The most important goal though is to love Emma more than life itself, to shower her with attention, and to do my best to keep her safe, healthy, and happy."

I saw the corner of Dr. Birk's mouth turn up, but I didn't want to get my hopes up. When I glanced over at David, he nodded his head once at me.

Dr. Birk looked down at the ground and then back up at me. "Son, I can't tell you how glad I am to hear you say all of that. It's important to have goals in life. Simple or not, they are our driving force to better ourselves. I have goals of my own as does Mr. Bauer over here."

David nodded his head and placed his hands in his pockets.

"Now, I'm not saying I'm okay with my daughter coming home one day and saying she is dropping out of college. I think it is very important for her to get an education, and the same goes for you."

I wanted to say something, but he held up his hand. "Garrett, I know what it took for you to walk away from your scholarship, and I know why you did it. I commend you for being the man you've become. But...you want something that is mine, and there is no way I'm going to give her up without some negotiations."

My heart was pounding so loudly that I was sure everyone could hear it. "Negotiations?" I asked.

Now, it was David's turn to talk. "Garrett, you know your father and I were best friends since we were ten years old. I respected him more than anything."

I nodded my head. "Yes, sir."

He cleared his throat and continued, "This past year has been hard on all of us, especially you and your mother. I've tried my best to be there for both of you, and...well, something has been happening over the last few months."

I already knew where David was going with this. I'd seen him and my mother together. I'd noticed how he was the only other person besides me who could make her smile. For the last two months, whenever David had walked into a room, my mother would light up.

I nodded my head and smiled. "I've seen y'all together, David. I see how happy you've been making her."

Relief spread across David's face. He smiled and then looked away before quickly looking back at me. "Yes, your mother makes me very happy as well, Garrett. I'm happier than I've been in years. We've been talking the last few weeks, and with Billy going to college and planning on moving to Austin, I've been doing a lot of thinking about my own ranch. It's much smaller than the Mathews' ranch. Your father and I had actually talked about him buying me out."

I tilted my head. "Buy you out? You mean, he was going to take over your ranch?" I looked at Emma.

"Yes, the deal was that I would sell but remain on as a ranch hand to help your father until you were out of school and could begin taking over full-time."

My head was spinning. That would make our ranch one of the biggest cattle ranches in Mason County. I smiled at the possibilities that could bring to our ranch.

David let out a chuckle. "Garrett, I can see your mind already working. Yes, that would make the Mathews' ranch the biggest cattle ranch in the area."

Dr. Birk smiled. "Garrett, I have a proposition for you. Right now, you don't have the monetary means to buy out Mr. Bauer, but I do. We talked this morning with your mother, and we've all come up with a plan."

Emma reached for my hand and stood up next to me. "Daddy, what kind of plan?"

"Now, I want you both to just listen to me before you say anything."

Emma and I both nodded our heads. I didn't even realize that I had been holding my breath until I slowly let it out as I waited for Emma's dad to tell us his plan.

"I will help with buying out Mr. Bauer's ranch, and in exchange for buying him out with cash, Mr. Bauer will come on as the ranch hand for the Mathews' cattle ranch. He will be in charge of running the ranch daily while you and Emma are attending school at the University of Texas."

Emma and I both said at the same time, "What?"

Dr. Birk took in a deep breath and slowly let it out. "Garrett, I've never thought that you were not capable of taking care of my daughter. I knew you didn't get into Texas A&M just on a football scholarship. I've seen your grades, and I know you were third in your class in high school. Son, I want to see you succeed to the best of your ability. It's very clear to me that my daughter is in love with you. I want the best for her, and I want the best for you. I want to see the two of you fulfill your dreams, but I firmly believe you both need to have college educations—not only for you but for my grandchildren."

Emma sucked in a deep breath and said, "Daddy—"

Dr. Birk held up his hand and shook his head. "My grandchildren that y'all will be giving me *after* you graduate from college."

I quickly said a prayer that Emma wouldn't get pregnant because of my stupid mistake last night, but if she did, we would deal with it. Right now, I was just trying to take everything in.

"Dr. Birk, I don't…I mean, I can't afford to go to school. All the income coming in goes right back into the ranch."

"I know that, son. I consider this an investment. I'm investing in you and your future," Dr. Birk said as he looked at Emma and winked.

Emma let out a squeal and ran into her father's arms.

My legs felt like they were about to go out. *Emma's father is going to pay for me to go to college on top of buying David's ranch? Why would he do that?* I slowly shook my head and ran my hand through my hair, trying to process all of this. "Dr. Birk, I do not mean any disrespect, sir, but why would you do all of this for me?"

Emma's father smiled as he looked me in the eyes. "I want to do this for you, Garrett, because my daughter loves you, and I believe you have a very bright future ahead of you."

"Sir, if I do this, then part of the deal must be that you will allow me to pay you back for everything."

I looked at David, who seemed to be beaming. He was smiling from ear to ear.

When I glanced back over at Dr. Birk, he was smiling bigger. "Garrett, you were truly raised as a gentleman. You should be very proud of your parents. Yes, I agree to your part of the deal, son."

Dr. Birk reached his hand out to me, and when I reached out to shake it, he pulled me in and quickly hugged me. I stepped back, and David stuck his hand out for mine.

As we shook hands, he pulled me in and whispered in my ear, "Your father would be so proud of the man you have become. We'll talk about last night after Charles leaves."

I stepped back and smiled. "Thank you, sir, and, um…okay."

Emma jumped up and down and then ran into my arms. "Garrett, we'll be together and in school!"

I smiled as I hugged her.

"There is one more thing," Dr. Birk said.

Emma quickly turned to face him. "What, Daddy? I'll do anything."

"I want you both to promise us that you will not get married until after you finish school," Dr. Birk said.

David nodded his head. He was quickly becoming more and more of a father figure to me, so his agreement spoke volumes to me.

Emma started to argue with her father, "Daddy, what? Why? I don't see—"

I stepped in front of her and nodded my head. "Although I want nothing more than to make Emma my wife, I do understand why you are including this condition."

Emma pushed me out of the way and placed her hands on her hips. "Excuse me, I don't seem to understand." She glared at me and then looked back at her father. "Why does it matter if we get married now or if we wait until after we graduate?"

Her father smiled. "Emma, let's just slow down and take things one day at a time. I think Garrett understands our reasons."

"Well, I don't, Daddy."

"I want you both to focus on school. Your first year is almost over, and Garrett can take summer classes to catch up. I'm not asking you to wait a long time. All I'm asking is for you both to wait a few years."

I walked up next to Emma and took her hand. When her eyes met mine, something happened between us. We didn't have to be married to know we belonged to each other. After what we had shared last night, I would wait forever for her. I gave her a smile, and when she smiled back, I felt the ground move.

Without looking back at her father, Emma said, "Okay. As long as we are both at the same university, I think I can wait a few years to become Mrs. Garrett Mathews."

I pulled her to me. I began kissing her, and I wasn't sure where my head was until David put his hand on my shoulder.

He pulled me back. "Garrett, I'd like to see you live another day, so mind your manners when it comes to kissing Dr. Birk's daughter, especially when he is standing right next to you."

Everyone let out a laugh, and I watched as the blush moved across Emma's cheeks.

"Come on, let's head back to the house. Your mother made potato soup, and it smelled like pure heaven. We will get you registered and all taken care of with the school by the end of the week," Dr. Birk said.

I wasn't about to ask how many strings he was fixin' to pull to get me into the University of Texas for the spring semester. I had been offered a football scholarship there, but I'd turned it down to go to A&M. Now, I was wishing more than anything that I had accepted it.

We spent the rest of the afternoon sitting on the porch, making plans for Emma and me to go to school together. Dr. Birk had walked inside to use the phone at least a dozen times. The last time he walked out onto the porch, he had a smile on his face as big as the Grand Canyon.

He cleared his throat and looked down at my mother and David before turning to me. "Garrett, I hope you've kept in shape, son. Starting this coming season, it looks like you'll be playing football for the University of Texas."

Emma and my mother stood up and began jumping up and down as David stood up and shook Dr. Birk's hand. I just sat there, stunned.

What in the hell just happened?

This morning, I was a cattle rancher, and now, I'm walking on the UT football team and getting my business management degree.

I shook my head and started to laugh. I looked up and silently thanked my father for continuing to look after me.

10 Emma

August 1958

I stood outside Moore-Hill Hall, waiting for Garrett to come out. He had been so busy all summer with taking classes to get caught up that we had hardly spent any time together. With all the football practices he'd had, we'd barely had time to say hi, but Garrett had made sure that we snuck in time to be alone together. I thought I would go insane if Garrett didn't make love to me at least once a week.

I smiled as I thought back to last night. He hadn't had a condom with him, so he'd refused to do anything. Ever since our first time together when he'd forgotten to use one, he had made sure to always have plenty of condoms with him, so he had been beyond frustrated that he had forgot one last night.

I closed my eyes and thought of how I'd finally gotten the nerve to take him into my mouth. Margie had been going on and on about how much she always loved giving Billy blow jobs. Garrett had seemed to like it, but honestly, I could never do it again and be happy.

"Hey, Emma. Did you run over here or something? Your face is flush."

I looked up to see Rick Manly standing there. I placed my hands over my cheeks and smiled as I shook my head. "No, it must be the heat."

Then, my whole body came to life as I felt arms around me.

Garrett turned me around and searched my face. He leaned down and whispered in my ear, "What are you thinking about, you naughty girl?"

I let out a giggle and whispered, "Last night."

"Which part? My lips on you or your lips on me?"

I hit him on the chest, and he started laughing.

"Hey, Rick. How's it going?" Garrett asked as he grabbed my hand and pulled me next to him.

"Good. With the look on your lovely girlfriend's face, I'd say things between you two seem to be heating up more and more."

Garrett laughed. "My goal is to keep her happy. We have to run though. We have a long drive ahead of us."

Rick and Garrett shook hands, and then Garrett and I turned and made our way to his truck.

We were heading back to Mason for the weekend to attend his mother and David's wedding. Garrett had been stressing out over the speech he had to give. The whole way to Mason, he kept practicing it over and over while moving around like he just couldn't sit still. At one point, I even offered to drive.

"Garrett, stop stressing. It sounds lovely. Why are you so nervous?" I asked.

He pushed his hand through his wavy brown hair. I slowly took in a deep breath. I wasn't sure why, but whenever he did that, it would turn me on. The pit of my stomach began to tighten. I was wishing we were already married, so we could just stay together this weekend and make love as much as we wanted to without having to sneak around to do it. I placed my head on the back of the seat and closed my eyes as I thought about this past month.

My parents had been in Europe the whole month, celebrating their anniversary, so Garrett and I had been going to my parent's house every chance we got. The things he would do to me—

Oh Lord.

I snapped my head forward and shook my head. I needed to stop thinking about it, or I would be forced to put my hand down my knickers. I glanced over at Garrett, and he was tapping the steering wheel. When I reached over and placed my hand on his arm, he jumped.

"Gosh, Garrett, what in the world is wrong? You're a nervous wreck."

Garrett smiled. "I'm just thinking about my mom getting married again. It's going to be weird. I mean, I've always thought of David as a second father, but at the same time, it will be weird to see my mother with a man besides…" His voice trailed off.

My heart broke.

He yawned and shook his head, like he was trying to wake himself up.

"Do you want me to drive? You look so tired," I said as I ran my fingers through his hair.

He let out a small moan, and I instantly wanted him inside me. I quickly glanced down between us.

The quilt.

I looked to see where we were, and I let out a giggle. Mr. Martin's old place wasn't too far down the road. I peeked over and saw Garrett yawning again.

"I know a place where we can pull off, and you can rest for a bit," I said as I adjusted myself in the seat to ease the throbbing.

Garrett let out a laugh. "Buttercup, we're almost into Mason. We only have about thirty minutes to go."

"I need to stop. I have to go pee." I slid my hand down next to me and crossed my fingers.

"Where are you going to go, Em? On the side of the road?"

I smiled and shook my head. "Nope. I know of an old farmhouse that has been abandoned. My father used to go and check on the older man because he lived alone. It's been empty for about five years now. My friends and I used to go and hang out there."

I saw the corners of Garrett's lips lift. He was smiling, and that made me smile.

I looked back out the window and said, "It's just up the road about another mile or so if you want to pull in. It will be on the right."

"You naughty little girl. Em, we'll be trespassing on private property," Garrett said with a chuckle.

I pulled my legs up underneath me. "Oh, come on, Garrett. Let's do something naughty."

He quickly looked at me and then back out onto the road. "We've been doing something naughty for the last eight months."

I let out a giggle and pointed straight ahead. "There it is! Garrett, pull into the driveway. I can't believe no one has put up a gate yet."

Garrett headed down the driveway. He drove for about a mile before we finally saw the old house. I let out a gasp and threw my hands up to my mouth. All the windows were broken, and the house looked like it was about to fall over.

"No," I whispered.

Garrett parked and turned off his truck. He got out and stretched. Looking at me, he said, "If you think I'm going into that house for one minute, you're crazy." After closing his door, he walked around to my side of the truck and opened the door for me.

"Are you afraid, Mr. Mathews?"

He was staring at the house and slowly nodded his head. "Yes, I am."

I jumped into his arms and took in a deep breath. He smelled heavenly. I needed to feel him inside me. I pressed my lips to his, and our kiss quickly heated up.

I barely pulled away from his lips and panted. "Please tell me you have a condom in your pocket."

He let out a laugh as he spun around and pushed me against his truck. I instantly hoped he would take me up against the truck. Garrett was always so gentle with his lovemaking, and for once, I wanted him to be rough. I wanted to have sex like Margie and Billy did. Those two had sex like rabbits every chance they got and everywhere they could.

Garrett reached into his pocket and pulled out a condom. I wanted to ask him if he kept them in every pair of pants he owned. He slowly slid me down, and then he reached inside the truck to grab the quilt. He intended on making love to me in his truck, but I had other plans. I quickly began undressing while he messed with spreading out the quilt. The other day, I had gone shopping with Margie, and I'd bought a new pair of lace knickers that I really wanted Garrett to see, but right now, the only thing on my mind was getting him to take me up against his truck.

When Garrett stepped back and turned around, his mouth dropped open. I was standing completely naked in front of him. I bit down on my lower lip.

Garrett whispered, "Jesus, Emma."

Come on, Emma Rose. You can do this. "I believe it was on New Year's Day, Mr. Mathews, when you promised me a good fucking up against a tree. That never happened, so I'm thinking your truck would make a nice substitute. Don't you?"

"I, um...I-I, um...I can't, um...can't think."

I smiled and put my finger inside my mouth. Margie had told me that if I stuck my finger in my mouth and either bit down on it or sucked on it while I moaned, it would certainly lead to sex. I decided to go in for the kill. As I closed my eyes, I pushed my finger all the way in my mouth, and I sucked on it before slowly pulling it out with a moan.

Garrett muttered a few curse words, and when I opened my eyes, he had his pants off. After rolling on the condom, he picked me up and walked me back against his truck.

"Yes! Oh God, Garrett, yes!" I said as I put my hands on his shoulders.

"Emma, I'm not going to be gentle with you. I can't right now. I need you too much."

I shook my head. "Don't be. Garrett, I need to feel you moving inside me—now!"

I let out a small whimper as Garrett lifted me a little higher. He placed his tip at my entrance and then slammed into me. When he pulled back and pushed into me again, I felt the pressure building.

You have got to be kidding me! I've never had an orgasm this fast before.

"Harder," I whispered.

Garrett pulled out, and this time, he slammed back into me so hard and deep that it hit me instantly.

"Faster...oh God, Garrett, go faster!"

Before I knew it, I had been taken to heaven and back as Garrett moved in and out of me, hard and fast. If my mother knew how I was behaving, she would lock me away and never let me out. Being with Garrett like this was all I ever thought about. I couldn't get enough of him.

"Emma...I'm gonna come, baby." Garrett gasped for breath. "Ah..." he cried out as he pulled out and thrust back in one more time.

He dropped his forehead to mine and tried desperately to get air. I had my legs wrapped around him so tight. I didn't want him to leave me. I loved feeling him inside me, and I loved how just the smallest movement on my part caused his dick to jump.

"Garrett…" I whispered. "I love you so much."

He took in a deep breath. "Emma Rose…I love you more."

When he pulled out of me, I instantly missed his warmth. I went to say something, but Garrett put his hand over my mouth as he put me down. He put his finger up to his lips, signaling for me to be quiet.

That was when I heard the car driving up the driveway.

"Are you kidding me?" Garrett said as he quickly picked up my clothes. He put them in my arms and shoved me into the truck. "Get dressed, Em!" he shouted.

He then pulled his pants on and quickly grabbed his cowboy boots from inside the truck. He picked up the sneakers he'd been wearing off the ground, threw them into the truck, and successfully hit me right in the eye.

I let out a scream.

"Em, be quiet!"

He shut the door, and I saw him reach down and pick something up. He ran over to some trees and gave whatever it was a good throw. He slowly began walking back to the truck, and then he stopped dead in his tracks. I was almost dressed at this point when I looked to see—

"Mr. Bauer?" I said to myself as I pulled my pants up and buttoned them. I slipped my loafers on and pulled my hair into a ponytail.

Mr. Bauer pulled up and parked. He got out of the truck and walked over to Garrett. Smiling, Mr. Bauer reached out his hand for Garrett's. They started talking, and Garrett pointed to the truck. I looked down and acted like I was messing with my shoe.

The door opened, and Garrett said, "Emma, you'll never believe who stopped by Mr. Martin's old place."

I peeked up and looked at Garrett. He was giving me a I-can't-believe-David-drove-up-on-us-naked-again look. I tried not to giggle.

The last time Mr. Bauer had driven up with my father in the passenger seat, Mr. Bauer had known Garrett and I had just slept together. He'd met with Garrett later that afternoon, and Garrett had said Mr. Bauer gave him the whole sex talk even though Garrett had assured him that he was safe. We never told anyone that our first time together was completely natural with no condom at all. I wouldn't change it for the world. It had felt like heaven, and I'd been begging Garrett not to wear one, but he was afraid he wouldn't be able to pull out in time.

Garrett reached for my hand and helped me up and out of the truck. I smiled as David leaned against his truck.

"Hey, Mr. Bauer! Are you getting nervous?" I asked, my voice cracking.

He laughed and nodded his head.

Garrett slipped his arm around my waist, and the butterflies went off in my stomach. I was shocked that his touch still affected me even after all these months.

Garrett said, "I was telling David that I had to really go pee, and I was about to pull over on the side of the road when you remembered your dad had stopped by here with you before. Since it's abandoned, we pulled in, so I could use the bathroom really quick while you changed into more comfortable pants."

I nodded my head and turned back to look at the house. "Yep. It makes me sad that the place has been let go like this. When I was just a little girl while my father was the doctor in Fredericksburg, my father used to see Mr. Martin."

I looked back, and Mr. Bauer was smiling.

I tilted my head and said, "Mr. Bauer, what's going on?"

He looked at Garrett and then back at me. "I bought this place about a month ago. My plan is to restore it, and by the time y'all are finished with school, hopefully, Julia and I will be moved into our new home."

I let out a squeal. "Oh, golly! How exciting, Mr. Bauer!"

Garrett was smiling from ear to ear. "Does Mom know?"

Mr. Bauer shook his head. "It's a wedding present. I was just coming to check on things, and here you kids were. It's almost like a sign."

I nodded my head in agreement. "Oh, it's a wonderful sign, and I have a feeling y'all are going to be very happy here. I can't wait to help restore this old house when we come home for visits."

"I'm going to hold you to that, young lady. I'm sure we will need all the help we can get," Mr. Bauer said as he took another look at the house.

We talked for a few minutes more before everyone piled back into the trucks. Once Mr. Bauer began driving off, Garrett and I looked at each other and started laughing.

"Holy shit! That's twice that bastard has almost caught us naked," Garrett said.

We both laughed again.

The twenty-five minute drive to the ranch went by pretty fast. Garrett was now rambling on and on about everything and anything he could think of. I couldn't believe how nervous he was about his mother getting married. I would almost think it was him getting married.

When he pulled up and parked, Mrs. Mathews came running down the porch stairs. Garrett got out and ran up to her. He picked her up and spun her around a few times as she let out a small scream.

"Garrett Thomas Mathews, you put me down right now," she said.

He gently put her down and kissed her on the cheek. "Damn, I've missed you, Mama."

"Mind your manners, young man. Don't be cursing in front of ladies."

He let out a small laugh. "Yes, ma'am."

Mrs. Mathews looked at me and smiled. "Emma Rose, darling, come here and hug me."

I walked over and gave her a hug. She held on to me tightly. The last time I'd hugged her, she had been so frail. I was glad to see that she had put on a bit more weight. She looked breathtaking. She was as tall as me with light brown hair and the bluest eyes I'd ever seen. Garrett looked so much like his mother, but he had his father's smile. Garrett was tall with wavy dark hair and eyes so blue, like the color of the sky after a rainstorm.

I had asked my father about the chances of our children having blue eyes.

He'd laughed and said, *Pretty darn good, sweetheart.*

I hoped our children had Garrett's vibrant blue eyes and not my bluish-gray ones.

"Are you excited, Mrs. Mathews?" I asked as we made our way into the house.

She smiled. "Emma Rose, please call me Julia."

The love in her eyes caused me to tear up.

"Thank you…Julia."

I peeked over at Garrett. He was smiling so big that I couldn't help but giggle.

As we walked with his mother into the kitchen, he took her in one arm as he pulled me closer to him with his other arm. "My two favorite women. I love you both so very much. I would be lost without you."

Garrett leaned down and kissed his mother on the cheek, and then he let her go and turned me to face him. He laid the most passionate kiss ever on me. I was soon lost in his kiss until I heard Julia laughing.

Garrett barely pulled away from my lips, and he whispered, "You are my entire world. You're the most precious thing ever to me."

My heart melted, and I was pretty sure I turned into Jell-O in his arms.

"Oh, you poor thing, Emma Rose. This boy is so much like his father," Julia said.

I peeked around Garrett and looked at her. "How so, Julia?" I gazed back into Garrett's sparkling blue eyes.

"Romance flowed through his father's blood. The things he said to me would make my cheeks flush in an instant."

Garrett smiled bigger and winked at me. "I have a surprise for you."

I did a little jump and clapped my hands. "Oh, Garrett, I love surprises."

He kissed me on the lips and then pulled away, too quickly for my liking. "I know you do, Buttercup, but you're going to have to wait until tomorrow afternoon."

"Tomorrow afternoon? As in, after the wedding?" I tried to give him my best pout.

His eyes turned from love to lust in two seconds flat. He leaned down and gently bit on my lip. Then, he placed his lips on my neck and moved them across my skin and up to my ear. Everywhere he touched was on fire, and the dull ache in my lower stomach began to intensify.

"I have a surprise for you tonight, too, but that one is our little secret."

Before I could even take in what he'd said, he turned and walked out of the kitchen and onto the front porch. I placed one hand on my stomach as my other hand grabbed on to the counter to steady myself.

Julia began laughing. "Yep, he's just like his daddy."

11 Garrett

I leaned against the wall and watched my mother and David talk to their guests. I couldn't help but smile every time my mother smiled. I hadn't seen her smile like that in a long time.

Billy walked up to me and said, "Well, it looks like we got our wish."

I gave him a questioning look. "Our wish?"

Billy was watching his father and my mother. "Yeah, you remember when we were little, we used to wish we were brothers. Our wish came true. Your mom makes my dad really happy."

I nodded my head. "And your dad makes my mom happy."

We both looked at each other and started laughing.

"Welcome to the family!" Billy said.

I shook my head and punched him on the arm. Then, his smile faded, and he looked down at the floor.

"What's with the long face, Billy?" I asked.

He took in a deep breath and then ran his hand through his hair. "I did something I regret."

My heart dropped, and I looked away. *So help me God, if he says what I think he is going to say, I will kill him.*

I slowly turned and looked at him. "If you are about to tell me that you cheated on Margie, you should probably think twice before you do it."

Billy's face dropped, and he took a step back. "*What?* I would never cheat on Margie, you stupid fuck."

I let out the breath I had been holding in as I ran my hand through my hair.

"Thank God. I didn't want to kick my new brother's ass." I winked at him.

"Fuck you," Billy whispered.

I started laughing and punched him on the arm. "What did you do that you regret?"

"I bought Dad tickets to a Johnny Cash concert," Billy said as he glanced at our father.

I looked at him with a confused expression on my face. "Why would you regret that?"

Billy looked at me. "Because that's his wedding gift."

It took a few seconds for it to sink in before I started laughing. "Holy shit! I just moved into the top position as favorite son, and they haven't even been married for two hours!"

Billy rolled his eyes and gave me a push. I couldn't stop laughing.

"You want the tickets, don't you?" I said in between bits of laughter.

"Do you really want a knuckle sandwich, Mathews?"

I held up my hands and tried to stop laughing.

"Garrett Mathews, are you rattling your brother's cage?" Emma asked as she walked up and wrapped her arms around my waist.

Billy smiled and shook his head. "You are so lucky you're my best friend, you jerk."

I watched as he turned to Margie and asked her to dance.

The moment I heard Elvis singing "Don't," I grabbed Emma and led her to the dance floor. "Have I ever told you how much I love Elvis?" I whispered in her ear.

She giggled. "Maybe once or twice."

I held her closer to me and took in how she felt in my arms. As we glided across the dance floor, I memorized her smell, her laugh, and her touch on my body. I began singing the words to her as she held on to me tightly.

"Garrett," she whispered as the song ended, "I love you." She pulled back and smiled.

I smiled back. "I love you more."

Right when I thought I wanted to take her right there, "All Shook Up" started playing.

"Ah, hell yeah," I said.

We took off, doing the jitterbug. Emma started laughing as I spun her around the dance floor.

This was my song to Emma, and she loved it when Elvis sang *buttercup*. When Emma and I danced, we commanded the floor. We fit together perfectly in more than one way, and I was totally lost in her. When the song changed to Nat King Cole's "Send for Me," Emma smiled as she raised her eyebrows. As we moved across the dance floor, I closed my eyes and thought about this afternoon.

"I love you, Em," I whispered in her ear.

I looked over at her father. He nodded his head and winked at me. I got a sick feeling in my stomach as my heart started pounding, and I swore the room was spinning.

I'm going to throw up.

"Garrett, I love you so much," Emma whispered back.

My nerves were immediately settled.

When I looked at Billy and Margie, they had huge smiles on their faces. Margie gave me a thumbs-up, and I smiled at her. They had both helped to set up my surprise for Emma. I was surprised Margie had been able to keep it a secret, but I'd made her swear on Billy's life that she wouldn't even tell Peggy.

Emma pulled back and looked into my eyes as she smiled. That crazy feeling I got in my stomach took off, and I wondered if my body would always have such a reaction to her.

"I wish we were alone," she said in a hushed voice.

I quickly looked at the clock. My mother and David would be leaving any moment now, and then I was going to whisk Emma out of here and to our special place. I took her hand and led her over to my mother and David.

"Darling, you look so handsome," my mother said as she placed her hands on my face. She gently kissed my cheek.

David was talking to Emma, but it was like I was standing in a tunnel. I couldn't hear a thing.

"Are you nervous?" she asked as she pulled away.

I smiled and nodded my head. "Yes, ma'am, I am."

My mother touched my arm. "Garrett, have one dance with me before David and I leave?"

I held out my arm for her and led her to the dance floor. "Sincerely" by The McGuire Sisters was playing as I took my mother in my arms. We danced in silence for about a minute.

"Garrett, I want you to know that I will never love another man like I loved your father."

I looked down into my mother's eyes. "I know that, Mama. I just want you to be happy."

She gently smiled and said, "I am happy, sweetheart, so very happy, but not just because I married David. I'm happy because of the man you are becoming. Your father would be so proud of you, and I want you to know that."

I nodded my head and looked away. It was still hard for me to talk about my father. I missed him so much, and there had been so many times I wanted to ask for his advice on something.

"Garrett, don't ever be afraid to talk to David. More than anything, he wants to be a father to you. He would never want to take the place of your daddy, but he is here for you. Please don't hesitate to ask him for advice with anything."

I held my breath as I looked at her. It was like she had read my mind.

"I'm not naïve, Garrett. I know that you and Emma have...well, that the two of you have been together. I'm not going to say I approve or disapprove, but I do want you to be careful. Please treat her with respect and never do anything she is not comfortable with. Now, I know I raised you right, but I want you to always put Emma before anything, even the ranch."

I nodded my head. "Yes, ma'am. I would never, *ever* hurt Emma, Mama. She is my entire world. I'd do anything to make her happy."

She smiled at me and let out a small chuckle. "I know you would, and from just watching the two of you together, it is evident how much you love each other. Hold on to that, darling, because that kind of love comes along only once in your life. Never take it for granted, and thank God every morning and every night."

Her voice cracked, and I knew she was thinking of my father.

"Mama," I said as I brought her closer to me and held on to her.

"I miss him, Garrett, and I feel so guilty for feeling happy."

It was tearing me apart to hear the hurt in her voice. "Mama, Daddy would want you to be happy, and I know he trusted David with his life. He would want the two of you to find each other. Please don't feel guilty. Be happy, Mama. Please be happy."

She pulled back and quickly wiped her tears away. "Garrett Thomas Mathews, God has blessed me with you for a son. I hope you know that. Now, back to you and Emma. Make it special for her tonight. Make it a moment she will never forget, a moment she will tell your children about. When I close my eyes at night, Garrett, I see you and Emma surrounded by your grandchildren, telling them about your amazing love story."

I smiled and nodded my head. "I will, Mama. I promise, I'll make it special for her."

My mother raised her eyebrows. "Just be careful, Garrett Mathews. Now, I'm going to go back to my little world I created where I have no idea as to what is going on between you two."

I laughed and pulled my mother in. I gently kissed her on the cheek, and when I stepped back, I held her hands and looked her up and down. "You are the most breathtaking woman I've ever laid my eyes on. You look beautiful, Mama."

Her cheeks flushed, and she rolled her eyes. "Liar," she said as she held her arm out for me to take.

As I walked her back to David, I caught sight of Emma standing off to the side. She was laughing at something Margie and Billy were saying to her. I looked back at David, and as my mother and I came to a stop in front of him, I handed my mother's hand to him.

He took it and kissed the back of it, and then he looked at me. "Thank you, Garrett."

I nodded my head and said the one thing I had been determined to say before they left, "Take care of her, Dad. I love her more than the air I breathe."

I heard my mother let out a sob, and David's eyes glassed over. He reached out, grabbed me, and pulled me in for a hug.

He slapped me on the back and gave me a small push. "You will never know what it means to me to hear you call me dad. I promise you, son, I will always take care of her and you and Billy."

David and my mother had left about thirty minutes ago, and I was frantically looking around for Emma. She had disappeared on me about ten minutes ago, and we needed to leave.

Someone walked up behind me and put their hand on my arm, causing me to jump. "Shit, Mathews. Calm the hell down, will you?"

I ran my hand through my hair and then down my face. "I'm a fucking nervous wreck, Margie."

She threw her head back and laughed. "Nice language in front of a lady, you ass."

I looked at her, confused. "You just swore in front of me. What's the difference?"

"Listen up, you need to get your ass out of here now. Everything is all set up."

"You used the quilt I gave you, right?" I asked as I continued to look around for Emma.

"Yes, and let me just say, I was slightly disgusted by touching it."

I spun around and looked at her. "Why?"

She put her hands on her hips and tilted her head as she gave me a look. "Please. Emma has told me about the nastiness y'all do on that thing."

I let out a chuckle and looked up. I had to catch my breath when I saw Emma standing across the room. I'd never seen anyone so beautiful in my life. She made my heart pound in my chest and my stomach flip around like I was on an amusement ride.

"By the look on your face, I'm going to take it that you've found Emma. Go get her, and get out of here," Margie said as she turned to follow my gaze.

"You don't have to tell me twice, Marg. I'm leaving." I gave her a good-bye kiss on the cheek. "Thank you, Margie. I appreciate everything you and Billy did to help me with this."

She smiled. "She loves you, Garrett. She loves you so much. Don't ever forget it."

I nodded and began walking toward Emma. Right before I got to her, Dr. Birk stepped in front of me.

Oh, great, like I'm not nervous enough.

Emma's parents had gotten back in town yesterday, and I had this fear they would find out that Emma and I had been going to their house.

"Garrett," Dr. Birk said with a smile and nod.

I reached out for his hand and shook it. "Dr. Birk, I haven't had a chance to ask you. How was the trip to Europe?"

He smiled bigger. "It was nice and relaxing."

"Did y'all get to visit all the places Mrs. Birk had hoped to see?"

He threw his head back and laughed. "Yes, she got to see all the places she had hoped to see." Then, he looked at me and shook his head. "Son, are you nervous?"

I let out the breath I'd been holding and nodded my head like a fool. "Sir, I'm so nervous that I feel like I'm going to throw up. What if I don't make it special enough for her? What if she says no? What if…" I wasn't sure why I'd decided to express every fear I had about asking Emma to marry me at that moment and to her father of all people.

He put his hand on my shoulder and relaxed his smile. "Garrett, my boy, take a deep breath. Slow that heart rate down, or you're never going to make it through this."

I pushed both hands through my hair and then ran them down my face. *I can't do this. There is no way I'm going to make this special enough for her. She deserves so much more.*

"Garrett, look at me," Dr. Birk said. "She is going to say yes because she loves you. I see the two of you together, and I see the way you both light up when the other enters a room. She was ready to walk away from college to be with you. You could ask her with a paper bag over your head, and she would say yes. Stop stressing over this. Now, Emma tells me you doubled up on classes this summer. Garrett, I want you to take it easy and not stress yourself out. Like we've talked about, I want you to eat, drink lots of water, and take it easy on the football field this summer. Do you understand me?"

I just stood there and stared at him. One minute, he had been talking to me about my proposal to his daughter, and the next, he had been worried about my health. In that moment, it all hit me. I'd lost my father, but in losing him, I'd gained two more fathers who both truly cared about my future and me.

I smiled as I nodded my head. "Yes, sir. I'll be sure not to take a heavy load in the fall. Yes, I'm eating like you said, and I will be sure to stay hydrated."

He smiled and slapped my back. "That's my boy. I'm not going to lie, son. I can't wait to see you kicking ass on that football field."

I laughed and nodded my head. "Yes, sir."

"Daddy, are you talking football again?" Emma asked as she walked up and hooked her arm with her father's.

"Yes, darling, I am. I think Garrett is going to make a hell of a good linebacker for the university. Number eighty-eight—that's a solid number."

"Yes, it is, and I'll be his own private cheerleading section, cheering him on at every game."

I grinned and shook my head. I was disappointed that I wouldn't be playing for A&M, but there was no way I was going to tell Emma's daddy that.

"Well, I hear Garrett has a surprise planned for you, so I will let the two of you go. Your mother wanted me to ask if you could both come over for dinner on Sunday night?"

"Yes, of course. Five o'clock?" Emma asked.

Her eyes met mine. She knew something was up because her parents hadn't invited us over for a formal dinner before. I shrugged my shoulders and nodded my head.

"Five o'clock indeed. We will see you kids then." Emma's father leaned down and kissed her cheek.

Then, he reached his hand out for mine. We shook hands, and he winked at me before walking away.

I took in a deep breath. "You ready?"

She gave me an innocent grin. "My father didn't ask where I would be staying this weekend."

I took her hand in mine and began leading her out to the car. "He didn't have to. David told him that a bunch of us are staying at my house and that the girls would be upstairs while the boys stayed downstairs. I don't think your dad liked it too much, but David said it would be just like the coed dorms at school, and your dad didn't really say anything after that."

I opened up the car door and held her hand as she got in. I shut it, took a deep breath, and said a silent prayer to God that I wouldn't mess this up.

12 Emma

As Garrett drove back to the Mathews' ranch, I could tell something wasn't right. He was a nervous wreck. If his hand went through his hair one more time, I was going to crawl over, sit on his lap, and make him release this tension building in the pit of my stomach.

He pulled up and parked the car. Looking over at me, he asked, "Do you want to change into something more comfortable?"

I nodded my head. "Yes, I need to get out of this dress as soon as possible!"

I waited for Garrett to get out and come around to my side of the car. He would get upset if I didn't let him open the door for me, so it was just easier if I waited. He opened my door and reached for my hand. The moment our hands touched, I felt the jolt of electricity move through my body. I looked into his eyes, and they were sparkling. He slowly gave me that crooked grin of his that just melted me on the spot. I looked at the house and then back at Garrett. I raised my eyebrows up as I bit down on my lower lip.

He began laughing. "Oh no. Don't even think about it. I have somewhere I need to take you, and we are running out of time." He opened the back door of the car and pulled out my suitcase. He carried it into the house.

When he started to make his way up the stairs, I stopped short of the steps. "Garrett, are we not staying together this weekend?"

He turned around. "Of course we are. Why are you asking me that?"

I shrugged my shoulders. "Well, you're taking my suitcase upstairs, and I thought we would be staying down here in your parents' room."

His mouth dropped open. "In my…you want to…stay in my parents' room?" he asked, stumbling on his words. He shook his head like a five-year-old boy who had just been told he did something wrong. "Oh, hell no. There is no way I'm making love to you in the same bed where my parents conceived me. No way. No. That is not happening."

He turned and started back up the stairs as I let out a giggle.

I sat in Garrett's truck with a hanky covering my eyes. Since we were in his truck, I knew he was taking me somewhere on the ranch. Why he wouldn't let me see where we were going was beyond me. As we drove in silence, I tried to guess what my surprise would be. My stomach was in knots, and I wasn't sure why. I'd tried to see if Peggy knew what the surprise was, and she had been a dead end. Margie had seemed to know what was going on, but she had been locked up tight like Fort Knox.

The truck came to a stop, and I heard the driver's door open.

"Don't move," Garrett said.

I chuckled. "Okay!"

Then, my door opened, and I was about to get out, but then Garrett scooped me up and began carrying me.

I let out a little squeal and wrapped my arms around his neck. "Mr. Mathews, where could you be taking me?" Then, a thought occurred to me. "Garrett, if you even think of throwing me in the river, I will never talk to you again. Do you hear me?"

He didn't say a word. His silence was killing me.

"Garrett? Garrett! I'm going to rip this thing off my eyes if you don't talk to me."

Then, I felt him slowly lowering me down onto solid ground. I let out a sigh and tried to reach for him.

"Garrett, where are you? Stop with this silly silence game and tell me where you are right now."

"Take off your blindfold, Em," Garrett said, his voice sounding different.

I couldn't tell if he was upset or if it was because he hadn't really talked to me the whole way here.

I reached up and took off the blindfold, but I kept my eyes closed. I wasn't sure what I was afraid of. Maybe I was nervous. Whatever it was, I stood there with my eyes closed.

"Emma..." Garrett whispered.

I snapped my eyes open. I looked down to see Garrett on one knee...on our quilt...under our tree. My eyes instantly filled with tears as I stared at him while he held a small box in his hands. I quickly looked around at everything. Small bouquets of daisies had been placed all over. Daisy petals and a few rose petals covered the quilt. I brought my hands up to my mouth and attempted to hold back the tears. I looked to the other side of the quilt, and a basket was sitting there. I was instantly taken back to the moment when we had gone on our first date—the picnic where Garrett had given me my first orgasm and when I'd fallen even more in love with him.

I looked down into his eyes, and he smiled so big and beautiful.

"Emma Rose Birk, the first time I saw you in that drugstore, I knew...I knew I would love you for the rest of my life. You captured my heart the moment your beautiful eyes met mine. I can't tell you how many times I've dreamed of this moment along with all the other ones—making you completely mine, making love to you under the stars, marrying you, and living in the house my father built for my mother. I just want to make all your dreams come true, Emma. I want to love you like I've never loved anyone. I want to make you laugh. I never, ever want to make you cry because it would destroy me if I hurt you. I want to see your belly swell up with our children. I want to tell you every chance I get how much I love you and how beautiful you are."

He opened the box, and I wiped the tears from my eyes and face. In a very unladylike fashion, I used the back of my right hand to wipe under my nose.

When my vision finally cleared, I let out a gasp. "Garrett..." I whispered.

"Em, I want to spend the rest of my life with you and only you. I promise to always be faithful to you and to love you and take care of you to the best of my ability. Will you do me the honor of becoming Mrs. Garrett Thomas Mathews?"

I let out a sob and fell to my knees before throwing myself into his body. "Yes! Oh my God, yes! Yes! Garrett, I love you so much."

I held on to him as tight as I could, and he wrapped his arms around me.

Nothing would ever top this moment. *Nothing.*

"Thank God," Garrett barely said.

I couldn't help but giggle. Now, I knew why he had been so nervous for the last few days.

I pulled back, and he took my left hand in his. Before he took out the ring, he kissed the back of my hand and looked up at me. He smiled, and my heart melted on the spot.

He slipped the ring on my finger, and I got a good look at it. It was beautiful. I had to take in a deep breath as I looked at the most beautiful ring I'd ever seen in my life. It was a round cut diamond surrounded by a halo of diamond accents. Two smaller diamonds on the side led to more accent diamonds that moved down the band. The way the ring sparkled in the sun was amazing.

A sob escaped my throat as I looked up at Garrett. The moment I saw a tear moving down his face, my whole world stopped.

"It's the most breathtaking ring I've ever seen," I said as I reached up and wiped away his tear.

He slowly took in a breath of air and let it out. "My father designed it. It was my mother's engagement ring."

I placed my hand over my mouth and began crying harder.

Garrett pulled me into his arms. "No, Buttercup, please don't cry. I don't want you to cry."

"I'm not crying because I'm sad. I'm crying because I've never been so happy in my life. For this to be your mother's ring just makes it all the more special. I swear, I can feel your father with us at this very moment."

Garrett pulled me even closer to him, and he just held me. As I kept my face buried in his chest, I was pretty sure I could hear him crying as well. Nothing needed to be said between us. It was almost as if this was a healing process for Garrett. He'd held it together for so long after his father died. I thought it was finally all coming to the surface. If this was where it needed to happen, then I would be here for him. I would always be here for him. I could feel Garrett's body as he slowly let it all out.

"I miss him so much, Em. I wish he were here, so I could tell him how much I love him, how proud I am of the things he built for my mother and me...for us. He would have loved you so much, Em."

He began crying again, and I held on to him as tightly as I could. If I could crawl into his body right now, I would. I didn't say anything. I remembered my father had told me that sometimes, words were not needed to comfort those who had lost so much. Instead, the loving touch of someone who cared would be all the comfort needed.

After a few minutes, Garrett released his hug on me and pulled back. I frantically began kissing his face as if I could kiss away hurt.

He placed his hands on the sides of my face and brought my lips to his. "You're mine, Emma." He pulled away and looked into my eyes.

"Yes, I'm yours, Garrett. Please..." I said, knowing he would know I needed to feel his body become one with mine.

"Buttercup...here or home?" he asked me as he searched my face.

As much as I wanted to make love to him right this very second, I wanted him to take me back to our future house.

"Home," I whispered.

He quickly stood and helped me up before lifting me and carrying me back over to the truck. "Emma, I'm taking you home and making love to you."

As Garrett opened the door to the truck, I looked back at our quilt and smiled. "Garrett, don't forget our quilt."

He placed me on the seat and kissed my forehead. "Never."

He ran back over and grabbed the basket and the quilt. Then, he reached for one bouquet of daisies. He walked back to the truck, and the smile I saw on his face was one I would never forget. Garrett Thomas Mathews would be forever mine. He handed me the flowers and put the basket in the back of the truck.

He quickly folded up the quilt and gave it to me. "This quilt, I do believe, is our good-luck charm."

I laughed. "I thought it was our sex quilt."

Garrett shrugged. "It's both."

I'm never, ever getting rid of this quilt.

13 Garrett

I walked into the house, carrying Emma in my arms. The next time I did this, she would be my bride. I wanted to run up the steps two at a time, so I could get inside her faster. I kicked open the bedroom door and then shut it with my foot. I didn't think Billy or Margie would be here anytime soon, but it was better to be safe than sorry.

I walked up to the bed and dropped Emma on it, causing her to let out a laugh.

"Undress yourself, Em," I said in a seductive voice.

Emma's smile faded, and she quickly began taking off her clothes. I smiled slightly, knowing that I probably had the sweetest, kindest fiancée in the world, but she sure had a side of her in the bedroom I loved. She was completely nude in less than a minute. She slowly lay back on the bed and began rubbing her legs together. My dick was harder than a rock, and I couldn't wait to be so far inside her while she screamed out my name.

"Your turn, Mr. Mathews," she purred.

I stripped out of my clothes faster than I thought I ever had. I reached into my pocket, pulled out three condoms, and threw them onto the bed.

Emma looked at them and laughed. "Feeling lucky tonight?"

I silently prayed I could keep up with Emma as I nodded my head. I slowly lowered my body down and on top of Emma. I covered her body in kisses as she let out sweet moan after sweet moan. I loved making her feel good, and hearing her call out my name was one of my favorite things ever. As I kissed her nipple, I moved my hand down and began touching her. She bucked her hips and whimpered as I pushed two fingers inside her. She was always so ready for me. I moved and began teasing her with my tip.

"Garrett…I can't wait until we are married, and we have nothing between us. I just want to feel you inside me. Please, just once," Emma said as she wrapped her legs around me.

I closed my eyes and did the one thing I knew I shouldn't do. I pushed myself into Emma. She arched her back and let out a moan that shot through my whole body.

"Oh…God…" I didn't move at all. I tried to take in how it felt to be inside her with nothing separating us.

"Garrett…move…please move."

I shook my head. "I can't, Em. If I move, I won't want to stop. This is a dangerous game we're playing."

I looked into her eyes, and I knew I would never put our future at risk for just a moment of pleasure. *Pure fucking pleasure.*

"Just a few times...please."

I slowly pulled out and pushed myself back into her. "Oh God..."

She made the sweetest sounds.

This time I pushed as far into her as I could possibly get.

"Garrett! Oh God..."

I shook my head and pulled all the way out of her. Cursing the entire time, I quickly reached for the condom and ripped it open. I was about to put it on when Emma sat up.

"Shh...I think someone is in the house," she said.

I was breathing like I'd just run a damn marathon, for Christ's sakes. "It's just Billy and Marg. Don't worry. They won't—"

"Garrett? Emma?"

"David?" Emma and I both said at the same time.

Emma busted out laughing and covered her mouth.

"Are y'all upstairs?"

"No. Fucking. Way." I pulled the covers out from underneath Emma and made her get under them. I looked around, and for some reason, I couldn't find my damn clothes anywhere. I saw a towel folded up on the chair, so I jumped up and quickly wrapped it around me. I picked up Emma's suitcase and threw it on top of the bed.

"Ouch!" Emma said.

"Be quiet!"

Just then, I heard the doorknob turning on my bedroom door. "He's not opening the door," I whispered.

I quickly ran to the door, but David swung it open, and I ran right into him.

"Garrett?"

"David? Um...Dad? Ah, shit. I don't really know what to call you right now."

David looked around the room. "Where is Emma?"

"She's, um...um...I don't know. With Margie? I was just getting ready to take a bath, and I...I, um—Jesus, David...do you not know how to knock?"

Billy was walking up the stairs, and he must have heard me because he started laughing. "Dad has a theory, Garrett. Tell him your theory, Dad."

David smiled and nodded his head. "An unlocked door is an open invitation."

I nodded my head. "I'll be sure to remember that, sir. Uh…what are you doing here? Aren't you supposed to be heading into Austin with Mom?"

"Yes, but she forgot one of her suitcases, so I told her we would come back for it. I heard someone upstairs, so I thought I would see who was here. I thought the guys were camping out downstairs?"

I looked over David's shoulder, and that bastard best friend of mine was laughing his ass off.

"We are, but my clothes and stuff are up here. Well, let me help you with that suitcase, so y'all can be on your way." I ushered David out of my room and down the stairs to my mother's room.

"There it is," I said as I picked up the suitcase. I handed it to him, and we made our way to the door.

Peggy and Margie busted in through the front door and ran upstairs. Billy came walking down the stairs, and he had the biggest shit-eating grin on his face.

"Now, boys, no parties, no getting crazy, and for the love of God, try to keep your snakes in your pants, please," David said. He turned and walked out of the house.

When I turned and looked at Billy, I was pretty sure his expression matched mine. Then, all I could hear was screaming.

Billy smiled. "Sounds like they found Emma."

I rolled my eyes and started making my way back up to my bedroom. I turned and pointed to Billy. "No one takes the master bedroom downstairs."

Billy made a motion like he was going to throw up. "Agreed."

I walked into my room, only to have Peggy whistle and tell me to take it off. I gave her a dirty look. I glanced down at the towel and then back up. My eyes caught Emma's. She looked so happy. She was still under the covers, but she had on one of my T-shirts. Just seeing her in my shirt caused my dick to start getting hard again.

"It's beautiful. Oh my God, it fits your finger perfectly. You know what that means, don't you?" Margie asked.

Em shook her head. "No. What does it mean?"

"Oh, Emma Rose, it's good luck. It means you're a fit for life." Margie looked at me and made a face because I was practically naked with only a towel wrapped around my waist. Then, she turned back to Emma. "Nothing will ever come between the two of you."

"Except for our dad." Billy let out another laugh and leaned against the doorjamb.

"Okay…y'all have seen it, and you've screamed." I looked at Billy. "You've had your laughs. Now, can I get back to my girl, please?"

Peggy stood up. "When the cat's away, the mice will play."

Margie let out a yelp and ran into Billy's arms. "Take me. I'm yours."

"Ew," Emma said as she covered her ears.

When Raymond walked up, it was Peggy's turn to let out a squeal.

"What in the hell is going on here?" He took one look at me in the towel and Emma in the bed. "I take it, we didn't give you enough time."

I shook my head. "No, y'all didn't. Now, get the hell out of my room!" I shouted as I began pushing Billy out. I slammed the door shut.

I started walking toward the bed when Billy called out, "An unlocked door is an open invitation."

Emma started giggling as I turned around and locked my bedroom door.

When I turned back around, Emma had taken the shirt off, and she was standing at the end of the bed waiting for me with a condom in her hand. I took the towel off and let it drop to the floor. I walked as fast as I could to get to her. I slammed my body against hers and began kissing her. I picked her up and placed her back down on my bed.

"You're gonna have to be quiet, Buttercup."

She nodded her head and put her finger up to her lips. I slowly kissed her neck and whispered how much I loved her.

"I'm going to make love to you all night long, Em," I said against her neck.

"Yes," she said as she lightly trailed her fingers along my back.

I loved to feel her touch. I loved to touch her. I ran my fingertip along the side of her face, down her chest, around her nipple, down her stomach, and found my way to heaven. As I slipped my fingers inside her, I let out a low moan. I sat up and ripped open the package before sliding the condom down my shaft.

"Garrett, I need to feel you so badly. Please go slow," Emma whispered.

I began pushing myself in. I moved in and out slowly. Emma's hands were all over my body as I kissed her neck and chest. I picked up the pace just a little.

"Feels. So. Good," she said.

I moved myself in a way that I knew she loved, and before I knew it, I was kissing her to muffle out the sounds of her moans of pleasure. When she finally came down, I began moving in and out gradually again.

Emma caught her breath and pulled my head closer to her. She put her lips up next to my ear. "I want you to fuck me harder."

Oh, holy shit. After two pumps, I was coming. "Ah…oh shit…I'm coming, Em…oh God," I whispered.

She smiled from ear to ear. I collapsed on her, and she continued to trail her fingers up and down my back.

"I like it when you just lie here, still inside me. It feels like we are one."

I lifted myself and smiled at her. "We are one, Em."

"This evening couldn't get any better," Emma said. She leaned up and kissed me.

I was just about to agree when I heard Margie and Billy.

Emma's eyes grew in horror as we heard Margie calling out, "Yes! Harder…go faster!"

I jumped up and covered my ears. "Mother of all things good! Oh God, my ears. I'll never recover from that mental image…ever!" I shouted.

Emma jumped up and quickly began looking for her clothes. She soon gave up and opened one of my drawers. She threw on a pair of my sweatpants that I usually wore to football practice. She reached for a T-shirt and slipped it on. I stumbled back when she turned around.

She just looked at me. "What's wrong? Oh God, did you hurt yourself or something?"

"Yes! Yes!" Margie called out again.

"No! No!" I yelled as I quickly got dressed. "Jesus, you look amazing in my clothes. Grab the quilt, and let's go!"

Emma chuckled as she skipped over and grabbed the quilt. She followed me out the door.

As I walked by the bedroom where Margie and Billy were staying, I banged on the door. "Not cool, y'all. So not cool."

I practically pulled Emma down the stairs and dragged her to the barn. After feeding the horses, we spread the quilt down in the foreman's office.

We spent the rest of the night talking about all the plans we had for our future together.

It was the best night of my life. Nothing would ever top this night.

14 Emma

May 1961

Garrett spun me around on the dance floor to Elvis's "Stuck on You." We both laughed and enjoyed not having to go back to our dorms and study. We'd finally graduated, and we were ready to start our lives together.

He pulled me into his arms and shouted, "Tell me you love me!"

I smiled and shouted back, "I love you, Garrett Mathews!"

"Marry me!"

I threw my head back and laughed. Then, I held my ring up and said, "I do believe I already said yes."

"Too Much" started playing, and Garrett yelled out, "It's an Elvis marathon!"

He spun me around, and by the time the song ended, I was exhausted.

"Garrett, I need to take a quick rest and have a drink."

He nodded his head as he took my hand and led me off the dance floor. I scanned the room, trying to find Margie and Billy. When I finally found Margie, she was talking to some guy I'd never seen before. I watched them as Garrett got us something to drink.

When he handed me my drink, I asked him, "Do you know who Marg is talking to?"

Garrett looked to where I was pointing, and he shook his head. "I've never seen him before." He looked around. "Where is Billy?"

I watched as Margie batted her eyes, and she kept putting her hand on this guy's arm.

What in the hell is she doing?

"I don't have a very good feeling about this, Garrett." I turned and looked at him. "Maybe we should go before she does something she regrets."

He nodded his head in agreement. "You go get Marg, and I'll go find Billy." He leaned down and kissed me. "I love you, Buttercup."

I smiled. "I love you more."

I watched as he made his way to the other side of the dance hall. I turned back around and started walking toward Margie.

I knew the last two months had been hard on her and Billy. She had been hoping he would ask her to marry him before we all graduated, but graduation had come and gone three days ago. She had no idea he had planned on asking her this coming weekend. Margie had been offered a teaching position in Austin, but Billy was torn. He wanted to go back to Mason and help Garrett run the ranch, but he also wanted to move to Austin.

As I got closer, the guy leaned down and whispered something into Margie's ear. She nodded, and he took her by the arm. He started to lead her toward the door. My heart started beating faster, and I began pushing people out of my way.

I ran through the door and screamed out, "Margie!"

Margie and the stranger stopped, and she spun around. "Emma Rose, what are you doing out here without your knight in shining armor?"

"What?"

Margie shook her head. "Never mind."

She turned to keep walking, but I grabbed her arm.

"Where are you going? And who is this guy?"

"Just go back inside, Emma, to your perfect fiancé and your perfect little world. Don't worry about me," Margie said, slurring her words and pulling her arm from my hand.

"Oh my God, are you drunk? Did you get her drunk?" I took a step closer and grabbed her arm.

The guy came closer to me and pushed me. I lost my balance and fell backward. I landed so hard that I screamed. Then, I saw someone run by me.

"You motherfucker!" Garrett said.

Billy reached down and picked me up as he yelled out, "Garrett!"

Everything was happening so fast, and I couldn't think straight.

"Emma, grab Margie," Billy said as he ran toward Garrett and the guy.

It took me a few seconds to see that Garrett was punching the guy over and over. I threw my hands up to my mouth. *Please stop. Oh God, please stop.*

I grabbed Margie and pulled her back. Then, out of nowhere, four more guys showed up. Two of them grabbed Garrett and held him while the guy who had been walking with Margie started to hit him.

"Stop!" I began screaming. "Please stop!"

I turned to look at Margie, and she was crying.

"Go get help, Margie!" I yelled.

I looked back, and both Garrett and Billy were being beaten.

"Margie!" I screamed. "Get help!"

I ran toward them, screaming for the guys to stop. One of the guys reached out and slapped me so hard across the face that I fell back.

"Fucker!" Garrett yelled, breaking free of the other guy's grip.

I'd never seen Garrett hurt anyone, and the way he was punching this guy scared me. The other guy got up and grabbed something from a car. When I saw he had something in his hand I screamed for Garrett to watch out, but the next thing I knew, he'd hit Garrett over the head. I watched as Garrett fell to the ground. I screamed out as loud as I could, and then I saw the lights. The police were pulling up from everywhere.

One of the guys called out, "Jimbo! The fuzz are here! We've got to go."

I watched as one guy hit Billy three more times before finally letting him go. He dropped to the ground and began crawling over toward Garrett.

I jumped up and ran to Garrett, calling out, "Garrett! God, please no. No!"

All of a sudden, people were everywhere, and Garrett was being put into an ambulance. Billy had blood all over him, and Margie was standing off to the side, talking to the police. I started to make my way to the ambulance. A police officer grabbed my arm.

"Please let me go with him. He is my fiancé. Please," I begged.

They shut the doors, and I watched the ambulance drive off.

"Miss, I promise, I will drive you to Brackenridge myself. I just need you to answer a few more questions. Did you know any of the other men?"

I wrapped my arms around myself to try to calm my shaking body. I shook my head. "I've never seen them before in my life."

"So, you've never seen them before at this dance hall?" the officer asked.

Then, I remembered one of them had said a name. I spun around to face the policeman. "Jimbo—that was what one of the guys called out. Jimbo was the one who walked out with Margie."

The police officer shook his head. "You just gave me everything I needed. I know exactly who they are. Jimbo Duran has been causing trouble for us for the last six months. We didn't have anything to use to put him in jail, but with the assault on your fiancé and his brother, we do now."

Margie walked up. "He told me he was taking me to a frat house."

I glared at her. "This is your fault."

She went to open her mouth to talk, but she shut it.

I shook my head and started pointing my finger at her. "I will never forgive you for this—ever!" I screamed.

Billy came up and took me in his arms. "Emma, it's okay. Garrett is going to be okay."

I tried to push Billy away. "He is not waking up, Billy. He. Is. Not. Okay!"

Margie began crying. "Em, I'm so—"

"Don't call me Em! Only Garrett calls me that. Don't you dare call me that."

The officer took me gently by the arm and began walking me to his car. I looked back and shouted, "I hate you, Margie. I hate you!"

I jumped when I felt someone touch my shoulder.

"Daddy!" I said as I jumped up and into his arms. "Oh, Daddy, no one is telling me anything, and they won't let me in there to see Garrett. Please just tell me he is okay."

"Emma Rose…calm down, okay? Garrett is going to be all right. He does have some big injuries, but he'll be okay."

I began crying as I nodded my head. "What kind of injuries?"

"Well, he is very lucky that he didn't really get injured when they hit his head. Billy said Garrett moved at the last second, and they barely caught him, but they did hit him again when he was down."

I tried to think back to when it had happened. "Daddy, I don't remember them hitting him when he passed out." I thought for a second and then looked at my father. "I did look away at Billy though."

My father nodded his head. "Emma, I need you to sit down, okay?"

I started shaking from head to toe, and then I felt someone grab a hold of me. I turned around. "Julia!" I threw myself into her arms.

"Shh…honey, calm down. Garrett is going to be okay."

I couldn't even talk. I was crying so hard. When I finally settled down, Julia had me sit on the sofa. I glanced up to see my mother walking up, and she took a seat on the other side of me.

She grabbed my hand and gave me a weak smile.

Why do I get the feeling they are about to tell me something very bad? "You're all scaring me," I whispered.

My father bent down. "No, sweetheart. I promise you, he is okay. Now, I need you to listen carefully. Garrett does have some serious injuries, so he will be in the hospital for a while."

I slowly nodded my head. "Tell me, Daddy."

My father took a deep breath and glanced up. David was standing on the other side of the waiting room with a battered and bruised Billy.

When my father started talking again, I looked into his eyes and held my breath.

"Garrett has four broken ribs. His right arm is broken—"

A loud sob escaped my mouth, and my mother squeezed my hand.

"And his left leg is broken as well. He has stitches across his forehead from where the bat hit him."

I let out a gasp. "Bat? He was hit by a bat?"

My father nodded his head. "Yes, Billy said it was a bat they used to hit Garrett. Emma, we're going to have to cancel the wedding. There is no way Garrett will recover in a month."

My mouth dropped open, and I shook my head. "No, Daddy, no. We've been waiting for so long to get married and start our lives together. This isn't fair!" I shouted.

"I know, sweetheart. Believe me, I know. Garrett is going to have a long recovery ahead of him, and he will need your help," my father said.

I sat up straighter and squared off my shoulders. "I'll do whatever it takes, but I'm not putting off my marriage to Garrett for another second. The justice of the peace can marry us, and then once Garrett has recovered, we will have the wedding." I held my breath and waited for the four of them to start arguing with me.

My father smiled. "Garrett said the same thing."

I jumped up. "He's awake? Daddy, I want to see him right now! Why didn't you tell me he was awake? I need to see him right away."

My father stood up and placed his hands on my shoulders. "You will, Emma, but Garrett wanted you to understand how serious his injuries are before you go in to see him."

Julia stood up and turned me toward her. "I'm not surprised at all that the both of you would say the same thing. Your mother and I will take care of getting the justice of the peace up here. Garrett has asked that the two of you be married as soon as possible."

I gave her a confused look.

"Emma Rose, they won't let you stay with him in the room unless you're married," my mother said.

"Oh...well then, yes. What do we have to do?"

My mother smiled and said, "You've already applied for the marriage license, so that is taken care of. Don't worry. We'll take care of the rest. Now, I need you to take a deep breath and prepare yourself for what you are about to see."

I looked at Billy and then at my father. "Does he look worse than Billy?"

"Thanks, Emma," Billy said with a chuckle.

My father nodded his head. "Yes."

I took in a few deep breaths. "I'm ready."

We began walking, and I got a glimpse of Margie.

I stopped and looked at her. "You're not welcome here. Please leave."

"Emma Rose Birk," my mother said, "that is your cousin."

I looked over my shoulder at my mother. "No, she's the reason Garrett is lying in that hospital bed and why Billy is standing there, looking the way he does." I turned back to Margie. "Please leave."

Margie started crying. "Emma, I'm so sorry. I don't know what came over me. I was so mad at Billy, and I just...I just..."

I walked up to her and got right in her face. "You just wanted to go and screw someone. Is that it, Margie? I should have let you leave with him."

She shook her head. "No. I wasn't going to...I just wanted Billy to be jealous and—"

"What about the hurtful things you said to me? You're so stupid. He was going to ask you to marry him, but you couldn't be patient, and now, you cost me my wedding and possibly Garrett's future. I have nothing else to say to you."

I turned and walked back up to my father. We made our way to Garrett's hospital room.

"I arranged for Garrett to have a private room."

I looked at my father and wiped a tear away. "Daddy, thank you so much. You didn't have to do that."

"Hey, what are the perks of being Chief of Staff if I can't pull my weight sometimes?"

I tried to laugh, but I just couldn't. I stopped outside of the room, and I could hear music playing. I smiled when I heard Elvis singing.

"Elvis always makes him feel better," I said in a soft voice.

"I brought up the record player and some Elvis sides from my office."

I hugged my father as tightly as I could. "Thank you, Daddy, for loving him so much."

"He's like a son to me, Emma Rose. There isn't a thing I wouldn't do for him. It was very hard for me to work on him in the emergency room."

"Oh, Daddy."

He kissed me on the forehead. "Go on. I know he really wants to see you."

I quietly pushed the door open and heard "Loving You" playing. I put my hand up to my mouth to hold back my sobs. As I moved closer to him, I couldn't tell if his eyes were open or shut. His whole face was swollen and black and blue. Garrett was softly singing, and I stopped and listened to him. He had such a beautiful voice. He was singing so softly, and I knew it had to hurt his ribs. The song ended, and another song began.

"Will you turn it off, Em?"

I quickly walked over and picked up the needle. I turned, and he was looking at me.

"How did you know I was in here?"

He smiled, and my heart broke. His beautiful crooked smile on his bruised and battered face still made me weak in the knees.

"I felt you...and I smelled your perfume."

I smiled and walked up to him. As I took his hand in mine, I gently bent down and kissed it. I was trying so hard not to cry, but he looked so banged up.

"Tell me you love me, Em."

I shook my head, and a sob escaped my betraying mouth. "Garrett...I love you more than the air I breathe. I love you so much that it hurts."

"Marry me."

I giggled. "When?"

"Tomorrow."

I smiled as that familiar feeling moved over my body like a blanket. "It's a date."

My mother fussed with my hair as I looked at my reflection in the mirror. My hair was pulled up with a few curls hanging down. I had put on a simple white skirt and a light blue collared shirt along with my favorite blue pumps that my mother had bought me.

"You look beautiful, Emma Rose. Are you nervous?"

I smiled and turned to my mother. "A little. I've waited so long to become Garrett's wife, and well..." My voice trailed off, and an overwhelming sense of sadness washed over me.

"What is it, darling?"

I tried to smile, but it was forced. "I just wish none of this had happened, and we were having our dream wedding next month, and—" I tried to hold in the sob, but it slipped through my lips.

My mother grabbed me and pulled me closer to her. "Shh...don't cry. It's okay, darling."

"I'm so mad at Margie, Mother, that I can't even see straight. What was she thinking? Look at what she did!" I began crying harder.

My mother pushed me away and looked into my eyes. "Emma Rose, Margie did not cause Garrett to end up in that hospital bed."

"But—"

She held up her hand and tilted her head. "Margie made a mistake. We all make them, Emma Rose. She is riddled with guilt, and the fact that you are treating her so poorly is not making her feel any better."

I swallowed and whispered, "Good."

"Emma Rose Birk, I am shocked at you. Where is this coming from? Now, I know you are upset that Garrett is hurt and that the wedding is being put off, but you should not carry around such hate in your heart. It does no one any good. Do you hear me? You need to forgive, Margie.

You're best friends and cousins. Would you want someone to hold a mistake against you like that?"

I thought about the biggest mistake of my life—pushing Garrett away. *What if Garrett held it against me when I'd gone out with Michael that one time?*

I slowly shook my head. "No, Mother, I wouldn't. I'll work at forgiving Margie."

She smiled. "Now, let's fix your makeup. You have a wedding to get to."

I grinned as my mother fixed me up, and we made our way to Garrett's hospital room. When I pushed open the door, my father and David were standing in the corner, talking to the justice of the peace. Julia was standing next to a sleeping Garrett. My heart broke in two. He was on so many pain medicines that he could hardly stay awake. As I made my way closer to him, he opened his eyes and looked at me. The smile that spread across his face caused me to suck in a breath.

"Em, you look beautiful," he whispered.

I smiled and took his hand in mine as I leaned down. "I thought you were asleep," I whispered against his lips. I gently kissed him.

"He hasn't taken any pain medicine this morning," Julia said with a sad face.

I snapped my head at Julia and then back at Garrett. "What?"

He gave me that crooked smile of his. "I didn't want to fall asleep at my own wedding."

I felt the tear slide down my face, and I quickly wiped it away. "Oh, Garrett, please take something for the pain. The ceremony is going to be quick." I turned and looked at my father with pleading eyes. "Daddy."

He nodded his head, and he was out the door faster than I'd ever seen him move.

When I turned back and looked at Julia, she mouthed, *Thank you.*

I nodded my head and peeked back down at Garrett.

"Em, I don't—"

I leaned down and kissed him again. I pulled my lips back and said, "Shh…I love you, Garrett Mathews."

My father walked back in and gave Garrett some pain medicine as my mother introduced me to the justice of the peace.

He smiled at me and asked, "Are you ready, Miss Birk?"

I nodded my head and walked over to stand next to Garrett. My heart was pounding a mile a minute. I couldn't believe I was fixin' to become Mrs. Garrett Thomas Mathews.

Garrett held my hand and quickly rubbed his thumb back and forth across my skin. Each movement left a trail of fire in its place.

As the justice of the peace started the ceremony, Garrett and I stared into each other's eyes. I wasn't even sure what all was being said. All I knew was that we were getting married, and there would be no more sneaking around. We were free to be with each other. I could now take care of Garrett and help him with his recovery—in more ways than one.

Garrett gave me a smirk and lifted his eyebrow at me. My face instantly turned red. He must have known what I was thinking.

"I now pronounce you man and wife. You may kiss your bride, Garrett."

Garrett licked his lips, and my insides melted.

Oh, how I want him more than anything.

I leaned down, and Garrett slipped his hand through my hair. He held me close to him as we kissed. He moved his tongue along my lips, seeking entry, and I opened myself up to his passionate kiss. Soon, we were lost in each other…until I heard my father clear his throat. I smiled against Garrett's lips and pulled slightly away.

"I love you, Emma Rose Mathews."

My heart soared. "I love you more, Garrett."

15 Garrett

Emma stopped just short of the restaurant.

I turned and looked at her. "Em, what's wrong?"

Her eyes filled with tears. "I said such horrible things to Marg. What if she doesn't forgive me?"

I pulled her into my arms. "Trust me, Margie misses you like crazy. It's been four months since you've seen her. Now, come on. They're waiting inside."

We were meeting Billy and Margie in Fredericksburg for dinner. It was the first time the girls would be seeing each other since the night of the fight. I was still having a hard time moving around, but I was slowly making a go of things.

As we walked in, I saw Billy stand up. He was grinning from ear to ear, and I couldn't help but smile. We made our way to the table, and Margie jumped up.

"Emma Rose," she whispered.

It didn't take long before they were in each other's arms. Billy and I both let out a sigh of relief.

Thank you, God.

They had both been so unhappy during the last few months.

Billy smiled and winked at me as he held out his hand. "How are you feeling, Garrett?"

"Sore still in my ribs, and my leg is giving me a bit of trouble, but other than that, I'm slowly getting back to it. You?"

His smile faded slightly before it came back. "I'm a hundred percent now."

I nodded my head. "Good. I'm glad to hear that."

We all took our seats, and within seconds, Emma let out a small scream. Everyone in the restaurant looked over at us.

Emma said, "Oh, I'm so sorry."

I looked at Emma. She was staring down at Margie's hand.

I snapped my head up and looked at Billy. "Congratulations, Billy! When did this happen?"

Margie and Emma were lost in conversation—something about dress shopping and where the wedding would be held. They were making my head spin.

"I asked her a month ago. She didn't want me to tell you because she wanted to be the one to tell Emma." Billy glanced over at the girls and smiled. "They seemed to have just fallen right back into place."

I glanced over at the girls and smiled. I looked back at Billy.

He leaned back and asked, "So, when are y'all planning on having the wedding?"

Emma and Margie stopped talking, and they both turned to look at me. "Ah…"

Emma smiled as she gave me a wink. We hadn't really talked about when we would reschedule the wedding. Our focus had mainly been on my slow recovery from all my broken bones and the work on the ranch.

I shrugged. "I guess that's up to Em."

"I'd like for Garrett to be fully recovered and for things to settle a bit since he is taking over more and more with the ranch." She looked at Margie and took her hand. "Besides, we have another wedding to plan first."

Margie wrapped Emma up in a hug, and both girls began crying. Finally, things were getting back to normal.

January 1962

I slowly made my way down to the barn. I was still trying to recover from the fight I had been in last summer, and my leg was giving me hell this morning. I glanced up and saw my father standing there.

He smiled and said, "Leg giving you problems today?"

I shrugged and nodded. I didn't want to tell him that it was probably because I had taken my wife against the wall and then again in the kitchen.

"It's just stiff. I have to move around for a bit, and it will loosen up," I said. I walked over to Jack and gave him a scoop full of oats. "You ready for the wedding?" I asked as I looked over at David shoeing a horse. Every time I had to shoe a horse, I thought of my father, and I knew that was why David did most of the shoeing.

He laughed. "Yes, I am. Your mother is not looking forward to heading into Austin though."

I threw my head back and laughed. "Billy doing okay? The last time I talked to him, he sounded like he was taking something to make him talk stupid."

David laughed. "You wait until this summer, boy, when you get married."

I turned around and walked over to him. "I am married. The wedding this summer is going to be a piece of cake. Why would I be nervous?"

David looked up at me, and I could tell he was holding back his laughter.

"You don't think you will be nervous, son?"

I shook my head. "No, Dad, I really don't."

He chuckled. "Want to wager a bet on that?"

I smiled and ran my hand through my hair. "What are you suggesting?"

David stood up and appeared to be thinking before he smiled and said, "If you get nervous at all…during any portion of the wedding…at the reception, you have to stand up and give me a toast, saying how wise I am and that you'd be lost without my words of wisdom."

My smile faded. I said, "You're shitting me, right?"

He laughed harder as I looked over and saw my beautiful bride walking my way. She was carrying a tray with glasses of sweet tea on it. My heart began beating faster as she smiled at me, and I was instantly brought back to this morning when she had been on top of me, making love to me so slowly and sweetly.

She stopped in front of me, and I leaned down to kiss her.

She pulled back some and whispered, "I can totally tell you're thinking of either this morning or perhaps last night."

Lord, this girl kills me. My dick jumped in my pants, and I had to force myself not to drag her back to the house and have my way with her.

She bit down on her lower lip. "I'm going to work in the garden for a bit, but I wanted to bring y'all out some tea before it got too hot out."

She set the tray down. She turned and started walking out of the barn, but then she looked back over her shoulder at me once.

David walked up to me and used his finger to shut my mouth. "Flies are gonna get in there, son," he said with a chuckle.

I slowly shook my head and turned to watch him pick up a glass and drink the tea. "How do they do that? How can she just say one thing to me, and I go all pussy-ass pansy?"

He shrugged his shoulders. "I'm guessing y'all are still on the honeymoon?"

I reached for the glass and took a drink. "Something like that."

David downed his tea. "Ah hell, I forgot that I needed to take care of something over at the house. No one else is working today. You going to be okay, Garrett?"

I turned and looked at him. "Where is everyone?"

David shrugged and laughed. "I guess everyone needed a day off." He reached down and grabbed his cowboy hat. He walked up to me. "Take the day off, son. Enjoy it with Emma."

The next thing I knew, I was watching him drive away. I made my way into the house and to our bedroom. I smiled when I saw our quilt sitting on the chair in the corner. I walked over, grabbed it, and reached into the drawer to pull out a condom before I remembered that Emma was now on birth control. I was still leery about something so new, but Emma had insisted that it worked. My biggest worry was Em getting pregnant before our wedding ceremony.

I headed out the back door and smiled when I saw Emma leaning over and bitching at the weeds. I slowly opened the gate to the garden and made my way over to her. I grabbed her, spun her around, and quickly kissed her. Soon, we were both lost in the kiss.

When we finally pulled away for air, she looked down at the quilt and then back up at me. "Mr. Mathews, what do you have in mind with that quilt?"

"Hmm...burying myself so deep inside you that you feel my presence there for the next few days."

Emma's eyes burned with desire, and I couldn't help but smile. I knew how much it turned her on when I talked a little dirty to her.

She closed her eyes. "Garrett...I need you."

I quickly grabbed her hand and began pulling her out the gate.

She pulled me to a stop and said, "Wait!"

I turned around. "Emma, my dick is so hard that it's painful."

She smiled and looked over toward the barn before turning back and looking at me. "You said something to me once, and ever since then, I've been fantasizing about it."

I looked at the barn and tried to remember if I'd ever said anything about having sex in the barn.

Then, it hit me.

"The day you told me your parents were moving to Austin," I whispered.

She nodded her head and put her finger in her mouth.

I let out a small moan. "Shit, Emma."

She began walking backward, and as the flush moved across her cheeks, she smiled. "I want to be fucked against the barn, Garrett."

I dropped the quilt and quickly walked up to her. I picked her up in my arms, and she instantly slammed her lips to mine. I practically ran to the barn. I walked in and pushed an empty stall door open and set her down. I quickly began undressing her while she fumbled with my pants.

"Jesus, Emma...what you do to me." I ripped my shirt open and stripped out of it. I quickly pushed her hands away and pulled my pants down, exposing myself to her. I watched as her eyes widened with delight.

She shimmied out of her knickers, and before she had them off her feet, I was picking her up and pushing her against the barn wall.

"Garrett...please..." she said. Her breathing picked up, coming in and out faster and heavier.

I pushed myself into her, and we both let out a moan at the same time. She felt so good.

"Damn, it feels so good to be inside you with no condom," I hissed through my teeth.

"Yes! Garrett, please..." she said as she snapped her head and looked into my eyes.

"Tell me what you want from me, Emma," I said as I slowed down to almost a stop.

"Garrett, move...God, please move."

"Tell me, Em...tell me what you want."

Emma closed her eyes and bit down on her lower lip. Then, she opened her eyes and smiled. "Fuck me, Garrett. Hard. Please. I want to feel you for the next few days."

There was nothing sexier than my sweet and innocent wife telling me to fuck her hard. I gave her everything she'd asked for and more. As she started to scream out in pleasure, I let my release go. Pouring myself into her body was one of the most amazing things ever. I couldn't wait until the day we made a child together.

We stood there for a few minutes, attempting to catch our breaths. I rested my forehead against hers and let out a laugh.

She giggled. "What's so funny?"

I shook my head and looked around. "I just fucked you in our barn. Anyone could have walked in and seen us."

She bit down on her lower lip so hard that it was turning white. I reached up and pulled it out from between her teeth.

"You're so beautiful, Emma. You steal my breath away every time I look at you, and you make me want to be a better man."

"You're the most amazing man I've ever known, Garrett. I'd be lost without you," Emma whispered as she brushed her fingers through my hair. "Take me to bed, Mr. Mathews, and make love to me."

I smiled and gently put her down. As we slowly got dressed, I watched her every move. I still couldn't believe she was mine. I stopped and just watched her as she got dressed and attempted to fix her hair.

She looked at me and tilted her head. "What?"

I shook my head as I reached for her and pulled her to me. "The first time I ever saw you, I knew."

She smiled that sweet, innocent smile, and her eyes lit up. "You knew what?"

"That someday you would be my wife. I knew that I'd wake up every morning and roll over to breathe in your heavenly scent. I knew you would taste sweeter than honey and that you would invade my thoughts every waking moment. I dreamed of making love to you while your belly was swollen with our child."

A tear was slowly making a path down her perfect face, and I brushed it away. "I knew I would love you for the rest of my life."

"Oh, Garrett…" Emma choked back a sob. "If only I hadn't been so foolish."

I smiled as I reached down and picked her up. I carried her to our house while she buried her face into my chest.

She placed her hand on my chest and said, "I can feel your heart beating."

"It only beats for you," I said. I reached for the door, and pushed it open with my foot.

I carried Emma through the house and into our bedroom. After I placed her down on the bed, I closed my eyes and thought back to the very moment when I'd walked through the door to the drugstore, and I'd seen her. When I opened my eyes, she was already naked and lying on our bed.

"The first moment I saw you, Garrett Mathews, I knew my life would never be the same. Those feelings that rushed through my body that day still rush through my body every time you look at me. I've never in my life loved someone like I love you."

I gently moved onto the bed, and I began kissing every inch of my wife until she was begging me to make love to her. We spent the rest of the day in bed, talking and making love, only leaving once to eat.

"Tell me you love me, Em," I whispered as I ran my fingers up and down her back.

"I love you, Garrett."

"Marry me."

She pushed off my chest and let out a giggle as she looked into my eyes. "When?"

I smiled and looked up, like I was thinking. "How fast can you plan a wedding?"

"Are we going on a honeymoon?" she asked as she wiggled her eyebrows up and down.

"I'll take you wherever you want to go, Buttercup."

She smiled bigger. "July. Let's get married in July."

I quickly rolled her over and slowly slid inside her, and she let out a slow, soft moan.

As I gently made love to Emma, I whispered in her ear, telling her all the ways I would make love to her on our honeymoon. When she began calling out my name, I pushed in deeper, and I was so overcome with the most intense orgasm of my life that I almost cried. I stayed inside her for a good ten minutes before I rolled over and pulled her to me. I closed my eyes and began drifting off to sleep as I dreamed about Emma walking down the aisle dressed in white.

16 Emma

July 1962

"Emma, why are you so nervous? Y'all have been married for a year already," Margie said as she messed with my hair.

I looked down at my hands, and they were shaking. I closed my eyes and tried to calm my beating heart. It felt like it was going to beat right out of my chest.

"Emma?"

I turned around and saw my mother standing in the doorway. The moment I saw her, I jumped up and walked into her arms. I tried desperately not to cry, but the second her perfume hit me, I began crying.

"Oh, baby girl. Now, why are you crying? This is far better than your little bedside wedding last year." She winked as she pushed a piece of my hair back.

"Oh, Mother. This last year with Garrett has been amazing, but for some reason, this wedding makes it feel so real, like maybe before we were just playing house. Now…well, now—"

"You're truly going to be his?" my mother said with a smile.

I nodded my head and whispered, "Yes, that's how it feels."

My mother let out a small laugh as she guided me back over to the chair. I sat down, and Margie began messing with the curls framing my face.

My mother let out a sigh. "You look breathtaking, Emma Rose. Garrett is going to pass out when he sees you."

Margie let out a chuckle. "I'm pretty sure Garrett is going to want to, um…er…uh…" She looked at my mother and down at me.

I couldn't help myself. I wasn't going to let it go. "He's going to want to what, Marg?" I asked as I raised my eyebrow.

"Um…you know. I'm just so glad I'm here for this wedding. Aunt Maria, did you see how beautiful the flowers are? They're so fresh," Margie said in an attempt to cover up what she had been about to say.

I let out a giggle and rolled my eyes. I glanced down at Margie's stomach and placed my hand on it. "I'm so glad you're here," I whispered.

Margie placed her hand on top of mine and said, "So am I."

It hadn't taken me long to forgive Marg after the incident last year, and things had gotten back to normal fairly quickly. Now, Margie and Billy were expecting their first baby in six months.

"How are you feeling?" I asked.

She starting placing pins in my hair, and she let out a sigh. "Sick as a dog. I've never thrown up so much in my life, but I wouldn't change a thing."

My mother laughed. "It is all worth it in the end."

After a few more touches on my makeup, I was led over to the other side of the room where my wedding dress was hanging up. My mother had spared no expenses when it came to my wedding dress. It was fashioned after Grace Kelly's wedding dress, and I had to admit that it was beautiful, even with the rounded collar. In keeping with the whole theme, the full skirt was made of ivory peau de soie, and the fitted bodice was a Duchesse lace embroidered with small white pearls. The yards of silk taffeta making the dress still baffled my mind. I smiled when I looked at my petticoat. My mother and aunt had spent hours sewing blue satin bows onto it, again fashioning after Grace Kelly's petticoat.

After getting the dress on and Margie fussing over my hair, I slipped on my shoes and slowly turned to look at myself in the mirror. I let out a gasp as I stared back at myself. My blonde hair was piled on top of my head with curls falling loosely around my face. I tried desperately not to cry.

"Garrett is going to be over the moon," I whispered to no one in particular.

"Yes, he is," my father said from behind me.

My eyes caught his reflection in the mirror, and he smiled.

My father placed his hands on my shoulders. "You look beyond breathtaking, Emma Rose. I've never laid my eyes on such a rare beauty. Someone should probably be ready to hold Garrett up when he sees you."

I quickly spun around and went to talk when my father held up his hand.

"Wait. Before you say anything, let me speak first. I couldn't have picked out a better man for my little girl if I had handpicked him myself. The love in Garrett's eyes when he looks at you is evident. I see the way he can't pull his eyes off of you, and I know he would lay down his life for you and your safety at any given moment. I know with all my heart that he will love you, like I love you, for the rest of your life. I'm so proud of the man he has become, and I'm so proud of the woman you've grown to be. I love you, Emma Rose, and no one, not even Garrett Mathews, could ever love you as much as I do."

I threw myself into my father's arms and began crying as he held on to me.

He whispered, "No, baby girl, don't cry."

"Daddy," I whispered, "I love him so much."

My father pulled back and used his thumbs to gently wipe away my tears. "Your mother is going to be upset with me for making you cry and for ruining your makeup."

I shook my head. "I don't care."

My father laughed and then looked into my eyes. "I know you love him, Emma. I also know he loves you so very much. That is the only reason he is alive today."

I felt the heat move up to my cheeks as I looked down. I was pretty sure my father and mother knew I hadn't been a virgin when Garrett and I had gotten married last year.

"Charles Birk, did you make her cry?" my mother said.

When I looked behind my father, I saw my mother standing there with her hands on her hips, ready for all-out war.

"I have something else for you," Daddy said in almost a whisper.

I looked as he pulled a box out of his pocket.

"They were my great grandmother's. She wore them in her wedding and then passed them on to my mother. Your grandmother gave them to me the day before I married your mother. Now, it is your turn to wear them."

I let out a gasp as he opened the box and revealed the most beautiful set of pearl earrings I'd ever seen. There were hints of rose, green, and gold colors.

"These are a very rare pair of copper baroque pearl earrings. When I first saw them on your mother, I couldn't believe how beautiful they were. Now, to see them on my own daughter..." His voice cracked before trailing off.

I struggled to keep from crying again.

Daddy cleared this throat. "To see them on my own daughter is an even more rare gift."

I gently took one of the earrings out, and I turned to face the mirror. I put the earring on, and when I took the other earring out, I glanced over to my mother. She was now crying, but she smiled and gave me a thumbs-up. I couldn't help but let out a giggle.

Once both earrings were in, I just stared at my reflection. I looked like a princess.

My father kissed me on the cheek. "Okay, well, I'm going to go take my place now."

Peggy walked in with my veil and said, "Next step is the veil."

Margie and Peggy walked up and began pinning the silk and lace wedding veil on. I just stood there and dreamed of what Garrett's face would look like when he saw me walking down the aisle.

Margie gave me a smile. "He's gonna shit his pants when he sees you."

Peggy and I both started laughing.

Peggy reached for my hand. "Shall we make you Mrs. Garrett Mathews...yet again?"

I nodded my head and took a deep breath to settle my nerves. "That sounds like an amazing idea."

As I began to head out, I stopped at the door, and a huge bouquet of white daisies was handed to me. I smiled, thinking back to Garrett giving me the first of many bouquets of white daisies. Then, my mind began drifting.

Peggy whispered into my ear, "Stop thinking about him like that. You just let out a moan, you horny bitch."

I snapped my head over to Peggy and dropped my mouth open. "Oh my! Did I really?" I asked.

She nodded her head and winked at me.

I smiled and started walking. "I blame it all on Garrett Mathews."

Margie huffed. "Romantic bastard."

We all looked at each other and laughed.

I nodded my head and whispered, "Romantic doesn't even begin to describe Garrett."

17 Garrett

"Son, are you okay?" my father asked from the other side of the door.

Yet again, I splashed my face with cold water. "Yes, sir. Just give me a few seconds."

"Three times. Who throws up three times right before his wedding?" Billy said.

I rolled my eyes and looked into the mirror. "Lord, please...I don't want to throw up on my beautiful bride."

"What was that, Garrett? I didn't hear you," my father said.

I opened the door and tried to smile. "I was praying that I wouldn't throw up on Emma."

Billy was laughing his ass off.

I gave him a good shove and said, "Push off, you ass."

"Boys, that's enough. Billy, you're fixin' to be a father, so start acting like it," my father said as he turned and looked at Billy.

I peeked around my father's back and gave Billy the middle finger. I mouthed, *Candy-ass.*

His mouth dropped open, and he quickly said, "Dad! He's giving me the finger."

Our father walked away and said, "It's his wedding, son. If he gave you the finger, I'm sure you deserved it. Oh, Garrett, don't forget about my toast."

I smiled and felt triumphant...for a whole two seconds.

"Garrett, it's time," Pastor Spencer gently said as he placed his hand on my shoulder.

I swallowed hard. "I think I'm going to throw up."

Billy threw his head back and laughed as he walked into the sanctuary.

Pastor Spencer giggled. "Son, take a deep breath, and let's make our way."

As we walked down the aisle at St. Paul's Lutheran Church, I took everything in. I inhaled a deep breath and smelled the flowers as I took in the color of them. Light blue bows were tied on to the end of every pew. It all said Emma. I smiled as I pictured her here last night, putting on the bows and directing exactly where she'd wanted every flower to go. When I glanced up, I saw all the white daisies, and my mind drifted back to that warm day on the quilt under our tree.

I was snapped out of my daydream when Pastor Spencer said, "Garrett, take your spot."

Billy was standing there, grinning from ear to ear. I couldn't help but smile back at him. I shook my head as I thought about him becoming a father and making me an uncle. Even though we weren't blood brothers, he would always be a brother to me. I looked at Raymond standing next to Billy, and when he winked at me, I gave him a nod back. The only person missing was Wayne. He had joined the Marines right after we graduated from college, and Billy had said the only reason he had joined was to get away from Anna and her constant hounding about getting married. Now, Wayne was engaged to a girl from South Carolina, and he'd talked about bringing her home to Texas soon.

The music began playing, and all three of us stood up straight.

Billy hit me on the arm and said, "Look at how cute she is!"

Lily, our two-year-old little sister, began walking down the aisle. Rather, she was running while she threw rose petals in the air and laughed. Peggy was next, and she looked beautiful. I glanced over to look at Raymond, and he was beaming with pride.

"Holy shit," Billy whispered.

I turned and saw Margie walking down the aisle. She was glowing, and I didn't think I'd ever seen her so happy.

Then, the music changed, and my heart slammed in my chest. *Don't get sick. Don't get sick.* I closed my eyes, and when I slowly opened them, I saw the most beautiful girl standing at the end of the aisle.

"Garrett, breathe. You've got to breathe," Billy whispered as he nudged my arm.

"I've...never...so...breathtaking," I barely said.

I watched as Emma gracefully walked down the aisle on her father's arm. Nothing could have ever prepared me for this moment. My heart was so overfilled with love...and lust. I could hardly think straight. Everything was in a fog, and I couldn't even hear what the pastor was saying.

I did, however, hear when Charles leaned in close to my ear and whispered, "You ever hurt my daughter...I'll kill you, chop you up into a million pieces, and toss you in the trash."

I pulled back and swallowed hard. "I, um..."

I shook my head to clear my thoughts, but he just smiled and placed Emma's hand in mine. When I looked down into her beautiful eyes, I quickly forgot all about her father's threat.

"Em, you look stunning. You take my breath away," I said. I began to rub my thumbs across her hand in a rather quick and nervous fashion.

She smiled. "You look so handsome, Garrett."

When she bit on her lower lip, I wanted to lift her veil and take her lips against mine.

I leaned down and whispered next to her ear, "The things I'm going to do to you tonight are going to make your body shake with desire."

She sucked in a breath of air and dropped her mouth open as she pulled back and looked at me. She slowly smiled. "Two can play at that game, Mr. Mathews. I have my own plans for you."

The rest of the ceremony was a blur. I couldn't stop thinking about what plans Emma had. My whole body was practically shaking with anticipation at the idea of being with her on our wedding night. Since I had been in the hospital during our first wedding, our wedding night had consisted of me sleeping most of the time from the pain pills. Now, I had every intention of making it up to her tonight.

"Are you about ready to leave?" I whispered into Emma's ear.

She looked up at me, and her eyes spoke for her loud and clear.

"You have no idea how ready I am to leave," she whispered back.

I still hadn't told her where we were going. For the last three years, I'd been saving every spare penny I could to take her on this honeymoon. Her parents had wanted to pay for the honeymoon, but I'd said no. The fact that they had paid for our entire wedding was more than enough.

I placed my hand on the small of her back and looked at my watch. Our plane would be leaving tomorrow, but I really wanted to get Emma out of here. I looked around for Margie. When her eyes caught mine, I gave her a look, and she nodded her head. She had made sure that Emma was packed up with everything she would need for our honeymoon. One week in Venice would be just what the doctor had ordered. I needed to take a break from the ranch, and Emma had been dreaming of going to Italy. For me to be able to make her dream come true felt amazing.

Emma was talking to some people.

I politely interrupted and said, "I hate to pull the bride away, but we have a flight waiting for us in Austin, and we really need to leave soon."

The oohs and aahs coming from everyone when I'd mentioned the word *bride* caused me to roll my eyes. As I led Emma toward the front door, our guests kept stopping us.

"Where are you going on your honeymoon?" someone asked from behind me.

Emma giggled. "He won't tell me where we are going. It's a surprise."

"It's probably to a cheap motel in Austin, if I know Garrett!" someone yelled out.

If I weren't in such a hurry, I would have turned around and given whoever had said that a knuckle sandwich.

"Garrett, you're practically pulling my arm out," Emma said.

We stopped at the door and waited for everyone to line up. They were all opening up the small bags that contained the rice.

Emma and I both said at the same time, "Oh, great."

Emma had begged her parents to skip this part, but they wouldn't have it. Their little girl would not be sneaking off. She deserved a proper send-off.

"Are you ready?" Maria asked as she looked at Emma and then me.

We both nodded our heads, and before we took off, I leaned down and said, "Take off your shoes."

Emma snapped her head and looked at me. "What? Why?"

I was looking at everyone smiling. "We can run faster if you're not running in damn heels."

"Oh, smart thinking!" Emma reached down and slipped one shoe off and then the other.

I leaned in to her and said, "I have a plan. Before your dad gets done talking, we take off running. We'll catch everyone off guard that way."

Emma laughed. "I knew I married you for a reason."

Charles walked up. "It's time to send off the bride and groom! May I—"

I pulled Emma's hand, and we both took off running. Everyone began scrambling to throw the rice.

"Um…well, there goes Mr. and Mrs. Garrett Thomas Mathews!" Emma's dad called out.

We were more than halfway to the car when the first rice pellets began hitting us. Once we got to the car, they were still pelting us.

"Shit! Why aren't they stopping?" I yelled out.

Emma laughed uncontrollably.

"Ouch! Son of a bitch! Who threw the whole bag at me?" I shouted. I looked up and saw Billy smiling from ear to ear. I pointed at him and said, "I'll get you back for that, you bas—"

"Garrett! We should go," Emma said as she pulled me back.

I quickly opened her door as her mother walked up, and we helped Emma into the truck. I ran around to the driver's side and waved. "Thanks, everyone! See y'all in a week!"

I attempted to get the rice out of my hair before I jumped into the truck. Emma was still laughing, and she grabbed my hand as I took off down the road.

"Bastards! I think some of those people purposely hit me with full bags of rice," I said.

Emma began picking rice out of her hair. "Garrett, pull over, so I can let my hair down and get this rice out."

I looked over at her. There was no way in hell I was letting her take her hair down. That was my job. "We'll be home soon, and I'll get it out. I want to take your hair down."

She turned, and from the corner of my eye, I could see her staring at me.

"I thought we had a flight to catch. You told everyone—" She stopped talking and put her hand up to her mouth. "You lied to everyone!"

I threw my head back and laughed. "Yes and no. I won't deny it. I needed an excuse to get you out of there and in my arms. Technically, we do have a flight waiting for us in Austin…tomorrow. Do you know how crazy I've been, seeing you in that dress?"

Emma laughed and then let out a gasp. "Our dance. Oh my God, Garrett…we never had our first dance."

I slammed on the brakes and looked at her.

"How did we not have our first dance?" I asked.

She looked at me like I was stupid.

I glanced into the rearview mirror and said, "Oh, holy hell."

Billy pulled up next to us, honking his horn, and I rolled down my window.

Margie said, "The first dance!"

Emma yelled, "We're coming back right now!"

I shook my head and quickly turned the truck around, making our way back to the church. The reception was being held in the basement, and by the time we pulled up, everyone was already back in the basement.

When we walked in, everyone began clapping, and Emma and I both just smiled.

"I still don't see how we forgot to do the first dance," she whispered.

"I know why. Ever since we cut the damn cake, everyone has been talking to us. I've never fake-smiled so much in my life."

Emma hit me in the stomach and smiled as we walked to the middle of the room. "Oh, Garrett. Did you remember to tell Billy the song you wanted for our first dance?"

I smiled as I reached down and kissed the tip of her nose. "Yes, Buttercup, I did."

We were standing in the middle of the dance floor, and Charles was about to introduce us again.

"I don't think anything else needs to be said. Ladies and gentlemen, here is Emma and Garrett for their first dance as husband and wife."

Emma and I both laughed. Everyone knew we had been married for a year now, but it didn't seem to matter. Emma turned and gave me that smile that made my knees weak every time I saw it. Then, "Can't Help

Falling in Love" started, and her eyes misted over with tears. I pulled her into my arms and began singing along with Elvis. The moment I'd first heard this song, I had known it was my song to her. She held on to me like her life depended on it.

"Emma, your smile melts my heart and makes me weak in the knees at the same time. Your laughter is the most beautiful thing I've ever heard, and I plan on hearing it every day for the rest of our lives." I placed my hand on the side of her face and wiped a tear away with my thumb. "Your eyes…my God, your eyes cause me to lose my breath every time I look into them. Your lips are the sweetest things on your body, and I crave them daily. Every day I wake up next to you and hear your voice, my heart beats harder in my chest, and I fall in love with you more. I will give you everything, Emma. My entire world is yours—always and forever."

I moved my mouth closer to her ear as I sang the last verse of the song, and Emma began crying harder.

Once the song ended, I lifted her chin and gently kissed her. "I love you, Emma Rose Mathews."

She swallowed and closed her eyes before opening them again and whispering, "I love you more, Garrett Thomas Mathews."

Elvis's "Too Much" started playing, and we both laughed. I grabbed her hands, and we took off dancing. I knew how much my girl loved to dance, and no one could pass up an Elvis song.

18 Emma

By the time we were driving down our driveway, I was fighting to keep my eyes open. I leaned my head back and dreamed of getting out of this wedding dress. I couldn't breathe with how tight the corset was. Garrett would like it, that was for sure. And the fact that I had been naughty and slipped off my knickers had me going crazy all night. I had tried to tell Garrett at least five times that I wasn't wearing knickers, but every time I'd tried, someone had come up and started talking to me.

I slowly lifted my head and turned to look at my handsome husband. "I have a surprise for you," I said.

Garrett smiled. "I have a surprise for you, too." He drove right on by the house and started making his way to the west pasture.

I giggled and put my hand up to my mouth. I was nervous for what I was about to admit. "Garrett?"

"Yeah, Buttercup?" He looked at me sweetly.

I slowly licked my lips. "I haven't had any knickers on this whole time."

He brought the truck to a stop and put it in park. He slowly turned his body and looked at me. When the smile spread across his face, I couldn't help but smile back.

"I'm so glad you didn't tell me that back at the church because I would have taken you right then and there. I'm pretty sure the Lord wouldn't have appreciated me causing my wife to yell out in pleasure in his house."

My face blushed instantly.

Garrett turned and jumped out of the truck. "Wait here, and keep your eyes shut."

I smiled and nodded my head as I closed my eyes. When I felt the truck move, I knew he was in the bed of it. The next thing I knew, my door had opened, and his hand was up and under my dress so fast that I let out a gasp.

"Spread your legs, Em," he whispered against my neck.

"Garrett…" I let out a gasp when his fingers moved up my thigh.

He snapped my garter belt against my leg, causing me to open my eyes and cry out as I hit him. Then, his fingers moved across my lips, and he moaned as he slipped his fingers inside me. I closed my eyes and dropped my head back as his lips moved along my neck.

"I can't wait to taste you, Emma," he said in such a deep voice.

I could feel my insides clenching down in anticipation. My eyes snapped open, and I looked into his eyes. "Garrett," I whispered.

He quickly pulled his fingers out of me, and when he put them up to his lips, my mouth dropped open. Before I knew what was happening, he had me out of the truck. He carried me to the back and set me down on the tailgate of the truck. He placed both hands on my face and gently kissed me on the lips. He reached for my hands and helped me down to the ground. I stepped onto a small blanket that he must have placed there.

"Turn around, Em," he whispered.

My heart practically pounded out of my chest. I slowly turned around, and when he touched my neck, I jumped.

As he began unbuttoning my dress, he said, "You looked like a princess today. There wasn't a man in the room who couldn't take his eyes off of you. You are so incredibly beautiful that I have to pinch myself every day just to make sure this isn't all a dream."

I closed my eyes and let his words wrap around my heart. "Garrett…" I whispered as I placed my hands on the tailgate to keep myself standing.

"Em, can I let the dress fall to the ground?"

I nodded my head. The last thing I cared about was the dress. I turned and watched as he picked it up and gently folded it over. He walked to the passenger side, opened the door, and laid the dress on the seat. I'd never in my entire life met anyone like Garrett. The way he paid attention to the little things was what made me love him so much.

I turned to face him as he walked back to me, and his eyes moved up and down my body.

"Take off the petticoat," he said with that deep voice that rattled my insides.

I quickly took it off and kicked it to the side. I stood before my husband in a light blue corset with a matching garter belt.

He reached his hands up and began taking down my hair. Piece by piece, my blonde hair fell loosely around my shoulders.

"So. Damn. Beautiful." He dropped to his knees, and then he unclipped my stockings and slowly began rolling them down my leg.

"Garrett…everywhere you touch is on fire," I whispered.

He peeked up at me and smiled. His eyes were on fire, and his smile had a touch of wickedness in it.

He removed my garter belt and placed his hand on my stomach. "That corset is beautiful."

I licked my lips and then bit down on my lower lip. I wanted to tell him that it was cutting off my breathing, but he seemed to be turned on by it. When he lifted my leg and placed it over his shoulder, I smiled. Then, he buried his face between my legs. He ran his tongue between my lips and then began tormenting my clit.

I grabbed on to the tailgate, and I couldn't control myself as I pushed my hips into his face.

"Garrett!" I called out as I began to feel the familiar buildup.

He quickly pulled away, and I practically shouted, "No! Don't stop!"

He stood up, and the smile on his face caused me to smile.

"I love to taste you, Em."

My chest was heaving up and down. "Why did you stop?"

"Get up on the quilt, Emma."

I turned around to see our quilt had been laid out in the back of the bed. I'd never moved so fast in my life.

"Garrett…please do that again. Please," I begged.

He crawled over me and pressed his lips to mine.

I ran my hands through his hair and gave it a hard tug as I pulled him away. "Don't make me beg."

He began kissing my neck and moved his way down to my nipple. The way he sucked and pulled on it was driving me insane. Then, he began kissing down my stomach, and I could feel my body starting to tremble with anticipation.

"Emma…you're so wet," he barely said.

I grabbed his head and began pushing him down between my legs. I heard him chuckle.

He asked me, "What do you want me to do, Em?"

I lifted my head and looked at him. "What?" I said in an exasperated voice.

"Tell me what you want me to do."

I dropped my head and thrashed it back and forth. "Kiss me, Garrett. God, just kiss me again."

He quickly licked my clit before he looked back up at me. "Kiss you where, Emma?"

I looked into his eyes, and they were on fire with desire.

Does he want me to talk dirty to him? Can I talk dirty to him? Shit, I just want to feel his lips on me again.

"Garrett…kiss me. Please just put your lips on me."

"I love your innocence, Em. It drives me insane with desire."

I was just about to talk when he buried his face and began sucking on my clit. The moment he slipped his fingers in, I started screaming out his name. I'd never had an orgasm hit me so fast and so hard. It lasted for so long.

I was just beginning to see the light of day again when I felt Garrett moving on top of me.

He brushed his lips along my neck and up to my ear where he gently bit down on my earlobe. "I've always wanted to make love to you in the back of my truck, Buttercup."

I pulled his body closer to mine and whispered, "I need to feel you closer."

Garrett slowly and gently entered my body, and he made love to me like never before. He whispered how much he loved me over and over. Right before he came, he placed his hands on my face and looked into my eyes.

He whispered, "You're mine—forever."

"Yes," I whispered back.

He softly called out my name. He stayed inside me for the longest time as I gently ran my fingertips up and down his back.

"You own my heart, Emma. I'm nothing without your love."

I wrapped my arms around him as tight as I could while I softly cried. My heart was so full of love that I was sure it was going to burst.

Garrett finally pulled out of me and rolled over onto his back. The sun had begun to set, and the stars were starting to dot the night sky.

"Every wish has a star," I whispered.

Garrett turned and looked at me. "I want to make all your wishes come true."

I turned and smiled. "You already have."

He slowly shook his head. "No, there's still another wish."

I rolled onto my side and began running my fingers down his chest. Garrett would go running every day before he began work on the ranch, and his amazing body showed it. Just looking at his perfect body about drove me crazy with lust.

"Oh, yeah? What's the other wish?" I asked with a giggle.

Garrett looked back up at the sky and whispered, "A baby."

My heart dropped to my stomach, and the butterflies began fluttering.

Garrett rolled over and looked into my eyes. "I'm washed away by the feelings I have for you. My love grows stronger and stronger every day, Em. I can't imagine what it's going to be like when you're carrying my child. I'm going to go insane from worrying about you both. I'll spoil the hell out of you, and I'll do everything I can to be the best husband and father."

I moved my eyes down to his lips and ran my tongue along the bottom of my lip. Garrett's eyes lit up, and the moon was beginning to reflect in them. I sat up and placed my hands on his chest as I pushed him onto his back.

When I crawled on top of him, he let out a laugh. "I don't think he's ready to play yet."

I gave him a wicked smile as I moved myself against his body. The friction between the two of us felt like heaven. I leaned down and began kissing him. When I pulled back, I sucked his lower lip into my mouth and gently bit down on it. He let out a moan as his eyes closed, and I let go of his lip.

He whispered, "Jesus, Emma...you're my Aphrodite."

I smiled when I felt him getting harder. I began rocking back and forth until I lifted and slowly sank down on him. I threw my head back and let out a moan. Nothing felt better than being one with Garrett.

I looked down at him as he sat up and pulled me closer to him. He began kissing me, and I was lost in our lovemaking, taken to a high with his kiss.

He barely pulled his lips away from mine. "When do you want to try for a baby, Em?"

My heart was beating so hard at just the idea of having a child with Garrett. "Would it be selfish of me if I said I wanted to spend a few years with just you and me? Maybe two or three more years?"

The smile that spread across his face made me giggle.

"I take it you're okay with that idea," I said.

"I want nothing more than to have kids, but right now, I want to be able to take you up against a barn wall or make love to you in the back of my truck...anytime I want to. I want to make you call out my name in the middle of the night...often."

I raised my eyebrows. "I like this plan."

I began moving again, and I quickly felt the buildup of my orgasm. "Garrett...I'm going to come," I whispered.

Garrett looked into my eyes as he let his own release go. I could feel his warmth entering my body.

He said, "Emma...baby, I'm coming."

He fell back, bringing me with him, and we lay next to each other. Garrett wrapped us up in the quilt, and he slowly began humming to me before he fell asleep. I moved my head to his chest, and before I knew it, I was dreaming. Garrett was running around, chasing a little boy, as I sat under our tree with my hand on my swollen belly.

The Venice afternoon sun was shining down, warming my face, as I sat on the private balcony of our suite at the Hotel Cipriani. I smiled as I thought back to when Garrett had told me he was taking me to Venice and how excited I had been to go to Italy. I lifted my head and opened my eyes. I stared out at the Venetian Lagoon. I'd never seen such a beautiful place in my entire life.

I felt a shock run through my whole body as Garrett placed his hands on my shoulders.

He brushed his lips across my neck. "Good morning, Buttercup."

I laughed. "It's afternoon, Mr. Mathews. You have given new meaning to the words *sleeping in.*"

Garrett sat down and smiled at me, and then he looked out over the water. "Well, when your wife keeps you up all night, demanding you make mad, passionate love to her, it tends to wear you out."

I raised my eyebrow. "Are you complaining? Shall we have less sex on our honeymoon? Perhaps we should shop more?"

Garrett threw his hands up and said, "No! God, no more shopping."

I giggled and took a sip of water. "Garrett, we went shopping only one time, and it was for less than an hour because you wanted to come back to the hotel for more...playtime."

Garrett's eyes lit up as he reached down and adjusted himself. I knew what he was thinking about. We had been in a local shop when something came over me, and I'd told Garrett I wanted to please him with my mouth. He had us back to the boat and in our hotel room in record time.

"I like your version of playtime, Em—a lot."

I felt the heat move into my cheeks, and I quickly looked away. Garrett stood up and walked over to me. He held out his hand for me to stand up. I placed my hand in his, and instantly, I felt the butterflies in my stomach.

Garrett gave me the sweetest smile and brushed a piece of my hair back and behind my ear. "Don't ever be ashamed of what we share together, Emma. I'm not. I could taste you every day, ten times a day. You're my wife, and I'm your husband. What we share together is amazing, magical, and sexy as hell."

I bit down on my lip. I wasn't sure why, but when Garrett spoke like that to me, it did things deep in the pit of my stomach.

I looked into his eyes and whispered, "I'm not ashamed, Garrett. I...I enjoyed making you come like that."

The moment that familiar smile of his spread across his face, I couldn't help but want to drop to my knees and take him in my mouth again.

"I enjoyed it, too, more than you know. I see the look in your eyes, Buttercup, but we can't. We have to get ready to head into the city. I have a surprise for you."

My smile faded, and I couldn't believe how disappointed I felt. I smiled weakly and said, "A surprise, huh?"

He nodded with excitement. "Get dressed, Em. We don't have much time."

I watched as he walked away from me, his sleeping pants barely hanging on by his hips. The way his toned body moved when he walked gave me shivers. I thought about last night in the bathtub where he'd made love to me and whispered to me all the places he was going to make love to me. The bathroom alone was incredibly romantic with a massive oval tub and marble everywhere. I closed my eyes and let out a moan. I could almost feel his lips on my body.

I never, ever want to leave Italy.

19 Garrett

As we walked up to the gondola, I couldn't help but notice Emma's smile. The gondolier allowed me in first, so I could help Emma in after me. She was still grinning from ear to ear, and it caused me to smile.

"I've been wanting to take a gondola ride," she said with excitement.

We took our seats, and I pulled Emma closer to me as the gondolier began singing a barcarole while he moved us along the Venetian Lagoon. His voice was smooth as silk, and he held both Emma and I captive with the beautiful song.

"Garrett, I never want to leave," Emma whispered.

I kissed her forehead. "Neither do I, Em. Neither do I."

The gondolier smiled. "Tale bella sposa. Così felice in amore."

I laughed. "I got *beautiful bride* and *love* out of that."

We all laughed.

The gondolier said, "Such a beautiful bride. So happy in love."

Emma looked up, and when my eyes caught hers, my heart melted. Her eyes were filled with so much love and happiness.

"Yes, I am very happy in love," she said.

I leaned down and kissed her forehead. "And you're the most beautiful bride ever."

After the gondola ride, we slowly made our way to a small restaurant that Charles had told me to take his daughter to. One of his doctor friends, John, had moved to Venice after meeting a girl from here and falling in love. They had opened up the restaurant a few years back, and Charles and Maria had been the first ones to eat there. I'd taken advantage of the friendship when I made arrangements for dinner this evening. John had told me I was not only going to score points with Emma, but with her father as well.

As we walked in, Emma and I both let out a gasp. The restaurant wasn't very big, but it was completely empty. I had offered to pay John handsomely to have the restaurant somewhat private, but once he'd found out that Charles was my father-in-law, he'd said he would do it for an old friend.

"Garrett!" Emma placed her hand up to her mouth.

I really wanted to have the same reaction, but I had to play it cool. *Holy shit. He did exactly what I said I had envisioned, even down to the flowers I mentioned.*

She spun around and looked at me. "Did you arrange all of this?"

I smiled. "I had connections with the owner."

I glanced up and saw John and his wife, Mary, standing there. I nodded my head and walked up to them. I shook John's hand, and he brought me in for a hug.

"Is this what you had in mind?" he asked.

I pulled back and smiled. "It's perfect, beyond perfect." I turned slightly and kissed Mary on the cheek. "How in the world did y'all do this in one day?"

She laughed. "It's amazing what can happen with true love as the driving force behind it."

I looked back at John. "Do I owe you more for the flowers? They are covering the restaurant."

He shook his head and glanced behind me. I turned to see Emma smelling all the flowers as she walked around the restaurant. She stopped at a picture and spun around quickly.

"My parents! Oh my gosh!" Her hands came up to her mouth. "John? Mary?"

John and Mary both chuckled as they walked up to Emma.

"Emma Rose, the last time I saw your beautiful face, you were running around, playing princess," John said.

Emma smiled bigger. "Oh, I wasn't even paying attention to the name of the restaurant when we walked up. I was hoping to visit."

"Well, your husband here beat you to it. He stopped in yesterday and made all the arrangements for dinner," Mary said as she hugged Emma. "Let's get you seated, shall we?"

Emma nodded her head as we made our way over to a table in the middle of the restaurant.

Mary placed napkins down for both of us as she began to go over what we would be eating. "I've prepared baccalà mantecata with risotto and gnocchi. It's my mother's recipe."

"Oh my, that all sounds heavenly, Mary," Emma said.

She looked at John and smiled as he placed a Bellini down in front of Emma and then me. Emma had become addicted to the drink since having it the first night we'd arrived.

John cleared his throat. "I've been told the bride loves tiramisu."

Emma laughed and looked at me.

"Yes, she does indeed," I said.

"Then, I dare say you will have the best you've ever had this evening," John said.

He and Mary excused themselves and headed to the kitchen.

Emma took a sip of her drink and raised her eyebrow at me. She placed the drink back on the table. "Garrett Thomas Mathews, this is the most romantic thing ever."

I shook my head. "This isn't your surprise, Em. That is still to come."

Her eyes danced with fire as she looked at me. It took everything I had not to touch her right now. I wanted to pick her up and make love to her while surrounded by the beautiful candlelight and the smell of the flowers.

She looked down quickly but then looked back at me as she tilted her head. "Did you pick the flowers?"

I looked around and nodded my head. "I did."

"They're beautiful, Garrett," she whispered.

"The white daisies represent your innocence. The orchids are for your beauty. The tulips represent our love and passion."

Emma quickly wiped away a tear that had been sliding down her cheek. "The apple blossoms?" she asked.

"Good fortune with the ranch," I said.

She smiled.

I took a deep breath and continued, "The forget-me-nots represent our true love. The blue violets are for my faithfulness to you, always and forever."

A sob escaped Emma's mouth. She whispered, "Garrett…"

"Last but certainly not least, the stephanotis represent—"

"Marital harmony," Emma said at the same time as me.

I nodded my head. "Yes."

She began crying more. "Garrett, all these beautiful flowers must have cost you a fortune."

I reached for her hand and pulled it to my lips. "I'd do anything to show you how much I love you, Em. If I had to give up the ranch just to show you how much I loved you, I would."

Emma started giggling. "I can't wait to tell Margie and Peggy."

I laughed. "Yeah, I kind of just set the bar pretty high for myself in the future."

She shook her head and squeezed my hand. "All I'll ever need is your love. That is the only thing on earth that I need from you. I love you, Garrett."

"I love you more, Emma Rose."

"I'm never eating again," Emma said as we strolled hand in hand along the streets of Venice.

"Did you enjoy this evening?" I asked as I stopped and turned to face her.

She reached her arms up and around my neck as she stood on her tippy toes. "I've never had such an amazing and romantic evening in my entire life. I can still smell all the flowers."

My stomach began doing flips as I thought about what was coming up. I wanted to make this trip one that Emma would never forget. It wasn't just about locking ourselves away and making love. It was about making memories that she would remember for the rest of her life.

I kissed Emma, and thoughts of the first time I'd ever seen her filled my mind. I pulled back and asked, "Do you want to go dancing?"

She did a little jump. "Have you ever known me not to want to go dancing?"

We made our way to downtown Venice where the nightlife was really hopping. I'd never seen Emma smile as much as she was tonight. We met another American couple, and we were sitting and talking with them.

When Emma got up and excused herself, I made my way to the band. The gentleman looked down.

I asked, "Do you know 'Unforgettable' by Nat King Cole?"

He smiled and said, "Of course. We're from America, and Jessica has sung it many times."

I grinned from ear to ear. "Would you mind playing it? I'm here with my wife, Emma, on our honeymoon from America. This song reminds me of the first time I ever saw her."

When Emma walked back out, I led her to the dance floor.

Before the band played, Jessica asked for everyone's attention. "I've been told we have a couple from America here on their honeymoon."

Everyone began clapping as I pulled Emma closer to me. I winked as her face turned a beautiful rose shade.

"The husband would like for me to sing this next song for his beautiful bride, Emma. He said this is what he felt the first moment he saw you." Jessica smiled, and those familiar chords began playing.

Emma attempted to hold back her tears. As Jessica began singing the song, I smiled down at my girl.

God, how I love her so much.

Emma buried her face into my chest and held on to me as we danced. Nothing needed to be said between us. I wanted Emma to listen to the words and know how much she meant to me.

When the song ended, she looked up at me. "No one has ever made me feel so wonderful, like you have tonight. I didn't think it was possible for me to love you any more than I already do, but...but you just...you keep..." She broke down in tears.

I slammed my lips to hers, and everyone began cheering as I stood there and kissed Emma with as much passion as I could. We were so lost in each other that we didn't even realize people were staring at us.

As I pulled away from her lips, I whispered, "Are you ready for your surprise?"

Her eyes lit up. "Garrett! There's more? How could you possibly top that?"

I threw my head back and laughed. "Let's go, Buttercup."

I took her hand in mine and led her back to the table. We said good-bye to the couple we had met and wished them a safe trip home. We made our way back to the gondolas.

When we walked up, the gondolier from earlier today smiled and nodded. "Are you ready for your midnight gondola ride?"

I helped Emma into the gondola and then reached into my pocket for the hundredth time this evening. *It's still there. Thank God.*

As we softly and smoothly moved along the lagoon, Emma stared up at the night sky. I swallowed hard and reached into my pocket. I had no idea why I was so nervous to give her this gift. It wasn't anything big, but I just prayed she would like it. I pulled back some and turned to look at her. She gave me a sweet smile. She was about to say something when I pulled out the jewelry box. Her eyes moved to the box and then came quickly back to my eyes.

"Emma, the first moment I saw you in that drugstore, I knew I was going to love you forever. I took everything in about you—how you were dressed, what you smelled like, the pink ribbons in your hair, and your beautiful eyes and how they danced in the light. My God, how your eyes captivated me from that moment on."

She smiled as the tears began to roll down her cheeks. I brushed away the tears from her beautiful face as I smiled back at her. I held the box up and opened it, revealing a white gold charm bracelet.

Emma let out a gasp when she saw it and looked back up at me. "Garrett, it's…it's beautiful."

I smiled as I took it out and placed it on her wrist. I moved the bracelet around until I found the first charm.

"A milkshake?" she asked.

"That's what you were drinking when I first met you—a strawberry milkshake."

"I didn't think you noticed me at all since you were talking to Margie the whole time."

I slowly shook my head. "I noticed everything about you."

I moved on to the next charm—a heart. "Because you stole my heart the instant you smiled at me," I whispered.

She began crying harder.

The next charm was a quilt. "I had to have this one made. I don't have to tell you the meaning behind it."

She giggled as she wiped away her tears.

I moved on to the next charm. "Daisies because they are your favorite."

The next charm caused her to laugh. It was the University of Texas symbol. "Attending college with you was some of the best years of my life. I'll never forget that time for as long as I live."

She nodded her head and barely said, "Neither will I."

I smiled when I showed her the next charm.

"A sock?" she said with a giggle.

I nodded and said, "For the sock hop. When we danced, it was the first time in my life that I truly felt happy. I knew the second I took you into my arms, I would never want to let you go. Plus, you love dancing so much."

I watched as she wiped another tear from her eye. I moved along the bracelet and held the dog charm. She looked completely confused and tilted her head. The moonlight was catching her beautiful eyes just right, and I had to swallow hard because all I wanted to do was take her in my arms and kiss her.

"A dog?" she asked as she raised her eyebrow at me.

I laughed. "My favorite movie will always be *Lady and the Tramp*. Always."

Emma threw her head back and laughed. "Only you could make me laugh and cry at the same time, Garrett Mathews."

I winked at her. "One more." I spun the bracelet around and held up the cow. When I looked back up into her eyes, they were filling with tears again.

"My dream was to take over my father's cattle ranch and make it even better. You have no idea how much it means to me that you will be by my side, Emma. I'm looking forward to our future together."

She began sobbing harder as she threw herself into my arms, and I held her. The gondolier smiled as he began singing. I wasn't sure how long we just sat there, but with her in my arms, I had never felt so at peace before in my life.

When she finally pulled back, she began looking at all the charms. "I can only think of one other charm that will need to be added someday," she whispered.

My heart dropped in my stomach at the idea of Emma carrying my child someday. I pulled her back in and gently brushed my hand up and down her back.

"Garrett, I love you so much," Emma said as she looked into my eyes.

"I'll love you forever, Emma."

Her eyes burned with passion as she smiled. "Our love is a forever love," she whispered.

I placed my finger under her chin and brought her lips up to mine. "Yes, it is."

20 Emma

January 1965

I stood at the kitchen sink, looking out the window, while Garrett was talking to her. If he winked at her one more time, I was going to go out and kick him in the shin. The screen door opened, and David walked in. I turned around and attempted to give him a smile.

"Did y'all get all the cattle vaccinated?" I asked. I turned back around and stared at the brunette veterinarian, who wouldn't stop placing her hand on Garrett's arm.

"We did. Seems like the new doc might have a bit of a crush on Garrett," David said with a laugh.

I spun around and glared at him. I made my way across the kitchen and out the door where I stood on the porch and watched the rest of their encounter play out.

Garrett was laughing and having a grand ole time talking to her. I looked her up and down. She wore her pants about three sizes too small and her shirt even smaller. Her breasts were practically falling out of her shirt.

Garrett finally reached his hand out and shook hers. She waved good-bye and got into her truck.

David walked out and stood next to me. "I think I'll be taking off for home. Now, don't be hard on the boy, Emma Rose. He loves you more than life itself."

I slowly nodded my head. "Tell Mama I said hi and that I'll be making an apple pie tomorrow. I plan on making a few extras."

He shook his head and made his way to the barn but not before stopping and saying good-bye to Garrett. When Garrett turned around and smiled at me, I gave him a dirty look and headed back into the house. I quickly walked over to the stove and began stirring the beef stew. When I heard the screen door open, I took a deep breath and tried to calm my breathing. I had no idea why I was so jealous.

"Em, is everything okay?" Garrett asked.

I turned and said, "Oh, I don't know, Garrett. Did you enjoy your time with the good doctor? It sure looked like you were."

He let out a laugh, but when he saw I was being serous, his smile dropped.

"Emma, are you…jealous of her? What? Was I not supposed to talk to her? She's possibly going to be the new vet and—"

I let out a laugh. "Oh, how all the ranchers will love those tight-ass pants and her breasts spilling out from her shirt. You couldn't seem to wipe the smile from your face, Garrett."

I saw the anger in his eyes, and I instantly regretted saying what I had. Garrett and I had never once had a fight, not in all the years we had been together, and I wasn't sure what was coming over me right now.

"I don't really like what you're accusing me of, Emma. I was being polite to her. Did I notice her clothing? Yes, I did—along with every other guy helping today. I won't lie to you about that. Did I stare at her or try to talk to her because of it? No. I'm surprised by your childish behavior, Em."

I let out a gasp. "Childish? You're an asshole, Garrett Mathews!" I screamed.

Garrett tilted his head. "You really want to do this over something so stupid, Em?"

I knew he was right, and that pissed me off even more. "Fuck off, Garrett." I spun around and put my hand up to my mouth. *Oh my God. What am I doing? Why am I picking a fight with him?* I knew how much Garrett loved me and how he would do anything for me. I was just being a jealous little brat.

Garrett walked off to our bedroom, and I sat down on the chair and quickly wiped the tears away.

A few minutes later, he walked in, and when I glanced up and saw his suitcase, a sob escaped my throat. I slowly stood up.

"I'm going to go stay the evening with my parents. I'm not sure why or how this got started, but I think it's best if I just leave before something is said that we'll both regret," he said before turning to leave.

I placed my hand on my stomach and instantly felt sick. I watched as he walked to the door, and I began crying harder. I tried to talk, but nothing would come out. When he opened the door, I finally was able to say something. "Garrett!" I called out.

He turned around, and when our eyes met, I slowly started to slide down to the floor.

I whispered, "I'm so sorry. I don't know what came over me. Please…please don't leave me."

Garrett dropped his suitcase and had me in his arms before I even knew what was happening. "Emma, I'd never leave you—ever. Our love is forever. Don't you know that?"

I frantically began kissing him. "Yes! God, yes, I know that. I'm so sorry. I don't know what came over me."

I quickly began trying to pull Garrett's shirt up and over his head. Then, he began taking off his pants.

He pulled me against his body. "Emma, I only have eyes for you. I only love you," he whispered against my lips.

I reached under my skirt and pulled off my knickers. I kicked them off to the side as I said, "I know. Oh God, Garrett, I know. Please…I need you."

The instant he slipped inside me, I let out a moan. We'd never had such raw, passionate sex as we did that afternoon. Garrett took me hard and fast against our kitchen counter, and then he carried me into our bedroom where we made love two more times.

We lay in bed, wrapped around each other, for the longest time before either one of us spoke.

"I promise you, Garrett, I will never let jealousy into my heart like that again. I just don't know what happened. It was so weird how upset I was."

He rolled over onto his side and pulled me closer to him, so we were facing each other. "Emma, I want to have a baby. It's been a few years since we got married, and I really want to have a baby."

I let out a sigh and smiled so big. "I do, too, Garrett. I've been trying to figure out a way to tell you, but I was so scared that you weren't ready, and well…maybe that is where my behavior came from today. I don't know."

Garrett smiled. "A woman has the right to have her moods, just like a man does. Let's not ever let it go that far again though, okay, Em? I never want to see that look on your face again—ever."

I leaned in and sucked his bottom lip into my mouth. I gently bit down on it, and he let out a moan.

I let it go and said, "I promise. Never again."

He gently pushed me onto my back and crawled onto me as he smiled. "I think we should start practicing for that baby."

I let out a giggle and nodded my head quickly. "I like that plan."

I let out a sigh when he slipped inside me and began moving oh-so slowly. I was quickly swept away by his lovemaking. Deep in my heart, I knew that we were making something amazing.

As I closed my eyes and snuggled up against my husband, I whispered, "Garrett, you should probably start looking for that charm."

21 Garrett

October 1965

I paced back and forth in the waiting room.

"Garrett, please stop pacing," Margie said.

I looked at my best friend and his wife sitting there, smiling at me. I couldn't help but smile when I glanced down and saw Billy's hand on Margie's swollen stomach. They were expecting their third child in a few weeks.

I let out a sigh and sat down. "I don't understand. They said they would let me in the delivery room with her, and no one is telling me a thing. I'm about to punch a hole in the damn wall if they don't let me see my wife."

Billy laughed. "Garrett, with our first two, I wasn't allowed in until after Margie gave birth, so just take some deep breaths. The nurse will let you know. Y'all just got here thirty minutes ago."

I nodded my head and then dropped it down into my hands as I tried to calm down.

"Mr. Mathews?"

I jumped up and looked around. When I saw the nurse standing there, I practically ran up to her. "Yes! That's me!"

She chuckled. "I know. I checked your wife in. Are you ready to head into the delivery room?"

I instantly felt sick and turned back to look at Margie and Billy. They both smiled.

"Go on, Mathews. Don't miss the chance to see your child being born," Billy said.

I spun back around to face the nurse. "Yes, I'm more than ready."

As we walked into the delivery room, I couldn't help but notice how beautiful Emma looked. When our eyes met and she smiled, I had to remind myself to breathe.

I walked up to her and leaned down to gently kiss her on the lips. "You take my breath away. You're so beautiful."

The nurse walked up to the other side of Emma. I looked up at her, and she smiled at Emma and then at me. "Now, Emma, I want you to breathe through the contractions, okay? Just like what we went over."

Emma nodded her head and took my hand in hers. "Okay. As long as I have my husband by my side, everything is good."

Then, she squeezed my hand and began breathing quickly. "Oh my…oh…this one is…"

The nurse said, "Breathe, Emma. Breathe through the pain."

Emma smiled and nodded her head. She looked at me and winked.

Three hours later, I was ready to hurt someone. Emma was in so much pain, and I felt helpless that I couldn't do anything.

"Mrs. Mathews, just a few more pushes, and your baby will be here," the doctor said.

"Damn it!" Emma called out as another contraction hit her.

When Kathy, the sweet nurse who had been here the whole time, started in with her breathing reminder again, I knew she was in trouble.

Emma snapped her head and gave her a look. "I swear to God, if you tell me one more time to breathe through the pain, I'm going to punch you!"

I tried not to, but I laughed. Then, I quickly said, "I'm so sorry, Kathy. She doesn't mean what she is saying."

Kathy smiled and said, "I know, Mr. Mathews. I take it all with a grain of salt."

I nodded my head, and I was about to say something else when Emma grabbed my shirt.

"If you think for one minute that I'm going to let you do this to me again, you have another thing coming. Never. Again."

I swallowed hard and looked at Kathy.

She mouthed, *Grain of salt*, to me and smiled.

I looked back down at Emma and said, "I'm so sorry, Em. If I could—"

Then, the doctor said, "Emma, push with the contraction. We just need one more good one."

I helped Emma to sit up a bit as she pushed as hard as she could. She never once screamed out in pain. I was pretty sure that was because she was slowly and painfully breaking each of my fingers. She was on her way to breaking my hand.

Then, I heard our baby's cries as Emma fell back onto the bed.

As the doctor held up our child, he said, "It's a boy, Mr. and Mrs. Mathews."

I couldn't help the flood of tears falling from my eyes as I looked at our child for the first time.

"He's beautiful." Emma began crying.

I turned and looked at her and then back at the baby. Besides my wife, I'd never seen anything so beautiful in my life. When I looked back down at Emma, I smiled as I reached down and wiped her tears from her face.

"You did it, Em. He's breathtaking…like his mother." I leaned over and kissed her lips gently. I whispered, "I love you, Em."

She pulled me closer to her and deepened the kiss. As she let me go, she whispered back, "I love you more."

I walked into the room and stopped immediately. Emma was in bed, holding our son. Seeing the two most important people in my life before my eyes, my heart couldn't possibly swell up any more.

"Hey," I said in a hushed voice.

As I walked up to the side of the hospital bed, Emma smiled big. "Hey back. He just finished eating, and he's out like a light."

I reached down and kissed her on the forehead and then kissed my son. "Have you given any more thought to his name?" I raised my eyebrow.

I knew Emma was torn between naming our son James or Jack. Jack was my favorite name, and I would love to see my son named after my beloved horse, but James was Emma's father's middle name. I could see the indecision on her face.

"You want to know what I think?" I asked.

She smiled. "Of course I do."

"Once upon a time, a great man had faith in me. He trusted me to do right by his daughter and to love her and treat her like she deserved, being the princess that she was. He gave me a once-in-a-lifetime opportunity to better myself, so I would be able to take care of that princess. If it weren't for this great man, our son wouldn't be here today. I think we owe it to him to name our first son after him—Charles James Mathews."

Emma tried to contain the sob, but it escaped her lips, and the moment she closed her eyes, the tears began to slide down her face. I reached over and kissed them away. When I pulled back, she attempted to talk, but she began crying again. Her little body was bouncing up and down as she cried, so I quickly slipped my hands under the baby and picked him up. I held him to my chest as I walked around. I peered down at him. When I looked up, I saw Charles and Maria standing at the door. It wasn't lost on me that Charles had quickly wiped a tear away before glancing down at Emma.

Maria walked up to me and asked, "May I?"

I chuckled. "Of course. He's been waiting to meet his grandparents."

I handed the baby to Maria. She sat down and began speaking baby talk to him as I sat down next to her. Charles was standing next to Emma, talking to her.

He turned around and looked at me, and then he cleared his throat. "Garrett, I heard what you said, and well...I couldn't be more honored to have you as a son-in-law. Thank you so much for loving my daughter like you do."

I tried desperately to hold back the tears building in my eyes. This had been an emotional day with the birth of my son and me wishing like hell that my father were here to hold him. With Emma's dad saying what he had said, it had just about pushed me over the edge.

"Thank you, sir. I'll love Emma until the day I die."

He nodded his head and held out his hand. I placed my hand in his to shake it, but he pulled me in for a hug.

He whispered in my ear, "I know you will, and I know how hard this is for you. Your father would have been so proud of you, son."

And there went the tears.

Charles pulled back and smiled at me as I quickly wiped away my tears.

He slapped his hands together and said, "Now, I don't think you should call him Charles."

Emma giggled and said, "What about Jim? It's short for James."

I nodded my head and looked at Maria.

She nodded her head and said, "I like it. It gives him his own name in a way."

Maria stood and walked up to Charles. She placed Jim in his arms. When I saw the tear slowly moving down his face, my heart stopped briefly. I glanced at Emma, who was now crying again. I walked over to her and leaned down before kissing her gently on the lips.

After Charles and Maria left, my father and mother came in.

"David, Julia, you made it," Emma said.

I walked up and hugged my mother and shook my father's hand. "I didn't think y'all would be able to make it tonight," I said.

With one look at Jim, my mother broke down in tears. "Oh. My. Lord. He is the most beautiful baby I've ever seen."

"Hey!" I said. I scooped Jim up from his bassinet and placed him in my mother's arms.

She tried not to, but she began crying as she sat down on the sofa next to David.

"Mother, please don't cry."

She let out a sob. "I'm so sorry. It's just...I just wish your father could hold him."

David wrapped his arm around my mother and gently kissed her on the forehead. My heart was beating faster, and I had to excuse myself from the room. I heard Emma call out for me, but I needed fresh air.

As I sat on the bench outside the hospital, I looked up. "Dad, why did you leave us? I really wish you were here." I placed my face in my hands and tried to concentrate on my breathing. It felt like someone was sitting on my chest.

I felt a hand on my shoulder, and when I looked up, I saw David standing there.

"Do you mind if I sit down?"

I shook my head and slid over just a bit. We sat in silence for a good ten minutes before he took a deep breath and let it out.

"After your sister was born, I felt the same way you feel right now, son. Oh, how I wished my mama and daddy could see her. She is a true gift from God. I remember Billy sitting on this same exact bench when his first child was born, feeling the same way you're feeling. I didn't have the words to make him feel better, just like I don't have the words to make you feel better. We all suffer losses in our lives. Some suffer greater than others, but each loss is significant to the person left behind. Your father has been with you this entire time, son. He's never left your side, and I'm pretty sure if I asked you right now, if you've ever felt his presence, you would tell me yes. It's unfair in a way."

I looked at him and asked, "What's unfair?"

"Being left behind and still feeling the pain for those who we have lost."

I nodded my head. "Yes, it is. Just when I think I'm okay, something happens, and I miss him. I'll smell the same cologne he wore, or a memory will pop into my head, or...or knowing my children will never know their grandfather."

David let out a giggle. "They will know him, Garrett. You will make sure that they know him. You'll talk about him often, and you'll share stories and advice he gave you. They might not be able to physically know him, but they will know him."

I quickly wiped a tear away and smiled. "David, I don't think I've ever really thanked you."

He turned and looked at me as he raised his eyebrow at me. "Thanked me for what?"

"Everything you did for me and Mama after Daddy passed away. Thank you for helping with the ranch while I was in school and for showing me everything my father would have shown me. Thank you for loving my mother. I really am glad you two found each other, and I know Daddy would want her to be with someone he trusted and loved."

I held my breath as I saw David's eyes fill with tears.

He reached for me and pulled me in for a hug. "You'll never know how much that means to me, son."

He slapped me hard on the back, and then he sat back and wiped away his tears. "Now, Garrett, I'm going to give you some advice my daddy gave me when Billy was born."

I nodded my head. "Okay, I'm listening."

"Help Emma out as much as possible. This baby took two to make, and it will take two of y'all to raise. You do your part in helping out with everything. That means, if you have to scrub your own britches, you scrub your own britches, so she can rest."

I nodded my head. "Yes, sir."

"Now, here is the big one—write her a letter."

I pulled my head back and looked at him with a confused expression. "A letter? What kind of letter?"

He smiled a crooked smile. "A letter telling her how you've felt—from the moment she told you she was having your child to watching her belly grow, and most of all, to holding your child in your arms for the first time. Write it down while it is fresh in your memory, son. Then, after you get home, when it feels like the right time, you give her that letter. Take the baby and go for a walk, so she has some time alone when she reads it."

I smiled and asked, "Did you write one to Mama after Lily was born?"

He chuckled. "Yes, I did. And let me just say, when I got back with Lily, your mother was…well…some things are best kept to oneself."

I shuddered. "Oh Lord, thank you for not sharing."

We both started laughing.

David stood up and put his hand on my shoulder. "My advice is to write it as soon as possible."

I stood up and reached my hand out for his. "Yes, sir. I'll do it right away."

As we made our way back into the hospital, I stopped at the nurses' station and asked for paper and a pen. I made my way back up to Emma's room. When I walked in, my mother was saying good-bye to Emma, and Jim was sound asleep in his bassinet.

"Are you leaving already, Mama?" I asked. I looked over at Emma, who seemed to be struggling to keep her eyes open.

My mother giggled. "Yes. We are staying the night with Charles and Maria, so we will be back tomorrow. I think Emma needs some rest."

My mother gave Emma a good-bye kiss on the cheek and then made her way over to me. She brought me in for a hug. She moved her mouth up close to my ear and whispered, "Just speak from your heart."

I pulled back and smiled. I was sure she knew David had told me about the letter. "Always, Mother. You raised me right."

She winked. "You bet I did."

I walked my mother and David out into the hall and talked to them for another five minutes.

When I walked back into the room, Emma was sleeping. I walked up to her and gently kissed her on the lips. I whispered, "Sleep, Buttercup."

I took the pad of paper and pen and sat down to begin writing my letter.

My dearest Emma,

I always thought that the day you said yes when I asked you to marry me would be the most amazing day of my life, but I was so wrong. Then, I thought the day you became my wife was surely the happiest day of my life. Yet again, I was wrong. Then, the day you walked into the barn, I knew from the look on your face that our family was about to get a bit bigger. Oh, yes, I thought, this was the happiest day of my life by far. I was proved wrong again. Watching your stomach grow day after day with our child—I thought nothing would ever top that. I was wrong again.

Today—the birth of our son—is one of the happiest days of my life by far, but it is not the happiest day. It finally dawned on me why. Every night, when I lay my head down next to yours, I thank God for another day with you. Each day I'm with you is the happiest day of my life, Emma. Every waking moment we are together, I'm the happiest I've ever been.

When we make love and we are completely one with each other, when you laugh at my silly jokes, or when you hold me as I feel like my world is about to come undone—these are the happiest moments of my life. When I walk in and see you standing at the kitchen sink, doing a little dance while listening to the radio and fixing dinner— my God, Em—I feel like my heart is going to burst from happiness.

Thank you, Emma, for giving me so many moments that I will treasure forever. Thank you for loving me. I pray every night that I make you as happy as you make me.

I'm sitting here right now, looking at our son, and I'm already thinking of our grandchildren. We are going to be kick-ass grandparents, Em. I'll teach them all there is to know about the ranch, and you will teach them to love one hundred percent with their hearts.

I can't wait to see what our future holds together. Always know you are my love, my life, and my forever.

Now, I'm going to stop writing this letter, so I can watch my beautiful wife sleep. I'll love you forever, Emma Rose Mathews. Never forget, our love is a forever love.

Love,

Garrett

22 Emma

"Should we wake him up, Mrs. Mathews?" the nurse asked.

We both looked down at Garrett sleeping in the chair.

I shook my head as we made our way out of the room. "No…let's let him sleep for just a bit."

I walked the halls of the hospital and tried like hell not to show the pain I was in. I was sure my son had ripped me open from one end to the other, but no way would I tell Garrett that. He would treat me like I couldn't do a thing if he knew I was in so much pain.

"The walking will help, Mrs. Mathews. I know it hurts. Would you like more pain medicine?"

I shook my head. "No, thank you. I don't like the idea of taking it while breastfeeding the baby."

She smiled slightly at me. "I promise you, it won't hurt the baby."

I bit down on my lower lip. "Well, I am in a lot of pain, so maybe—"

"You're in a lot of pain? Should you be walking, Emma? Maybe she should be resting," Garrett said as he walked up alongside me and held on to my arm.

I let out a laugh. "Garrett Mathews, you will not treat me like I'm incapable of doing anything. Of course I'm in pain. I just pushed a watermelon out of a hole the size of a grape. Now, don't harass the nurse. Walking is very good for me, and the faster I can get out of the hospital and home with you and our son, the better."

Garrett nodded his head and smiled. "Yes, ma'am. Ladies, I do believe I'm going to go peek at my son through the nursery glass again."

I let out a giggle. "Tell him I love him."

Garrett leaned down and kissed me on the cheek. "I will, Buttercup."

After a few more minutes of walking, I turned to the nurse and said, "You know what? I'll take that pain medicine now."

She chuckled and led me back to my room. "I have a feeling you will be heading home soon, Mrs. Mathews."

Garrett pulled up, and we both let out a sigh of relief. "Jesus, that was the most stressful few hours of my life. Tell me why we decided to have the baby in Austin?"

I laughed. "Because my dad insisted we have the baby at *his* hospital."

He shook his head. "I'm sorry, Em, but the next one will be born in Mason."

Garrett jumped out and ran around to open my door. He helped me out of the car and then took Jim in his arms. We walked up the steps with our son for the first time. We stopped right outside the door and looked at each other.

"Garrett, are we going to be able to do this? I mean, he's so small. What if I drop him or he slips when I give him a bath? I can't bear the thought of hurting him."

He let out a chuckle as he handed Jim to me. "Em, you're going to be the most amazing mother ever. You're not going to drop him or hurt him. You're going to love him and protect him always."

I nodded my head. "Okay. Well, let's do this then, shall we?"

We walked into the house, and the smell of freshly baked bread hit me almost at once.

"Is that fresh bread?" I asked.

Garrett turned and walked backward as he said, "I asked Margie to organize it. She, Peggy, Mama, and Lily all pitched in and made a few days' worth of meals. Mama said she would be by in a few days, but she wanted us to get settled first."

I tried to hold back my tears, but I finally just let them fall. I couldn't possibly love this man any more than I did in this very moment.

"Garrett, you always think of every little detail," I said.

He reached over and kissed my nose. "Emma, I love you so much. I just want you to be happy."

My heart began beating harder in my chest, and I was sure it would wake up Jim. "Garrett," I whispered, "I couldn't be any happier than I am right now."

He gave me that panty-melting smile of his. "Come on, let's put Jim down and get you into a hot bath."

Oh my. Yes, I could get used to this.

After my bath, I was so relaxed. I made my way over to our bed and crawled under the covers.

Garrett walked in with Jim. "My little guy wants something to eat. Then, I thought I would take him out for a bit of fresh air."

"Garrett, please don't take him into the barn or around any animals, not yet," I said as I reached for my little man.

Garrett threw his head back and said, "I'm excited about teaching him about ranching, Em, but I do think I can wait a few years."

After I fed and burped Jim, Garrett took him from my arms. "Now, rest for a bit while we go on a short walk."

I smiled as I watched Garrett walk away with our son. Nothing was sexier than seeing him holding our child. I closed my eyes and wished like hell we could be together. The doctor had said six weeks and no sooner. Margie had told me how much fun she and Billy had doing other things until they had finally broken down and had sex at four weeks.

I slid down and closed my eyes. I opened them again and turned to look at the nightstand. There was an envelope with my name on it. I sat up and reached for it. I began to open it.

It was a letter…from Garrett. I sat back some and began reading it. The more I read, the harder I cried. I had to stop a few times since I couldn't read through my tears. Twice, I had to put the letter down to try to control the crying. When I finally was able to finish, I folded the letter and carefully put it back into the envelope.

I got up out of bed and quickly made my way over to my dresser. I opened up my lingerie drawer and searched for the sheer black baby doll lingerie that Margie had given me for my birthday. I had been pregnant at the time, and I had been so pissed that she gave it to me then. When she'd told me it was for after the baby was born, I'd hugged her and told her she was the best cousin and best friend in the entire world.

I rushed into the bathroom and slipped it on. *Ugh.* I hated that I was bleeding so badly, but all I wanted to do was make Garrett happy. Wearing this would be just the start.

"Em? Are you okay?" Garrett called from the other side of the bathroom door.

I smiled and did a little hop as I looked at myself in the mirror. Just a few pinches to each cheek, and I was good to go.

"Is Jim awake?" I asked.

Garrett laughed. "Hell no. The country air knocked him out cold. I think he is going to take one hell of a good nap."

I opened the door and leaned against the doorframe. "Good. I'm going to need time to make sure my husband has one hell of a good orgasm."

Garrett's eyes traveled up and down my body, and he swallowed hard. "Em, what are you…where did you…what…what's happening?"

I giggled as I walked up to him. I began lifting his shirt up and over his head. "Mmm…your body drives me insane with lust, Garrett."

171

I placed my hands on his chest and began moving them up and down as I licked my lips and looked up into his eyes. They were dancing with passion, and I couldn't help but smile, knowing I was making him feel this way.

He closed his eyes and then opened them as he let out a long sigh. "Em, we can't, not for six weeks."

I began pushing him, so he had to start walking backward.

I slowly shook my head. "Oh, Mr. Mathews...this is all for you."

His legs bumped the bed, and I quickly moved my hands down to start getting his pants off. I pulled them down, and when his erection sprang free, I let out a moan. I dropped to my knees, pulling his pants down all the way. I took him into my mouth, and Garrett pushed his hands through my hair as he let out a loud moan. I began moving, barely grazing my teeth along his hard shaft.

"Fuck," he hissed as he looked down and into my eyes.

I could feel him getting bigger in my mouth, and I closed my eyes as I let out a moan. I would have given anything to touch myself or have Garrett touch me. I let out another moan, and that was Garrett's undoing.

"Jesus, Em. I'm going to come."

I took every last ounce of what he gave me. When he reached down and pulled me up to him, he was panting. I quickly wiped my mouth and smiled at him.

"Thank you, Em. That was...amazing."

"Garrett...thank you. Thank you so much for loving me and for treating me like a princess."

He kissed my nose. "You are a princess, and I do it because I love you so much. Let's get cleaned up, and then we'll try to get a bit of sleep while Jim is sleeping."

A few minutes later, I was lying next to Garrett as he held me tightly.

"You read the letter, didn't you?"

I smiled even though he couldn't see my face. I nodded and said, "Yes, I did. Garrett, that has to be the most romantic thing you've ever done. Thank you so much."

I rolled over and faced him. We both lay on our sides and looked at each other. I watched as Garrett's eyes slowly began closing. He rolled over onto his back and pulled me to him. I rested my head on his chest and listened to his breathing slow down. I'd never been so content in my life as I was right now.

As I thought about our future, I couldn't help but think about more kids. If Garrett were to ask me right now how many more kids I wanted, I would have to say one more. I thought about the ranch being filled with grandkids running all around and how I would teach them all about gardening. Garrett would teach them about cattle, horses, ranching, and so much more.

I snuggled deeper into Garrett and drifted off to sleep. I dreamed of two little boys running around, being chased by Garrett. I dreamed of our oak tree where Garrett had made me his. I dreamed of a wedding, a beautiful country wedding, and a young couple standing under our oak tree. I couldn't see their faces, but I could feel their love in my dream. I dreamed of kids, lots of little ones running around on the ranch. I'd never had such happy dreams in my life.

When I woke up, I felt an empty space beside me. I sat up and looked around. I could hear Garrett whispering in the kitchen. I slowly got up and wrapped myself in my robe before making my way to the kitchen. I stopped just before I got there, and I listened to my husband softly singing "Love Me Tender" to our son. I placed my hand over my mouth and cried silently as I dropped my head against the wall. Garrett sang the entire song to our son as I tried to contain my sobbing. I dropped my hand from my mouth and quickly wiped away my tears. I pushed off the wall and made my way into the kitchen as Garrett started signing again.

Garrett kept singing as I walked in. He looked over at me and smiled. When he finished singing, he looked back down at the baby and said, "Charles James Mathews, you and your mother are the two most important people in my life, and I promise you, I'll love you both forever."

I walked over to Garrett, reached up, and kissed him with as much love and passion as I could. When we both pulled away, we looked into each other's eyes and smiled.

"A forever love," I whispered.

Garrett pushed a piece of my hair behind my ear and nodded. "A forever love."

Three Years Later

I looked down and silently thanked God for the blessing in my arms. It had taken Garrett and I longer than we wanted to have our second child, and I had been about to give up when we went on vacation. Two months later, I had found out I was pregnant. Garrett had been beyond-the-moon happy.

He'd felt even happier five weeks ago when the doctor held up our baby and said, *It's a son.*

I looked up when I heard the door to the bedroom open. Garrett walked in with a huge bouquet of white daisies. I was pretty sure my grin was from ear to ear.

Jim came running in behind Garrett, yelling, "Is da baby up? I want to hold da baby again, Mama."

Garrett reached down and scooped up Jim, and he began laughing.

I held up my finger and said, "Shh…Jack is sleeping. He needs his big brother to play quietly, so he can sleep and grow, and then he'll be able to play with you soon."

Garrett chuckled as he set the flowers down on the nightstand. He carefully leaned Jim over so that he could kiss Jack. "Gentle, buddy. Remember what we talked about in the barn."

Jim was focused on the baby and said, "Yes, sir. I will kiss da baby verwy softly."

I watched as Jim kissed Jack on the forehead, and then oh-so carefully, Jim began petting Jack on the top of his head.

Garrett laughed. "Son, he's not a dog."

Garrett set Jim down and leaned over to kiss me. "How are you feeling, Em?"

I nodded my head. "The second time around is a lot easier, that's for sure."

"Daddy, pwease can we go for a walk now?" Jim asked as he looked up at Garrett with pleading eyes.

There was nothing that child loved to do more than go walking with Garrett. My mother had said it was because Garrett had walked with him so much when he was a baby.

Garrett rubbed the top of Jim's head. "Yeah, buddy. Go pick out a toy to bring."

When Garrett looked back at me, he raised his eyebrow. "Two of them. This is going to be fun."

I let out a laugh and nodded my head. Garrett turned and took the old flowers out of the vase. He tossed them into the trash can and placed the fresh daisies in the vase. I glanced down at Jack, who was sound asleep in my arms with a nice full belly.

The next thing I knew, Garrett was taking Jack from my arms. He quickly kissed me on the lips. "I'm taking Jack for a walk with Jim. Try to get a few minutes of rest, okay, Em? I have a feeling you'll need it."

I chuckled. "Okay. Don't be gone too long. It's a bit breezy outside."

Garrett smiled down at Jack and mumbled something about it not being cold out and that they would be fine. I watched as he walked out of our bedroom.

I decided I wanted to throw the quiche I had made up last night in the oven. When I threw my legs over the side of the bed, a white envelope caught my eye. I couldn't help the butterflies that took off in the pit of my stomach.

I placed my hand on my stomach and said, "After all these years, Garrett Mathews, you still make me feel like a young girl in love."

My name was written across the envelope. I reached for it, took a deep breath, and opened it. I pulled the letter out and began reading it.

My dearest Emma,

I watched you sleep last night for the longest time. I was so overcome with love that I wanted to wake you up and tell you how much I loved you. You have given me so much, Emma—love, happiness, two beautiful sons.

You will never truly know how much you saved me all those years ago when you smiled at me in Mr. Horster's drugstore. I do believe that I can honestly say that was the best moment of my life—the moment I first saw you, the second I knew that we would be together for always.

No words will ever be able to describe that moment you told me we were expecting our second child. No words will ever be able to describe when Jack was born or the moment I saw you hold him for the first time. I will never fully be able to tell you how happy you continue to make me.

The only thing I know to say to you is that you, Jim, and Jack are the most important people in my life, and I will spend the rest of my life loving all three of you.

I believe you are still missing one charm, my love.

I love you, Emma Rose Mathews. I'll love you forever and always because our love is and always will be...

A forever love.

Love always,

Garrett

I picked up the small blue velvet bag and slowly opened it. I turned it over and let the charm fall into my hand. It was a round charm with a baby footprint in the middle. On either side of the footprint was each boy's birthstone. I instantly began crying. I quickly got up and made my way over to my dresser. I opened my jewelry box. I pulled out my charm bracelet and laid it across the dresser. I was going to have Garrett go to the jeweler first thing in the morning to have the charm added to my bracelet.

I made my way into the kitchen and pulled the quiche out from the refrigerator. I turned on the oven. I didn't even wait for it to heat up before I placed the quiche inside the oven and started the timer. I walked over to the phone and picked it up. I dialed Margie's number.

"Hello?"

"Marg?"

"Ah hell…he wrote you a letter, didn't he? That overly romantic bastard."

I couldn't help but giggle. "Yes, he did, and I need to call in a favor."

She let out a sigh. "Billy will be over in a few minutes to pick up my precious little nephew. Make sure to pack up a bag. I'm sure Jim will want to spend the night with us."

I did a little jump. "Margie, I swear to you, I owe you big time."

"Hell yeah, you do. I'm going to be calling it in soon, too. I can't even remember the last time Billy and I had a good fucking."

I placed my hand over my mouth and laughed. "I've got to go, so I can get Jim's stuff ready." I started making a mental note of everything he would need.

Margie laughed. "I'll send Billy right now."

"Perfect. Love you!" I said.

"Love you back."

I rushed around the house to get everything ready.

Billy and Margie had moved back to Mason two years ago, and it had been a blessing for both of us. I'd missed her so much, and now, with her teaching here in Mason and Billy working for Garrett, we got to see each other all the time.

I heard Garrett and Jim talking on the front porch.

"Well, did you go poo in your diapers, Daddy?"

Garrett chuckled. "Yes, son, everyone starts off going potty in their diapers."

Garrett opened the door, and I was standing there, holding a bag. He looked around and then glanced back at me, confused. Jack was fussing, so I set the bag down and walked up to Garrett. I took Jack from Garrett's arms and sat down on the sofa.

"Jim, Uncle Billy and Aunt Margie wanted to know if you would like to spend the night with them tonight."

Jim let out a small scream and said, "Oh, pwease, Mama. Pwease can I go over and play?"

Garrett and I both laughed.

I said, "Of course you can. I packed you a bag and put your favorite toys in there. Mommy and Daddy will be over first thing in the morning to pick you up."

Jim ran over and grabbed his bag. He started heading to the door.

Garrett bent down and stopped him. "Hey, where do you think you're going?"

Jim looked at him with a serious face. "To Uncle Billy's to play, Daddy."

There was a knock on the door, and Billy came walking in. Jim ran up to him. Billy quickly dropped down and took Jim into his arms.

He looked at Garrett and then at me as he smiled. "Well, I'm going to safely say the little guy wants to play."

I was sitting on the sofa, feeding Jack, as I nodded my head. "Just a little."

Garrett clapped his hands. "Well, not to rush you out the door, brother, but..."

Billy laughed and scooped up Jim as he grabbed the bag. "Well, hell, if that isn't a hint, I don't know what is."

Garrett slapped Billy on the back. "Make plans to take your wife somewhere romantic in a few weeks. Between us and Mom and Dad, we've got you covered. Y'all deserve it."

Billy stopped and looked at Garrett. "Oh, man, that would be awesome. If you're serious, I know Margie has been talking about going to the coast. I'd love to take her there, just us two."

Garrett nodded his head. "Consider it done. Make the plans, and I'll talk to Mom tomorrow. I'm sure Lily would love to spend some time with the kids."

Billy thanked Garrett again and headed out with Jim.

"Thanks again, bro!" Garrett called out.

When he turned around and shut the door, I saw the look in his eyes. He walked up and peered down at me.

I swallowed hard and stood up, holding a sleeping Jack. "I think he's out."

"Oh, he is out. He's my son, and he knows when Daddy needs alone time with Mommy."

I giggled as I walked into our room and placed Jack into his bassinet. I no sooner turned around before Garrett was picking me up and taking me over to the bed.

In no time at all, I was softly calling out my husband's name as he took me to heaven and back.

After returning the favor and making Garrett orgasm, we both took a quick shower where Garrett snuck in another orgasm for me.

Later, we wrapped ourselves up in our quilt and sat on the front porch. We hadn't had any alone time in so long that it was amazing to just sit and be with each other.

As I looked out toward the west pasture, I couldn't help but smile.

Garrett pulled me closer to him and said, "What is that smile for?"

I shrugged. "I'm not sure. I just see so many wonderful things happening on this ranch in the future."

He nodded his head. "I hope so. I really hope so."

I slowly turned and looked at him. "Thank you for my letter."

He smiled that smile that melted my heart. I knew that smile would forever melt my heart.

"I meant every word."

I pulled his hand up and kissed the back of it. "I know you did."

Garrett let out a long sigh and said, "I had a dream last night."

"Oh, yeah? What was it about?"

He shook his head. "I was sitting on this porch, talking to the boys, I guess. They were older, our age when we got married. I was telling them about our story."

I smiled as I thought back to the first time I'd laid my eyes on Garrett Mathews and how foolish I had been, fighting my feelings for him.

"Do you know what my hope is for our boys?" Garrett asked.

"That they find a love like ours?"

He looked back at me and smiled. "Yes. My hope is for them to find a love like ours."

I nodded my head and whispered, "That's my wish, too."

We sat there for a few minutes in silence before Garrett pushed the quilt off of him, and he stood up. He held his hand out, and I placed my hand in his.

"Where are we going?" I asked as I raised my eyebrows.

Garrett's eyes lit up with a fire I hadn't seen in a few months, and I couldn't help thinking of how badly I needed to feel him inside me.

"It just dawned on me that it's been five weeks, and I think I've waited long enough to make love to my wife. I'm taking you inside, and I'm going to make you feel like you've never felt before."

"Oh," was all I could say.

I let Garrett lead me into the house. After a quick check on Jack, Garrett gently laid me down on the bed, and he slowly began making love to me. He took his time, and I was so glad he did.

"Garrett...you feel amazing," I whispered.

He slowly moved in and out of my body.

When I felt the familiar buildup, I grabbed on to his shoulders and looked into his eyes. "Garrett...I'm coming."

Garrett closed his eyes and let out a long moan as he slowly came to a stop. He stayed inside me for a few minutes. Neither one of us wanted to break the bond we had. When he finally pulled out of me, he placed his hands on either side of my face and kissed me so tenderly. It didn't take long for me to be so overcome with emotion that I began to softly cry.

Garrett was resting his body on his elbows, and he slowly smiled as he wiped a tear away from my cheek.

"Emma Rose, will you marry me?"

I smiled. "I do believe I've said yes…a few times."

"Marry me again," he whispered.

"Only if you promise to love me forever."

As he slowly sat back, he pulled me up. He moved my body to where I was straddling him.

"Emma Rose Mathews, I promise to love you forever."

I smiled, and I was about to kiss him when I heard, "Emma? Garrett?"

Garrett's mouth dropped open, and he quietly said, "Are you fucking kidding me?"

I let out a giggle. "An unlocked door is an open invitation." I gently kissed my husband on the lips and whispered, "I love you, Garrett."

He moved his hand behind my neck as he smiled that smile that would forever be my undoing. He whispered back to me, "I love you more, Emma."

23 Garrett

Present Day

I couldn't help but smile as I watched all the girls sitting there with tears in their eyes—well, all of them but one. Ari was sitting with her arms crossed over her chest, and her mouth was dropped open.

"I knew it! I knew there had to be some reason you always walk in on us, old man," Ari said as she shook her head.

Emma let out a chuckle. Ellie glanced over at Ari and hit her on the arm before turning back and wiping away her tears.

Ellie took in a deep breath. "That was the most beautiful story I've ever heard, Garrett. I had no idea you were behind all the letters."

Emma reached for my hand. "It seems like it was all just a moment ago."

"Grams, Gramps…that was the most amazing story I've ever heard. Thank you for sharing it with us."

Jeff nodded. "I always knew that quilt was a good-luck charm."

Everyone began laughing as Emma and I looked at each other and smiled.

"It seems like it was just yesterday when Emma was handing me that quilt and we were going on that picnic. My bride is just as beautiful today, if not more beautiful than that day."

Heather cleared her throat. "I think it is pretty clear where Gunner got his romance from, but I have to say, I think you blow them all out of the water, Garrett. Oh my goodness…the charm when the boys were born."

Amanda blew her nose. "So beautiful."

Ari smiled. "The honeymoon and Nat King Cole's song. Swoon the hell out of me!"

Ellie nodded her head. "The honeymoon night!"

Amanda said, "Yes…in the back of the truck."

Josh started laughing. "Garrett, I'm pretty sure we learned from the best when it comes to the romance department."

I glanced over to Gunner, and he smiled and winked at me.

Jessie cleared her throat. "Garrett, I never knew about your father. That just breaks my heart." She broke down crying again.

Emma reached across and took Jessie's hand in hers. "The only way to truly appreciate the happy times in your life is to go through the bad times." She looked back at me and grinned. "Garrett and I learned that very early on."

She glanced back at the kids. "Kids, not everything in your life is going to be wonderful. You're going to get upset and fight with each other. We tend to make it much harder than we should. We question our love, and we place doubt in our minds, but you have to believe in the very thing that got you this far—love. It breaks down the walls we have built and shows us the light we've always known is there. Nothing is stronger than love."

Emma looked over to me.

I smiled. "Especially when it is a forever love."

The End

The Letters

The following section includes letters written from Gunner, Jeff, Josh, Brad, and Scott after the birth of each one's first child.

Gunner

Dear Ellie,

I'll never forget the day you told me we were expecting our first child. I can close my eyes and still feel the excitement I felt at that very moment. I think the months of trying so hard made it all the sweeter.

Watching your stomach grow with our child, Ells, I've never in my life experienced such emotions. Each morning, waking up next to the one person I loved more than life itself, knowing you would give me one of the most amazing gifts ever, filled my heart with so much love that it felt as if it would burst each day.

The first time I heard our baby's heartbeat, I was certain nothing would ever top that moment. I was proved wrong when I placed my hand on your stomach and felt our child move.

Then, the day came when we welcomed Alex into this world. Seeing the smile spread across your face the first time you saw our daughter was probably one of the most amazing moments in our marriage. To be a part of something so miraculous and to share it with you…words will never be able to explain how I felt. I'll never forget the sounds of her cries filling the air like the sweetest of love songs. I'll never forget your tears of happiness when you held her. I've always known you would be an amazing mother, Ells, and to watch that exchange between the two most important girls in my life was truly a gift from above.

I thank God every day that I was with Jeff the day I first placed my eyes on the most beautiful woman ever. Thank you, Ellie, for letting me love you. Thank you for giving me the greatest gifts ever—our daughter and your love.

I love you more.
Gunner

Jeff

My sweet, beautiful Arianna,

I don't even have the words to describe what I've been feeling the last nine months. I won't lie and say that I haven't been scared to death this whole time. I've prayed every morning and every night that God and our little angel would watch over you and keep you and the baby safe.

As I sit here and write this letter to you, I think back to the day you told me you were pregnant. The look in your eyes made me fall in love with you even more, if that were possible. I still remember what you were wearing, how you smelled, what your hair looked liked, and how your eyes danced with a light I hadn't seen in so long. It felt like we had been given the greatest gift of all, and I knew no other moment in my life would top it.

Then, you placed my hand on your swollen stomach, and I felt our son move. I tremble now as I think back to that amazing day. My heart was overflowing with love for you. Thinking back to what we shared while you were pregnant, one word comes to mind—magical. I was lost in every single second of watching your body change and watching the glow on your face brighten day after day. Something so simple as picking out the outfit for the baby to wear when he came home seems like it was just a moment ago.

All those moments, I said to myself, *Nothing will ever top this*. How incredibly wrong I was. The moment our son was born will forever be the most incredible moment of my life.

Thank you, Ari, for loving me and for giving me one of the greatest blessings of my life—our son, Luke.

I love you, baby.
Jeff

Josh

Dear Heather,

I had all these things I wanted to say to you in this letter, but as I sit here and watch you sleep, my heart is so filled with happiness that all I really want to do is pinch myself and pray that this isn't all just a dream.

I know the road that we took to get to where we are was filled with so many ups and downs, but I believe that is what has made our love so strong. We had to fight for it from the very beginning. One of the many happy memories along that road was the day I found out you were pregnant. So many emotions played through that day, but that very moment in time, when I knew I was going to be a father, has to be one of the best times of my life.

It seems some of our best memories have been mixed with so many different emotions. The day I watched on the monitor and saw two little peanuts, I wasn't sure if I should be happy or totally scared to death. I was so freaked-out, but at the same time, I was so blessed in knowing that you and I were not just bringing one blessing into our world but two.

Some of my greatest memories will always be watching your stomach grow with our babies. To see how strong you were the whole time makes my heart swell up with so much pride. The first time I felt them move or saw a tiny little foot move across your stomach will forever be etched into my memory. To see your eyes light up whenever you talked about the babies or made plans about their future. Even the day your hair was covered in paint when we were painting the twins' bedroom. Each moment has been a blessing that I will never take for granted.

Thank you for giving me those memories, Heather.

Thank you for being such an amazing wife and for loving me like you do.

I can only hope that I am able to show you each and every day just how much I love you, Will, and Libby. I love you more than the air I breathe, and I thank God every day, Heather, that he brought you into my life. You will forever be the love of my life, my entire world, and my reason for being.

I love you infinity.
Josh

Brad

Dear Pumpkin,

I wish I could fill this letter with amazing memories of the first moment I found out you were pregnant or the first time I felt the baby move. My mistakes do not allow me to do that.

What I can do is tell you that the first time I felt our child move, the day you forgave me and we started again, was one of the happiest days of my life. But then, too many things have happened to us these last few months, and I could title them all as the happiest days of my life. I've come to the realization that just being with you, being married to you, and experiencing these last few months of our pregnancy have been the happiest days of my life.

Something happened to me the day our daughter was born. A part of me healed. To hear the cries of our daughter move through my body like a warm breeze was probably one of the most magical moments of my life. I've never felt so complete as I did the moment she looked up into my eyes. I'm honored to be able to share this with you.

As I watched you this morning with Maegan, my heart was so overcome with so much love that I had to step out of the room. I took a walk outside and let the tears fall from eyes as I thought about how blessed I truly am to have a woman so amazing love me like you do. To watch you, Amanda, with our daughter, who is everything to me, is just the most wonderful experience I've ever had.

I thank God every single moment I can that he gave me the strength to put my mistakes behind me and that he gave you the courage to love me enough to forgive me. I love you so very much, Amanda. I promise you, I will always be there for you and Maegan. You both are my entire world. You're both my everything.

Thank you for believing in me.

Forever yours,
Brad

Scott

Dear Jessie,

As I sit here and look at our beautiful daughter, Lauren, I'm taken back to the day you told me you were pregnant. Nothing had ever affected my world like those words did. I went from feeling one emotion to a totally opposite emotion when you said the words, *I'm pregnant.*

As the months went on, I was blessed with being able to see your body change and watch your stomach grow. I realized that you had given me so many moments like that very day you announced you were pregnant.

I've never seen anyone so beautiful in my life as you were each morning. The glow on your face and the sparkle in your eyes caused my heart to drop every single time. The feel of our child moving inside your body was an experience I just can't put into words. Seeing a tiny little elbow move from one side of your stomach to the next while we sat there in awe was probably one of my most favorite moments. Your strange eating habits—well, maybe I should just leave that one alone.

What I'm trying to say is that the last few months have been the most amazing, miraculous, wonderful, delightful, enchanting months of my life.

Thank you for loving me. Thank you for being you, Jess. I will never truly be able to write down in words how much I love you and how much your love means to me. I hope you feel it though.

Thank you for being an incredible mother, and I look forward to seeing us both grow, not only as mother and father but also as husband and wife.

You and Lauren are the two most important people in my life. I promise to love you and protect you both. I promise I will do my best to be the husband and father you both deserve.

With all my love,
Scott

Thank You

I thank God every day for allowing me to be able to tell the stories that are in my head and put them down on paper.

Darrin—Thank you for just being you. Your support means the world to me, and I will never be able to thank you enough. You listen to me go on and on about my fictional friends, and you even help me brainstorm new stories. I am truly blessed to have you in my life. Thank you for loving me.

Lauren—Thank you for being on the cover of this book. You will never know what it means to me. Each day, you make me so proud, and I have such hopes and dreams for you. Always stay true to yourself. I love doo so very much.

Ari Niknejadi– Thank you for being you and for never filling my head with bullshit. This last year has been crazy. We are kindred spirits though—always. Remember that! RFB girl…R. F. B. Love you!

Gary Taylor—Thank you so much for your support and friendship. It has been an awesome ride, and I'm so glad you were along for it!

Heather Davenport—I know I always say this, but I really would be lost without you. You are amazing and keep me going. I've never known anyone who works as hard as you do and is so damn organized. Jesus H. Christ…I need to learn your skills. I love you, girl!

Kristin Mayer—My Special K. I don't know how I would make it some days if it wasn't for your positive attitude. You make me laugh, and you always keep it real. I'm so blessed to call you a friend. I've never met anyone with such a giving and caring heart as you. I can't wait to see what the future holds. Oh, by the way, you are one kick-ass author, too, I might add. Love you, girl!

Jemma Scarry—Thank you! Thank you! Thank you! Your beta-reading skills are like none other. Your friendship though means more to me than you will ever know. You are an amazing mother, wife, and friend. I am so very blessed to have you in my life. I hope you know that. I can't wait to see you in July! I love you, girl!

JoJo Belle—No one makes me laugh like you do. Seriously…you are probably one of the funniest people I know, and you are also one of the kindest people I know. Thank you for always dropping everything when I send you one of these silly books to read. Your comments make me laugh, and the fact that you take the time to do this means more to me than anything. I admire you, girl, and I don't know how you do it all. Thank you for your friendship. I cherish it! Can't wait to see you in July! Love you, girl!

Nikki Sievert—Thank you so much for taking time out of your life to read these books! You are the last person to see them before I hit publish, and for that…I have to say THANK YOU!

Molly McAdams—Girl, I love you! I love our lunch dates and our silly text messages. I don't know how I would do it without you! I miss your face so much when I don't get to see you. You are one of the most real people I have ever met. I love that about you. Never change! #PeasAndCarrots

Jovana Shirley—Thank you for all your hard work that you put into editing each book! You're the best!

My HIPAA girls—Thank you for your support! I adore you girls more than you will ever know. Thank you for spreading the word about my books and me. I'll never be able to thank you enough.

Kelly's Most Wanted—You are the best darn street team around! Gosh, y'all…thank you so much for all you do for me.

To all my friends and readers—I wouldn't be able to do all of this if it wasn't for y'all. Thank you for supporting me! I love you to the moon and back!

Mom—Thank you for raising me right. I hope that you are looking down, nodding your head, and saying, "Well done." Listening to the songs while writing this book flooded my mind with memories of you. I love you and miss you so much.

Playlist

"Unforgettable" by Nat King Cole—Garrett sees Emma for the first time.

"I Want You, I Love You, I Need You" by Elvis Presley—Garrett and Emma dance at the Halloween party.

"Love Me Tender" by Elvis Presley—Garrett and Emma dance at the wall party.

"Rock Around the Clock" by Bill Haley and His Comets—Emma looks for Garrett at the sock hop.

"Only You" by The Platters—Garrett is about to kiss Emma while they dance at the sock hop.

"Loving You" by Elvis Presley—Garrett and Emma are on their first date under the oak tree.

"Don't" by Elvis Presley—Garrett and Emma dance at Julia and David's wedding.

"All Shook Up" by Elvis Presley—Garrett and Emma jitterbug at Julia and David's wedding.

"Send for Me" by Nat King Cole—Garrett and Emma dance at Julia and David's wedding.

"Sincerely" by The McGuire Sisters—Garrett dances with his mother at her wedding.

"Stuck on You" by Elvis Presley—Garrett and Emma dance at a party after graduating from college.

"Too Much" by Elvis Presley—Garrett and Emma dance at a party after graduating from college.

"Loving You" by Elvis Presley—After getting beat up, Garrett listens to this song while in the hospital.

"Can't Help Falling in Love" by Elvis Presley— Garrett and Emma's wedding song. Garrett and Emma dance their first dance at their wedding.

"Unforgettable" by Nat King Cole—Garrett and Emma dance in the club on their honeymoon.

"Love Me Tender" by Elvis Presley—Garrett sings to Jim in the kitchen.

"That's What Love Is For" by Amy Grant—At the end of the story, Garrett and Emma talk to the kids after sharing their love story with them.

CPSIA information can be obtained
at www.ICGtesting.com
Printed in the USA
LVOW04s1949201016
509597LV00012B/954/P